The Voices In Between

Dear Lilly –

I hope you enjoy this book as much as I enjoy your wonderful mom!

All my best,
Beth

The Voices In Between

a novel by
Charlene Challenger

Copyright © 2014 Charlene Challenger
All rights reserved

Tightrope Books
167 Browning Trail
Barrie, Ontario. L4N 5E7
www.tightropebooks.com

Editor: Jessie Hale
Copy editor: Sèphera Girón
Typography: Dawn Kresan
Cover: Russell Challenger
Author photo credit: Laurie Bulchak

Printed and bound in Canada

We thank the Canada Council for the Arts, the Ontario Arts Council, and the Government of Ontario through the book publishing tax credit for their support of our publishing program.
Library and Archives Canada Cataloguing in Publication

Challenger, Charlene, 1978–, author
    The voices in between / Charlene Challenger.

ISBN 978-1-926639-79-6 (PBK.)

    I. TITLE.

PS8605.H3367V63 2014   JC813'.6   C2014-903016-9

For Russell

Chapter One

November wasn't supposed to be dreary. It was supposed to be exciting; a month dazzled by twinkling lights and silver and gold, thirty days of sharp winter weather, crisp with anticipation. It was supposed to rattle when the sun shone, and hum when the snow fell. Adoni looked at the people surrounding her on the bus ride home from school. She couldn't see a single smile; just the eyes of the other patrons, cast down to the floor beneath a veil of dingy, overcast light.

A light drizzle washed away the last traces of snow that had settled over the street the night before. Adoni was itchy and sweaty in her winter jacket. She fidgeted in her seat until she freed herself from its zipper and sleeves. Beneath the jacket was her uniform - the blue acrylic cardigan bearing her high school's crest, a rumpled white shirt that gaped between the buttons, and a pair of tight grey dress pants. She poked at her belly, at the two rolls of flesh her pants divided her into. She hated asking her mother for new clothes; the uniform pants, cardigans, and shirts were expensive, and the school didn't allow cheaper substitutions.

The bus halted at an intersection. A pudgy cop in a florescent green coat stood in the middle of the street, waving his arms to direct the traffic and glancing at his watch every now and then. Grumbles and clucks of impatience rose up all around her.

Driving with her mother was the same frustrating exercise, back when her mother owned and could drive a car. "Look at this guy, look, look, look," Ida quipped when she pointed to someone driving too slowly, tailgating, or refusing to change lanes despite signalling left or right. "I swear these assholes get their licenses out of cereal boxes." At fourteen, Adoni was still too young to drive, not that she had any desire to learn, given the way people around her reacted to traffic jams and inconveniences.

The pop and arch of an old-time crooner's voice, the sleazy wail of a saxophone, blared out from another driver's cheap car stereo. Adoni ignored the squeal and growl of the bus and concentrated on the melody. She recognized the song from trips to drug stores and supermarkets—a track from the late fifties, bumping along on a path of staccato horns and paper thin doo-wop. The lyrics, at first delivered one by one, beat by beat, were standard bubble-gum fare. Then the singer's cadence stretched into five long, loving notes, held high over a bed of "oooh"s and "aaah"s until they settled into the warmth and silk of a woman's name, Diana, and the sweetness of the sugar turned into the grit of the saxophone's refrain.

Adoni closed her eyes and dreamed of cruising along a country road in an old convertible with her arms stretched over her head.

Someone's cell phone rang right next to her ear, pulling the song apart. *Diana*, she thought, trying to ignore the interruption. *Pretty name.*

She wondered if her own name, laid against the bow of someone's devoted lips, would sound just as nice.

Adoni had never thought much about the origin of her name, but earlier that afternoon, Monica, the girl with oily skin and glasses who sat next to her in history class, had caused her to wonder. Monica had recently made a habit of following Adoni to the cafeteria after third period. Adoni didn't like Monica very much, but preferred sitting with her to sitting by herself in a room filled with hundreds of other students.

"My dad named me after his big sister," Monica said after popping a couple of gravy-drenched fries into her mouth and gulping them down with a mouthful of chocolate milk. "She died in a car crash when he was seven. He never really talks about her but I guess he loved her a lot because why'd he name his kid after her?" Adoni shrugged her broad shoulders and slumped in her chair, staring at Monica's lunch. "And they named my brother after my grandfather on my mom's side," Monica continued. She lifted her bangs out of her face with two grimy fingers. "He's dead too. Who are you named after?"

"I don't know," Adoni said. "Nobody. Unless my mom knew someone with the same name and never said it."

Monica dug her fingers back into the pile of fries and retrieved a particularly long and mushy one. She slurped it up like a strand of spaghetti. Adoni's ears filled with the sounds of wet, sloppy chewing. A buttery smile spread across Monica's pockmarked face. "Did you know Rob got suspended for spitting in the gravy?"

"No he didn't."

"Yeah he did. Jason's in his food prep class and he said Rob was spitting in the gravy."

"I see him whenever I'm here, so if he got suspended he must not have anyplace better to be."

"You're hilarious!" Monica roared. "But he did, though."

Shabnam had told Adoni the same story the week before, but instead the culprit was Jason and Rob was the witness. The kids at Assumption High School always questioned the sanitary condition of the gravy. The same story had floated around the cafeteria for years, with one name substituting for another as the student body changed. The texture of it made them wonder.

Monica rattled on, citing item after item of proof of Rob's guilt with the irritating finesse of a car alarm between noisy bites and swigs. Adoni said little to interrupt her, dividing her attention between listening to Monica and watching the second hand march around the clock on the wall.

When the first bell finally rang, the carton of fries was only half empty, with the remaining contents lying in a lukewarm, congealed mess. Monica wiped her mouth with a fistful of napkins and dropped them on the table next to her half-eaten lunch. "What class do you have now?"

"English, but I'm not going."

"Want the rest of my fries?"

"Sure."

Monica pushed the carton towards Adoni and grabbed her backpack. "Okay, I'll see you at lunch next Wednesday," she said, a hair too loudly. "Ha! You're my Wednesday lunch friend!" Adoni slid back against her chair and smiled as politely as she could. Monica swung the heavy pack over her shoulder and bounced out of the room.

Adoni reached for the clean plastic fork Monica hadn't bothered to use, and speared the rest of the fries into her mouth.

After lunch, Adoni trudged up to the second floor and peeked into the library to see if Shabnam was there. A pair of girls sat in front of one of the computers. "Do 298 Wilkins Street," one of them whispered. Her companion typed the address in. "Oh, sick! That's where Greg and Anton live!"

"Don't sit next to them in class, eh?" the other girl warned with a hiss. "That's nasty. They hide in your clothes and then jump off and get in your bag."

"Gross! What do they look like?"

Their giggles of amusement and disgust caught the librarian's attention. He sauntered over to them and asked what they were looking at. The slow shake of his head sparked a flurry of excuses. "It's for science, sir. Check it out, I'm gonna do a project on bed bugs."

"Okay girls; let's just keep the noise down. Science isn't supposed to be that much fun."

The girls fussed over the pictures until another student called them over and they abandoned their search. Adoni sat down at the newly vacated computer station and clicked back through the web pages until she found the original site the girls had been on. She typed in the school's address first, and a message flashed across the screen: No results.

She typed in her home address.

One match, she read, in bold red letters, next to a map.

Adoni slipped her coat back on as the bus neared her stop. She stood up and nudged her way through the crowd standing in front of the rear exit. When the door opened she plodded down the stairs and stepped into a deep puddle. She swore and pulled her foot out of the water, then headed left, towards the low-rise she called home, with her head bent forward to keep the rain out of her eyes.

Her heavy steps splashed water up the back of her pants and soaked the cuffs. Nelly's, the coffee shop Adoni popped into some mornings, had a string of blinking Christmas lights in the window. She caught a whiff of roasted beans and stopped to peer through the glass. A pair of old men sat at the table closest to the counter, their legs splayed and their canes held out to their sides, their skins a sickly shade of green beneath the fluorescent bulbs. A woman in a kurta sat a few tables away, watching the street with eyes set deep in a pair of dark rings. Adoni kept walking. She passed the house with the broken fountain in front—the house that told her she was only a minute away from home.

She clenched her jaw.

The white bricks of Adoni's building were covered with grey ash, and the short patch of grass out front sagged under the weight of too much water and snow. Stained concrete and wrought-iron balconies hung below every unit, some decorated with lights for the upcoming holiday. Adoni reached the front door and immediately smelled the building's pipes and drains. They rattled whenever someone took a long shower, and in the summer they gave off the rancid odour of boiled cabbage. The neighbours complained about it constantly, but the superintendent only stared them down and asked them, "What do you expect? The building's sixty years old."

Adoni climbed a flight of stairs, made her way to the splintered front door of the apartment, and put her ear to the wood.

Ida was playing Led Zeppelin.

Adoni opened the door and snuck inside. She slipped out of her wet shoes and leaned them up against the radiator. A single lamp was on in the furthest corner of the room. Ida's back was in shadow, and Adoni saw the white curl of smoke from her cigarette. She bent down and gently leaned her backpack against the closet. The dry air in the room tickled the back of her throat. She tried her best to stifle her cough, and failed. Ida turned her head. "Hey."

Adoni froze. "Hey."

"Come here and sit with me."

Adoni sat on the coffee table in front of her and waited. Ida's smile hung loosely on her flushed and puffy face. "How's your day?" she asked.

"Good."

"You learning?"

"Uh-huh."

"What're you learning?"

"English, math, history, and gym."

"Don't you know gym yet?" Ida laughed. "Dodge ball!"

Adoni cringed.

Ida took a long drag on her cigarette. "Yeah Donny. We're not long for this world." She leaned back. The couch springs creaked under her weight. "How're you supposed to know when you're young? I dunno. You tell them I did my best when they come. Because they're gonna ask you."

Ida leaned over and let Zeppelin's words evaporate in the bass and the thousands of strings. She held the bottle of beer she'd been drinking out to her daughter. "Finish that. I'm getting another one. Stay there."

Adoni swallowed the rest of the beer in one long swig and looked around the living room. In addition to spinning music, the old CD player served as a wedge to prop the window open and let in the night breeze. She shivered; the temperature was dropping. It would be a cold night, for sure.

Ida returned from the kitchen and held out the beer. "Twist that off." Adoni opened the bottle and handed it back. Ida put the beer to her lips and gulped. "God writes down the day you're born and the day you die in His book. He's got a system." Her loopy grin returned as she backed herself onto the couch again. "Getting pretty fat, eh?" She hooked a finger in one of the gaps in Adoni's shirt and tugged. "You gotta watch that. Maybe I'll put you on a diet. You don't wanna get fat, eh? I'm not getting you another shirt." Adoni shrugged. Ida poked out her tongue. "I mean it!"

She leaned back again as the song on the CD player changed and guitars started growling. "We're not long for this world, Donny. What're you gonna do? You know? But make sure you tell them I did my best. They're gonna ask you! But I'm just human. I'm good in my heart, you know? I'm good with it. I make mistakes, whatever. How're you supposed to know when you're young? That's what you tell them when they come. Right? Huh?"

Ida closed her eyes and sang along, off key. When she couldn't remember the lyrics, she hummed.

Adoni hadn't heard this song since the night Ida took her to the hamburger place around the corner from their old apartment. Faded by radio static, the melody crept around the room like a thief and tiptoed up the back of Adoni's neck. She held onto it, anchoring it down with her heels. In her head she wore black leather, and had smooth hair pouring over her back like an oil spill, and a flat belly with a silver stud in her navel, and the tops of her thighs didn't rub against each other when she walked through the streets in high heeled boots, and she could do absolutely anything she wanted to.

Ida returned to the table with burgers and fries, and when the first taste of pickles and salt had melted away, she told her they were moving again.

Pickles, onions, and florescent lights; they were as familiar to change as the changes themselves. That night Adoni added *Kashmir* to the list.

"It's never enough time, you know?" Ida said. "Sooner or later we're all alone. But I know how it's supposed to be like. Why should we sit around here when there's guys out there that go places every day and any time they want to? Huh? You tell me. You know, all I can think is maybe something I did way back in the day, you know? How're you supposed to know when you're young?"

"Mom."

"You tell me."

"Mom."

"What?"

"Where does my name come from?"

Ida laughed. "How the hell am I supposed to know? I didn't name you."

"Who named me?"

"Your dad did. I wanted to name you Jennifer."

"Why?"

"Jeez, why! I saw it in a magazine!" A string of mutes and skips interrupted the song on the player. Adoni stood up. "Where're you going?"

"The CD's messed up."

"Well yeah, turn it off and come here."

Adoni examined the CD under the lamp light. The disc was scratched up after spending nearly a year under the television stand. She wiped it on her sleeve.

"Because I make mistakes, eh?" Ida continued. "I do. I'm not gonna lie. Don't tell them the bad stuff, Donny. Because there's the bad stuff but there's good too, in me. You know? Huh?"

"Yeah."

"Yeah, you know."

Ida's smile slid off her face. The weight of her head pulled her over to one side. She started to snooze, but came to with a snort and straightened up. Her lucidity came and went for half an hour, until the threat of dropping the bottle in her hand woke her up once and for all. She looked at her daughter. "Want one?"

Adoni wiped her eyes, her cheeks, and her chin, with the back of her hand, with her sleeve.

"Huh?" Ida said, impatient.

"Yeah."

She went to the fridge and retrieved another beer. She tapped the neck of Adoni's bottle with the butt of hers.

Later, dressed in flannel pyjamas and a pair of thick socks, Adoni went to work on her room, pulling off her bed sheets, flipping her mattress, searching the corners, the doorjamb, the window sill. She looked for flat shiny bodies and spindly black legs, and the whiff of musty sweetness the website described. An infestation meant washing everything in the apartment with hot water and bleach. It meant load after load of laundry, boiled through twice and tied up in garbage bags. It meant throwing away everything that wasn't absolutely necessary, because there was no way to be sure where the dirty little monsters were hiding.

She picked up her overflowing laundry hamper, dumped the contents onto her unmade bed, and sifted through the pile of clothes, fully expecting to find a swarm of bed bugs among the tangled seams. There may have been a chance to exterminate the bugs if Ida had given her the usual weekly handful of loonies and quarters for the laundry machines. Instead the clothes were wrapped up and folded into each other for going on a month; plenty of time for laying and breeding.

"She stinks," she remembered one boy, an eighth grader, hissing when she passed him in the hallway. She remembered the way her cheeks burned when his friends clucked their agreement as they went into their classroom and took their seats. She asked Shabnam if it was true on the walk home.

"Yeah, you do a little," Shabnam replied in her haughty, mousy voice. "It's your clothes. Lots of people talk about it."

"The other kids talk about it?"

"Yeah."

"You could've told me!"

Shabnam frowned. "I didn't want to hurt your feelings. What do you want me to say, that you reek?"

"All the kids have been talking about me!"

"So I was doing you a favour!" she said. "God, you're a bitch!"

Adoni had been vigilant about laundry ever since.

Failing to find any evidence of an infestation, she stuffed everything back into the hamper and flipped the lid shut. Something in the next room hit the floor with a dull thud. Adoni heard jacket sleeves and zippers brushing against the back wall of the closet. Shoe boxes landed with a plop as they were tossed aside. Plastic and wire hangers clattered on the sagging rail. Ida was looking for one of the nearly dozen unfinished bottles of booze she kept tucked away in the back. After a few minutes of furious searching, the apartment went quiet again.

Adoni looked at the alarm clock on her night stand. It was 1:21 in the morning. She went to the door and put her hand on the knob.

Then she heard Ida rambling.

She scratched the back of her head with broken fingernails and leaned against the door. There was no way she was going out there now; not with Ida in another drunken stupor.

She turned back to her tiny room and was about to get into bed when, over the usual sound of night time traffic, she heard someone singing in the alley below. She went to the window and looked down.

A young man was crouched in the alleyway, next to the bricks and trash. Black clothes, cut and sewn at odd angles, swaddled his thin frame. He stuck two sets of skinny fingers into his thick blonde hair and fitfully worked them through. He shoved a bag of garbage with his foot and paced a small circle, sniffling and swinging his arms.

He leaned back against the wall and let out another string of lyric and melody. Then his voice divided into three.

Three voices that harmonized with each other, that rose and fell like animals. They crawled up Adoni's arms, brushed over her skin like warm, open palms. Instruments came from him next—a flute first, and then a bass. He sang in a language Adoni didn't recognize, yet, strangely, she still understood what the words meant. It was a song about hopelessness, about reaching out forever, about never being satisfied. It was a song about fear, about helplessness, about despair so deep it left a stain behind. He sang with conviction for a minute, and the music swelled with his breath.

But his voice—his voices—and his instruments faltered, and a gust of wind snuffed the music out.

He sniffled again and kicked the side of the building.

Adoni shouted at him.

"Hey!"

He jumped away from the wall and looked up. A streak of yellow light fell across his wet cheeks. He had a pair of diamond shaped eyes divided by a long and pointed nose. A dimple in each cheek edged his pinched lips. He crossed his arms over his chest and glared at her.

"Get your crazy ass away from my window!" she said.

He laughed, rankled and amused, and flipped her off with a flamboyant flick of his wrist.

She leaned on the sill and stuck her head all the way out the window. "How're you doing that?" she asked. He turned and walked face first into the wind. "I'm talking to you!"

"Fuck off!" he shouted back at her, before disappearing into the night.

Adoni ducked back into her room and climbed into bed with her socks still on. The young man's song soared through her, carried her away on a sumptuous spread of feathers and breeze. She hummed several bars of it into her pillow as if it were a secret. It reached back into her mind and shook a part of her she rarely touched—an untapped spring of courage. The tune carved into her thoughts so deeply she could remember its arc and swirl as if she'd been hearing it all her life. It kissed her temple and sent her to sleep.

She got an hour's rest before Ida's voice woke her up again.

"Donny!"

She glanced at the clock. It was past two in the morning.

Ida lay in bed on her back in a t-shirt and underwear, her legs propped up on a pile of clothes. An empty bottle of gin lay on the carpet next to the bed, and the bedroom reeked of the acidic funk of sweat. Adoni walked into the room on gingerly steps, picked the bottle up, and put it on the night table. "Mom."

"Open the window."

Adoni fought with the window for a minute, trying to get it to stick up in the jamb. Ida grunted and hooked a finger into her collar. "It's boiling in here!" Adoni finally used the bottle to prop the glass open.

Ida's brow twisted as she snatched a breath. Her head lolled from one side to the other until the breeze rushed in. "Why's it always so hot in here? Why do I have to be so hot all the time, and my kid?" She put her hand over her face.

"Mom."

"Hi baby."

The last time Ida called Adoni "baby" was last spring, a week before the move. Most of the old apartment had been packed away, aside from a few pots and pans, the CD player, and a few of Ida's favourite albums. Ida was playing Lynyrd Skynyrd and heartily singing along, off-key. The song, a waltz of guitar strings and piano keys, strolled leisurely around them as they crouched on the kitchen floor and taped the remaining cardboard boxes closed. Adoni sat on her haunches and concentrated on pulling the tape along and across every open seam. She caught Ida looking at her. A smile of pride crept up on her mother's lips. "Good job baby," she said, flashing her stained teeth. She ran her hand over Adoni's long black hair. "Nothing's gonna fall outta that, eh? I'm gonna need a blow torch to open up your boxes."

Adoni clung to that intimacy as the days got shorter and darker, as Ida lost her job and settled for another one that didn't pay as much, as cheques delivered to the landlord in good faith became certified cheques to battle an increasing wave of mistrust, as the bin under the sink in the new apartment filled with more and more silver tallboy cans, more and more green and amber bottles.

Adoni wasn't a baby anymore; she was old enough to take care of herself.

"Hi mom."

Ida put her clammy hand on Adoni's knee. "Because I think it's pretty," she said. "You know."

"What's pretty? Mom? What's pretty?" Ida stared at the ceiling. "What're you looking at?"

Ida squeezed her eyes shut. When they opened again, she was someone else.

"You," she said. "I'm looking at you."

"What did you want?" Adoni asked quietly.

"Where're my smokes?"

Adoni looked around the room and saw the empty pack lying next to the closet door. "You don't have any more."

"Go get my smokes."

"I have to go to the store to get more."

"Go get them."

"Can't you wait until tomorrow for your smokes?"

Ida grabbed hold of a hairbrush that was lying next to her and brought it down, slapping Adoni across the mouth. "Did I wait in the hospital for you?" she snapped. "Huh? 'Cause I didn't feel like it? I buy you all your shit!"

Adoni's eyes watered. "You're gonna fall asleep with one."

Ida wrinkled her nose and shook her head. She tried to raise herself up and swing her legs over the side of the bed, but after several futile rocks to the left and right she settled back down again. Her breathing came and went through her open mouth, on the tang of beer and gin. "My pants."

"What?"

Ida raised a heavy arm and flapped her hand towards the floor. Her jeans lay in a knot on the carpet. Adoni picked them up and retrieved her mother's wallet. Inside were two worn twenty dollar bills. She heard a clatter of loonies knocking into each other in the change purse. Judging by the sound, there were enough coins for several loads of laundry. Stealing them would be easy. Being caught later meant a harder blow across the face, and a blow delivered with much more accuracy too, since discovering the theft required a certain level of sobriety. Adoni picked out a twenty and put the wallet back.

"What size do you want? Mom? Mom? What size? I'm getting a large, okay?"

No answer.

Adoni went to her room to put on a t-shirt and a pair of jeans. Once dressed, she retrieved her running shoes, still wet, from the radiator and slipped them on. She pulled her jacket on and headed out into the street.

It finally felt like winter—frigid air sliced through her clothes, jolting her awake. The puddles of rain were already crusting over with ice. She turned her head against the wind, marched up the sidewalk, and popped into the all night convenience store on the corner. A thin man sat behind a counter piled high with lighters, condoms, beef jerky, and packs of gum. A foreign movie was playing on the tiny television next to the register. The speakers buzzed and crackled with static. Adoni stepped up to the counter and asked for a large pack of cigarettes. "ID," the clerk said.

"They're for my mom."

"Who's your mom?"

"The blonde lady who lives up the street," she said. "I come in with her all the time."

The man looked at her suspiciously. "Lots of ladies come in here," he said.

"My mom's gonna go to work soon and she needs a pack." He shook his head. Adoni let out a huff. "Seriously? Come on."

"I can't sell them to you without ID."

"Fine, I'm gonna tell her not to come back if you won't sell them to me."

He turned back to his television before she finished uttering the threat.

She returned to the sidewalk and looked up the street, searching for another illuminated sign, another trace of nightlife. Ida may have already drifted off to sleep and might not notice her missing cigarettes until well into afternoon the next day while Adoni was supposed to be at school. But there was also a chance of her waking up at the sound of the front door opening. Tonight it was a hair brush, but last week it had been a coffee cup, hurled at her from across the room. On other occasions a bottle, or a fork, served as the weapon of choice. The moments were creeping up on her more and more often. Adoni couldn't risk coming home empty handed.

She turned down a street and walked south, swallowing hard in the wind, towards the convenience store at the other end of the street. This time, when the clerk behind the counter, a younger guy with spiked hair and a cell phone wedged between his shoulder and ear, asked her for ID, she said "I forgot it," and tilted her head to one side, trying to make it look like a usual oversight. The clerk, too occupied with the voice on the line, tossed the pack across the counter. She grabbed them and headed back to the apartment.

She hummed softly to keep herself company on the way back home, something discordant at first, meant solely to keep out the cold, until it morphed into the young man's tune from earlier, and came out of her mouth like a stream of silk and lace. Somewhere deep within, its sadness was a part of her, its guileless yearning a welcomed scrap of truth; someone else knew what it was like to be outside in the cold with numb fingers and a head full of beer buzz. She cleared the sidewalk and made her way up to the front door of her apartment.

A voice shot out from the alley.

"Who are you?"

Adoni's head snapped to the right. The young man from earlier was standing there, half in light and half in shadow.

"What?" she said.

"The song you're singing."

"How'd you do all that stuff earlier? Do you have an iPhone or something and it makes your voice all crazy?"

He marched towards her. "Are you listening to me?"

"What?"

"Sylvester sent you, didn't he?"

"I don't even know who that is."

"You can't fool me. Tell Sylvester he'll have to be cleverer than that."

"Who the hell is that? I don't even know."

"So changelings can come through the agate now, eh?" he said. "Another gift from Ansgar? It doesn't surprise me." He stopped a few inches away from her. With a straight back he was easily six feet tall. "Where did you learn that song? Did Ansgar teach it to him?"

"I heard you singing it before."

"You know it too well to have just overheard me."

"I have a good memory for tunes."

"Do you know the words?"

"No."

He shoved his hands into his wide coat pockets and turned his nose up at her. "You'll do well not to sing that song again. You have no idea what it means. Consider yourself warned."

"What's wrong with you, man? You talk like an asshole."

He smirked. "Charming. Really. Anything else?"

She didn't answer.

He shuffled back a few paces, still grinning, still knowing something she didn't know, still smugly keeping it from her.

A moment later, the world split apart at his heels.

Adoni shielded her eyes as a crack of light became a searing white blast and ripples of blue and orange fire formed what looked to be a gaping doorway to a world beyond. The young man turned and walked into the centre of the flare, his body and black clothes now an iris, a cat's eye surrounded by a wily flame. Before Adoni could call him back to her side he was gone, sewn up beyond her reach when the air stitched itself back together.

"Shit..." she whispered, fumbling in her pocket for the pack of cigarettes, ripping the cellophane off with her chattering teeth. She put a smoke to her lips and set the end on fire.

Chapter Two

Adoni's alarm clock went off at 7:30 am. She curled away from the edge of the bed, reached her arm out from under the warmth of her blankets, snapped off the alarm, and closed her eyes again. She wanted to skip over the entire day and wake up when it was summer.

Next door, Ida was silent. No doubt she was sleeping off another headache and sour stomach. Hangovers meant Adoni had permission to skip school. Her mother would be grateful she was around, would ask her for a mug of soup and the quilt from the closet. They would go through old photo albums and laugh at the clothes and hairstyles and sepia-tinged memories Adoni's grandmother had handed down.

Adoni's grandmother, Janine, had been a tall woman, big and broad shouldered, with unruly hair and a mouth full of chipped teeth. Just like Ida, she was pale and blonde, and looked nothing like Adoni, whose brown skin and black eyes came from the other, unfamiliar side of her family. Janine died when Adoni was too young to remember much about her, so Ida filled in the blanks.

"There's Grandma," Ida said, on a spring day they both were hiding from. "She had some husband when I was born, some bald guy. I think his name was Eddie or something. Some stupid drunk she picked up and they got married and got drunk together a lot and maybe six months later she divorced him for being a stupid drunk, eh?" She laughed and sipped her alphabet soup. "Birds of a feather, you know. She got married again when I was fourteen or something, to a guy named Bill. He was an all right guy but, you know, he didn't want to put up with her forever, so he left. He used to do all kinds of stuff around the house, you know, he really tried, but she used to be... she was unreasonable sometimes. She'd scream at you for no reason. No wonder people wanted to get away from her, eh? So did I."

"Everybody looks nice," Adoni said.

"Yeah, sure they do. You know when somebody says 'say cheese' before a picture? It was like pointing a gun at us." Her fingers spread and formed the barrel of a gun. She poked them against Adoni's temple. "Say cheese! *Bang!*" She smoothed her daughter's hair back with a hearty palm, lifted the album up and squinted at the pasted-on smiles and polyester outfits. "I don't know any of these people. I guess they're relatives."

Adoni's excuse for skipping school that morning was what she had seen and heard the night before—the young man's accusation, his angry green eyes and barbed threat, his disappearance in a fantastic split of air and fire and light. Telling her mother might make her angry; exaggeration annoyed Ida, who took it as a sign of someone making fun of her. The only option left was to sit with last night's every moment, all throughout the day, to study and try to make sense of it.

Adoni heard the woman across the hall wearily responding to her four year old son's bawling. The boy, Tyler, was known as a wailing terror throughout the building. She couldn't remember seeing him happy a single time. The only thing he seemed to know how to do was scream. When Tyler wasn't screeching he was tugging on his mother's sleeve and demanding to be noticed, his voice pulsing like an ambulance siren. The more his mother ignored his pleas for attention, the more insistent he became. His father was hardly ever around. Adoni thought he was some kind of contractor or construction worker. Whenever she saw him his glare was sharp and cruel, and his knuckles were cut up.

Adoni had only had one interaction with Tyler. A few weeks before, just after Halloween, she came home from the drugstore with her pockets full of stolen perfume samples. Tyler was sitting alone in front of his apartment, wearing stained blue pyjamas that covered his feet. Adoni had never seen the boy without his mother before. "Hey Tyler," she said. "It's late, eh? Where's your mom?"

He turned his head and gawked at her as if she weren't quite real. "Where's your mom, Tyler?" she asked again. He didn't answer. She huffed and dug her keys out of her pocket. "Okay, so have fun out here."

Something fell from the jumble of metal in her hand as she reached for the lock. It knocked against the linoleum and bounced into the middle of the hallway—a bite sized chocolate bar left over from Halloween. Tyler rose from his spot on the floor and waddled over to it with a bent back and one hand outstretched. "Have it if you want," Adoni said when she saw his determination. He picked the candy up and turned it over and over, pinching at the wrapper with skinny fingers. "Want me to open it for you?" She bent down to retrieve it.

He whined and stepped back quickly, cringing and grasping the candy bar tightly around the middle. He stuck the end of it in his mouth and gnawed a corner of the wrapper off with his front teeth. He spat out the plastic and finally freed the chocolate by splaying his fingers through the hole he had created. The entire thing disappeared in his mouth, where it melted into a mound of sticky caramel and peanuts. The wider the mess spread over his tongue and between his teeth, the harder it was to keep behind his lips. A stream of chocolate and drool dripped from one corner of his mouth and oozed down the front of his pyjamas.

Tyler's mother yanked the apartment door open and bounded into the hallway, her eyes wide, her face wan. She grabbed him with one wide swoop of her arm—an action so familiar she could do it without looking—turned him around, and landed an open palm as hard as she could on his backside. His face twisted up and a howl erupted from his gaping mouth. The chocolate mush spilled out and landed on the floor. His mother snapped at him and disappeared behind her door with Tyler squawking in her arms.

The next morning the superintendent tacked a note onto the bulletin board, demanding the tenants keep their pets from defecating in the shared spaces.

"Someone's gonna call child services on them," Ida said one night over pizza. "She better watch it."

"Are you gonna do it?"

"No, I just know how they do it. She's gonna piss someone off, watch."

"I feel bad for her."

Ida finished off her crust. "Yeah," she muttered.

Adoni growled and stuffed her head into her pillow to drown out the noise. *Why the hell does he cry so much? Spoiled brat. His mom should put her foot in his ass and shut him up.*

Eventually Tyler's cries turned to quiet whimpering, and his mother's condolences faded into silence. Adoni fell asleep again, and the morning slipped into afternoon.

At twelve o'clock, she heard voices at the front door.

"… Two months."

"I know, and I'd write you a cheque right now only I ran out of cheques, right. But I have to go to the bank first thing Monday."

"Ida."

Tall, thin, and old, the superintendent's job consisted of ignoring requests for repairs, informing residents of complaints being brought against them, and demanding the rent. Seeing him, hearing him, meant something was wrong. Adoni got out of bed and opened her bedroom door a crack. Ida stood at the door, shifting her weight from one foot to the other. Adoni saw the bald crescent of the superintendent's head beyond her mother's matted hair. The hallway lights glinted off his scalp.

"You got NSF on your last cheque and you didn't give me one for the month before, so…" He let his sentence trail off.

"Yes, yes."

"I mean…"

"Yes."

"If it's another month you're gonna miss, I'm gonna have to change the locks."

"I have the money, though, like I said."

"I can't let you give another NSF cheque, okay? Get a certified cheque and bring it to head office on Monday."

"All right, yeah."

"No later than Monday."

"Yes, yes, I'll get a certified cheque over there as soon as I can."

"No later than Monday."

"Yes. Yeah. Like I said, I have the money."

"Okay, well, I can't dispute that with you."

"You know the guys upstairs are dealing, eh?"

"Well…"

Adoni shrank away from the door and grabbed her jeans and the last clean t-shirt she had out of her drawer. She stole into the washroom as Ida changed the subject from the dealers upstairs to the neighbours who dumped their garbage—a broken futon, a toaster, and ripped up baby clothes—in the back of the building when they thought no one was looking. The superintendent sniggered. "Well, those people, you know what kind of people those are," he said.

The water pressure in the building was so low showering was like standing beneath someone's leisurely stream of piss against a tree trunk. Adoni massaged a handful of shampoo into her hair and swayed back and forth beneath the shower head, waiting patiently for the suds to rinse away. She hummed a few bars of the young man's song, and once again it swam through her blood and seized the back of her brain. She was high on a hill, ablaze with lightning, wrapped in wind, bending the elements, squeezing them together into shiny nuggets and hurling them into space, where they hung as bright new stars in the sky.

She dried herself off, dressed, opened the bathroom door, and stepped into the hallway-

into Ida, who reeled back and slapped her daughter across the face.

Adoni backed away until her calves were pressed against the toilet. Ida landed another blow to her head, her shoulder, her ear. "What the hell are you still doing here?" Adoni braced herself and cowered against the wall, pressed her cheek against the pink and yellow wallpaper. "Why the hell aren't you at school? I bought you that stupid uniform for nothing!" Another slap on the cheek, on the back of her head when she bent to protect her face, two, three, four on her forearms, one to her belly. Ida stopped; her face was flushed and sweaty. Adoni hung her head and didn't move. "A hundred and twenty bucks!" Ida said. "A hundred and twenty bucks, you know! Just for a lousy sweater! Yeah? Why the hell do I even bother? Why do I bother?"

Ida stuck her finger in her cringing daughter's face. "You're not gonna sit around here all day, you know. You're outta here in ten minutes. Get dressed and get your ass to school. I have things to do." She slammed the bathroom door closed.

Adoni's mouth stretched wide, her bottom lip rolled over, and a thin sound, barely audible, leaked out of her. She covered her face with her hand and cried as quietly as she could as the streamlets of water dripped down the drain.

Adoni hated walking through the halls when other students were around. They were like packs of vultures perched over a fallen gazelle, waiting for the final twitch of life before springing and tearing out the insides. They braced each other and whispered, their eyes following her from one end of the hall to the other. Rumours went around Assumption like the flu, contaminating everyone, so it wasn't unusual for a bunch of students to band together against a common enemy, whether they knew her or not. The trick was figuring out who had started the rumour in the first place, and then forcing them to fight; losers always lost all their cred.

Adoni got to school during third period, when she was supposed to be in math class. Of all the subjects she had to take, math was absolutely her least favourite. She couldn't wrap her head around the numbers, the formulas, the theories, and word problems. It didn't help that she had to sit next to Caroline, a beautiful creature with blonde hair and creamy skin who loved to get into verbal altercations with the boys in the class. Being a girl, and a blonde one at that, Caroline made it a point to tell everyone who would listen how good she was at the subject, and how stupid the girls-aren't-good-at-math stereotype was. The boys who sat in front of her picked up on this and doubled their efforts to put her down, constantly pestering her with girl jokes and blonde jokes to get a reaction out of her. And react she did, to every single snotty quip they came up with. Occasionally they tried to engage Adoni in their arguments. Adoni didn't know whose side to take—she didn't want to make enemies out of the boys, and she didn't know how to prove Caroline right, even though she agreed with her, since she didn't understand the subject herself—so she kept her chin down and kept quiet.

She shuffled into class just as Mr. Peck was explaining a new formula. It must have had something to do with last night's homework, judging from the students' reaction when he spelled the answer out on the white board. "I *knew* it. I was totally gonna write that too, eh? I should've got that!"

It was always the same few kids humming and hawing and fussing about which answers they knew and which ones they should have known. *Liars*, she thought. *No way they'd've got the same answer.* She hadn't even attempted the ten problems Mr. Peck assigned the day before. Integers, square roots, equivalents; she'd never heard of a single adult needing to know any of it. Ida had never once mentioned trigonometry when figuring out how much money she had left in her bank account. All anyone had to know was how much money would be saved on a sale item in a grocery store, but they never taught anything as useful as that.

Caroline was at her desk, gnawing on the end of her pencil. Adoni slipped into her seat and immediately felt the strain of her pants on her belly. Ida was right; she had gained weight in the last few weeks. If she didn't watch it she'd outgrow the only pair of uniform pants she owned. Her mother had hissed through her teeth when she heard how much a pair cost through the official website. Caroline was slender, a sporty girl who played on the basketball and volleyball teams, and only wore kilts to school, since she had the long legs to carry off a skirt. Adoni stole a glimpse of the girl's flat belly, compared it with her own bulging flesh.

She bit her lip and stared ahead at the white board. Filled with green dry-erase markings, it looked more like an ancient scroll than a math lesson. Occasionally Mr. Peck paused from his swift, whirlwind style and asked the students if they had any questions. The smarter students snorted whenever a question was asked. They despised having to stop so someone could have something explained to them, especially if it was, as one student put it, "the same dumb kid every time." Adoni didn't want to be that same dumb kid. Instead of paying attention, she let her eyes glaze over and her mind wander.

There was the split in the darkness, opening wide, and the young man disappearing through it. Adoni had never seen magic like that before; all she knew of magic was sleight of hand and conjurers with black hair wearing leather pants, just practice made perfect by nimble fingers or, failing that, camera tricks. Adoni's leg bounced up and down beneath her desk. She wished she knew the young man's name, who he was, what he was doing, and where he vanished to when he stepped into that flame. She couldn't keep this to herself. She had to tell someone. Shabnam was the only choice.

She and Shabnam called themselves friends, even though they didn't have very much in common. Shabnam was pretty, at least to Adoni, and though she wasn't one of the popular girls at school she nevertheless enjoyed a blissful anonymity from the cliques and bullies. She and Adoni fought often, from little squabbles to full-fledged shouting matches, and pulled no punches when it came down to hurling insults that cut to the quick. There were times when they went weeks without speaking to each other. Adoni usually made the first effort to apologize, and they would tentatively resume their friendship. Shabnam was the only person who seemed remotely interested in what Adoni thought, and though she only listened to her out of vague curiosity, it was better than being ignored. Anything was better than being ignored.

Mr. Peck finished the lesson and gave the students fifteen minutes at the end of class to get a head start on their homework. His routine was to check everyone's homework at the start of the class—his way of logging participation marks—but since Adoni had come to class late he came by her desk, red binder and pen in hand, towards the end of the period.

She didn't have anything against Mr. Peck. He was a small man who spoke with a thick accent the students made fun of behind his back. He always slicked his hair back and wore tan suits to class. It wasn't his way to come down hard on any student, regardless of how clueless they were or how little they participated. All he did when one of his students disappointed him was shake his head, as if he were too tired to fight.

"Where's your homework?"

"I don't have it."

"Did you finish it?"

"Yeah," she lied, "I just don't have it."

"Where is it?"

"I left it at home."

"What good is it going to do you there?"

"Nothing."

There was the head shake, and the sigh. He made a mark on her record. The bell rang.

Adoni grabbed her things and headed for Shabnam's locker.

Fourth period was supposed to be English class, but she had no intention of going. The English teacher, Ms. Hanks, was a bland woman with a voice so low and calming it never failed to put Adoni to sleep. At first Ms. Hanks seemed amused by her student's failure to keep her eyes open. As time wore on, however, she became less and less tolerant. The last time Adoni had fallen asleep she let out a huge snore that set the other kids laughing and got her sent to the office, where the vice principal gave her a speech about getting the proper number of hours' sleep a night. He offered to let her rest on the cot in the health room during her lunch break if she needed to, but if she spent the period sleeping she couldn't bum a part of someone's lunch and would have to wait until she got home to eat again.

The halls were full of students rushing to get to their next class or shuffling out to the parking lot to smoke their cigarettes. Adoni leaned up against Shabnam's locker and waited. Shabnam walked everywhere as slowly as possible, her way of biding time and not being chastised for loitering. She rounded the corner just as the first warning bell sounded, her backpack drooping off her shoulders. The hem of her white shirt hung over her kilt, which made the uniform look a lot more jaunty and casual. She didn't look too excited to see Adoni, but she never looked particularly excited about anything.

"Hey," she said.

"Hey. What've you got for lunch?"

"I'm going home for lunch."

"Can I come with you?"

Shabnam kissed her teeth. "Fine." She unloaded her textbooks and lifted her jacket off the hook. Her hair was so black and shiny a blue tint bounced off of every strand. Adoni wished she had hair as thick and lustrous as Shabnam's. Instead her hair was dry, brittle, and frizzed out when it was humid or when it got wet. Shabnam's hands were still decorated with the intricate henna pattern for the wedding she had attended the weekend before; romantic orange and brown swirls, flowers, and teardrops gave a lucid poetry to her skin. She told Adoni the pattern would come off in a couple of weeks. "That sucks," Adoni said. "It's so pretty."

Shabnam secured her locker and muttered, "Come on." They left the building through the side door so Adoni wouldn't risk getting caught skipping.

Shabnam lived a block away from Assumption, in a brown stone apartment sandwiched between two houses. Adoni loved going to Shabnam's place. Her mother, Kirupa, was a stay-at-home mom who took care of her newborn son and cooked rich Indian dishes laden with fragrant spices and cream. She always insisted Adoni eat something while she was there. Kirupa was soft spoken and gentle, and the words she used were inexhaustibly elegant. Adoni wasn't just *welcome*; she was *most welcome*, and Kirupa *most definitely* looked forward to hosting her again.

Save for one evening a year earlier, Adoni never brought Shabnam to her apartment. Ida couldn't stand the girl and told Adoni she wasn't welcome back. "You wanna hang out with her, go to her place," she said. "That kid's using you, I can tell." Even if she had been welcome, Adoni wouldn't want to invite her over again. The place was a sty most nights. There was never anything to snack on. And last, but not least, there was Ida's ever-fluctuating temper.

Adoni smelled Kirupa's curry the moment she and Shabnam stepped up to the apartment door. Her stomach growled. She tried to cover the sound with a cough, but Shabnam's ears were too sharp to fool. "Oh my god, what was *that*? Don't you ever eat before you come over?"

"I missed lunch."

"We're always feeding you! Tell your mom to buy some groceries once in a while!"

She put her key in the lock and opened the door.

Shabnam's apartment was small but comfortable, with newly shellacked wooden floors and family photos hanging on white walls. The couches in the living room were covered with fleecy throws and pillows, and there wasn't a speck of dust to be seen on any surface.

Kirupa was singing to the baby in the next room, something soft and sweet. Shabnam dropped her bag on the couch and shouted, "Ma!"

"Lower your voice please, Shabnam."

Shabnam kissed her teeth and lifted the lid off of the skillet. "So I guess you're gonna want some?"

"If it's okay."

"Well, I'm not gonna just eat in front of you and make you watch me."

"Okay."

"Want some rice too?"

"Okay."

Shabnam grabbed a couple of plates out of the kitchen cupboards and filled them with two heaping scoops of rice and two ladles of curry. She put the plates on the kitchen table with a loud knock and sat down. Adoni joined her, tucking herself away at the other end. After a few mouthfuls she leaned over her plate and spoke to Shabnam in a low voice. "I have to tell you something."

"What?"

"Something freaky happened to me yesterday."

"Okay."

"And I wasn't drunk, so don't even say it, okay?"

"Fine, what?"

"The other day I was at home and I heard this guy. He was singing in the alley outside, and his voice was really weird, like he was a voice and instruments and stuff, all at the same time. Like, I don't even know how to describe it. Like he was magic or something."

Shabnam smirked. "Yeah."

"I'm serious."

"Sure."

"And I saw him later and he was really pissed off at me for some reason. He kept saying something about some guy named Sylvester and I don't even know who that is."

"What's this guy's name?"

"I don't know."

"Does he live around here?"

"No, because he said a bunch of stuff I didn't understand, and he turned around and, like…"

She stopped as Kirupa stepped into the kitchen. Dressed in a red and green kurta, her long braided hair swinging as she walked, she could have passed for a queen in a fairy tale. She saw the girls sitting at the table and smiled. "Good, you've helped yourselves. Hello Adoni, how are you this afternoon?"

"Good."

"Are you enjoying the dish?"

"Yes."

"Help yourself to as much as you like, you're most welcome to it. Shabnam, I'm going out to fetch some things, all right? Please look after your brother until I get back."

"You can't be too long, I've got class," Shabnam grumbled.

"I won't be longer than half an hour."

Kirupa slipped on a pair of boots and her long winter coat. Adoni waited for the latch to click shut behind her so she could resume her story. "So anyway..."

Shabnam's cellphone rang; a piercing jingle with heavily auto-tuned lyrics. She put the phone to her ear. "Hello?" Her grimace disappeared. "Yeah. I'm on lunch. No, I've got French after. Last period French sucks. Yeah it does!" She left Adoni sitting at the table and sat down in the living room.

Adoni finished off her plate and waited for Shabnam to end her call, although she didn't seem interested in speeding up the conversation. Instead she stretched out on the couch and switched the television on, tuning it to a popular soap opera. Adoni rose from the table and walked up the short hallway to the baby's room.

Shabnam's brother lay on his back in his crib, gurgling and stuffing his fists into his mouth. He had a head full of tightly curled black hair and a dimple in his chin deep enough to hold a dime. Adoni stood over him and inhaled the lovely clean smell of baby powder and fabric softener. She wasn't used to seeing babies so clean, so perfect. The babies in her neighbourhood were like Tyler; constantly screaming and dressed in soiled pyjamas and being pushed around in flimsy strollers with rusted or broken wheels.

Shabnam and her brother had it good, with a mom like Kirupa looking after their every whim. It would be nice to have a mom like her, she thought; someone sweet-natured and eloquent, someone who cooked and took care of things around the house, someone who was friendly to guests and didn't hide in her bedroom until they were gone.

Adoni smiled down at the little thing, admiring his toes, his nose, his chubby arms and legs. He coughed and let out a whine, and a moment later he was crying. She stuck her head out of the bedroom and called out to Shabnam. "Your brother's crying."

"What?"

"Your brother's crying."

"Just leave him, he always cries." Adoni heard her grunt a quick "sorry" into her cellphone.

Adoni returned to the side of the crib. The baby curled his legs up tightly against his chest, clenched his fists, and continued to weep. She frowned. Kirupa wasn't going to be back for a while; she couldn't let the poor thing wail himself sick. She reached into the crib and lifted him up into her arms. "Come on, your mom's gonna be back soon. It's okay." She paced around the room, bouncing him gently, trying her best to soothe him. For a while it seemed to do the trick; he sputtered and sucked back a breath, and eventually his crying dulled to a sniffle.

It had been so long since Ida had held Adoni, or given her one of her wonderful bear hugs. When Adoni was little Ida used to walk around the apartment pretending to be Captain Cuddle, the Hugging Pirate, with her arms spread out wide, hollering, "Whoever I catches I hugs!" Adoni used to dart back and forth in front of her, pretending it was a babyish game and she didn't want to be caught but relishing the moment her mother's arms closed around her and lifted her off the floor.

She looked down at the baby. He was still fussing, but at least he seemed to appreciate her being there. Adoni hummed softly to him, a haphazard melody she made up as she went along, something maternal and shapeless, until it occurred to her; she knew a tune that might take his mind off of whatever was troubling him. She leaned in close, nose to nose, and hummed the young man's melody.

Shabnam's brother cried out again, louder than before.

Adoni tried shushing him, tried singing, but he was no longer in the mood to be soothed. His screaming reached its zenith as Shabnam finished her phone call and stomped into the room. "What are you doing? Put him down!"

"He was crying."

"You probably made him start, coming in here! He was sleeping! You're not my sister, why're you picking him up?"

"You were on the phone."

Shabnam snatched him out of her arms and put him back in his crib. His legs curled up again and he wailed with even greater force. "You don't just go into someone's place and start touching things. You've got no manners, Donny! Doesn't your mom teach you anything?"

Adoni gritted her teeth. "Don't talk about my mom."

"Well who's supposed to teach you what's proper or not? She didn't tell you not to invite yourself over to people's places either, did she? You guys are low class!"

"Leave my mom alone!"

"Jeez, go back to school Donny, you've already had your lunch!" She put her hand on her brother's belly, trying to appear concerned and affectionate. "Poor baby! Were you sleeping?"

Adoni glared at Shabnam, locked her knees back and readied herself for a shouting match. "Yeah, you wanna talk about low class? Who stays on the phone when they've got someone over?"

"Someone who doesn't want a guest to start with!" Shabnam snapped. She lifted her cellphone, dialled a number, and put it to her ear. "Sorry. Yeah, so she goes right into my brother's room and, like, picks him up!"

Adoni hadn't realized she'd been the topic of Shabnam's conversation. Her jaw went slack, and she strained to hear what Shabnam was telling the person on the other end of the line. Shabnam went back to the living room and resumed her position on the couch, her relaxed posture an added insult to Adoni, whose shoulders had gone stiff. "Yeah, like she's family or something! Oh, and she finished off, like, half my lunch too! Because she's a mooch, that's why!"

The word stuck in Adoni's gut. It was bad enough having to pretend their friendship was anything other than a convenience, a relationship built on matching schedules and grim curiosity. It was worse to be called on it, with such hatred, as if Shabnam didn't know she was guilty of it too.

She grabbed the cellphone out of Shabnam's hand and threw it against the floor. The back of the case and the battery were knocked free and skidded across the hardwood. "Get out of my house, spaz!" Shabnam yelled. "You're buying me a new phone if it's broken!"

"Bitch!" Adoni snarled back. She grabbed her things and let the apartment door slam shut behind her.

Chapter Three

Adoni didn't want to return to school. She had no idea who had called Shabnam's cellphone, but they had plenty of time to spread a story about her before she got back to Assumption. There was no use going back to class, either. She hadn't done any homework and wouldn't be able to sit still knowing Shabnam was on a gossiping rampage. There was no way to predict how long this fight would last. She pressed her lips together tightly and headed to Nelly's.

She spent the rest of the afternoon in the coffee shop, dressed in her expensive school uniform, her running shoes, and her purple coat. At six o'clock it started to snow, tiny pellet-like flakes that stung her face. Still leery of bed bugs lurking in the linens, she hoped Ida had had the chance to get to a laundry during the day. By the time she reached her building the short flight of steps out front was covered in a thin layer of ice flakes that crunched under her heels as she climbed.

Adoni put her ear to her front door; no music tonight. She stepped inside and found the windows shut and the apartment especially muggy. She put her backpack and coat down on the floor in the closet and slipped off her shoes. Thursday was Ida's usual grocery day, and Adoni was familiar with the staples she brought home in plaid shopping bags. Canned soup was one of them, and crackers, and milk, and sliced white bread.

She went to the kitchen and opened the cupboards. Ida had indeed gone to the grocery store—her purse and wallet were still on the counter—but she hadn't brought back as many cans as she usually did; only three, compared with the usual six or eight. She opened a can of chicken noodle soup, poured it into her mug with half a can of water, and put it into the microwave for two minutes while she looked for the crackers. There was only one box of macaroni and cheese this time, only two tins of baked beans. She opened the fridge. Ida had remembered the milk but not much else; no bags of frozen veggies, no concentrated orange juice. The microwave shut itself off with a sharp beep. She took her soup mug out and held it in the dish towel in her palm.

On the side of the microwave, tucked away and half in shadow, were two bottles of liquor and a six pack of beer. The liquor was the hard stuff; whisky and gin. Her heart sank. Half of the gin was gone.

She felt Ida's fist before the soup mug dropped to the floor and shattered, sending chipped ceramic, hot liquid, and noodles everywhere. Adoni brought her shoulder up to protect her ear and shrank as Ida shoved her against the counter. "Where were you today?" she snapped. "And don't you lie to me!"

"At school."

"Yeah, I'm gonna believe you!"

"I was."

"Then how come that teacher Ms. Hanks called me and asked where you were at this afternoon, eh? And I had to say I don't know, huh?" Adoni didn't answer. "What'd I tell you this morning?"

Adoni's throat seized up. She thought Ida would be satisfied with a partial truth. "I went to Shabnam's for lunch."

Ida teetered back on her heels. "You know I hate that kid! I hate that kid! Why're you going over to her place? Her and her stuck-up mom!"

Adoni squinted and started to shake. "Her mom gave me lunch."

"Yeah, and she should, too! What'd you get that kid for her birthday?"

"A DVD."

"Yeah, *I* got her a DVD, it's my money. What'd she get you for your birthday, huh?"

"We were in a fight."

"Yeah, she's always in a fight with you when it's her turn, little user. Why do you hang out with that kid?" Adoni shrugged. Ida wasn't satisfied. "I don't want you hanging out with that kid, understand? With her smug grin, coming in here and judging us!"

"We're in a fight again."

"Good! Stay in a fight!"

"She's my friend."

"Huh?"

Adoni could barely speak. "She's my friend."

"Make some other friends!"

She blinked back a pair of hot tears. "I can't."

Ida rolled her eyes and turned away. "That's why nobody likes you! Because you're a doormat! What, you're gonna kiss her ass now?"

Adoni's body went hard as a rock.

Ida looked down at the broken mug and spilled soup. Her red cheeks, the sweat on her forehead, said it all. She pulled back and slapped Adoni's arm, her side, her neck, her cheek. The blows were so fast, so automatic and consistent, Adoni simply gave up, leaned back against the counter, and waited for her to finish.

Ida delivered her last smack into Adoni's ear. She muttered, "Clean it up," and trudged back to her room, slamming the bedroom door behind her.

Adoni picked up the larger pieces of ceramic, wrapped them in newspaper, and tossed them into the trash. She ran the faucet and soaked a tea towel with water, and soon the noodles and broth were on their way down the drain.

The hard stuff usually sent Ida over the edge. It was too strong. She'd tried it herself a few months ago, picking up the last swig of a bottle of cheap whisky her mother overlooked. She didn't like how it tasted but loved the warm feeling it left, a reassuring pang she knew anyone could get used to if they tried hard enough.

Adoni wrung the sopping dish towel into the sink and whipped it viciously against the tap.

Ida was trying hard enough. Adoni hated her for it.

She went into the living room and sat on the couch, listening, waiting. She remembered something Ida had muttered the night before—*why should we sit around here when there's guys out there that go places every day and any time they want to?*

The alcohol took away whatever eloquence there may have been in her words, but Adoni still understood what she meant. Other families had freedom. Other mothers were on the phone with friends and filled their homes with the joyful swing of laughter. Other daughters were surrounded by clean floors, comfortable clothes, and fresh scents, and had bellies full of food. They understood school and the things it was trying to teach, they understood what was important for their futures, and why.

She ground her teeth and bounced her leg up and down. She wanted to have regular conversations with normal people, people who didn't hold her heart in a vise's grip and squeeze when she was out of their control. She wanted an apartment on the other side of town, painted bright colours, smelling of oranges and vibrating with music. She didn't want to feel trapped anymore, didn't want to feel like she wasn't welcome.

Ida's wallet was still on the kitchen counter, unguarded. It wouldn't be long before she passed out drunk. Adoni waited until the silence was absolutely unbroken before rising from the couch and seizing the neatly folded bills.

Fifty dollars. It wasn't enough, but it would have to do.

She went to the front closet, slipped on her running shoes, her purple jacket, stepped into the hallway, closed the door behind her, and put her key into the lock.

The bolt gently slipped into place, and that was it. She was free.

She crossed the hall to the apartment entrance, down the steps and into the night.

It was eerie, standing in the cold and darkness, knowing her task now was to find a place to camp out, away from vagrants, away from the police. The women's shelter was a few streets over. She'd passed it a hundred times. Its façade was built with light grey bricks, and it had several bulletin boards covered with community listings for shared accommodations and homemade help wanted fliers. She didn't want to spend the night there if she could avoid it. The stories that came out of the place weren't pleasant; women being robbed in the middle of the night, drug addicts and alcoholics wailing in their sleep as they tried to kick their habits. She could last a night or two on her own, so long as she stuck to well-lit places that stayed open all night. Nelly's was the perfect choice, and she had cash in her pocket to buy something if she got hungry. She was on her way to the coffee shop when she caught a wisp of movement in the alley next to her apartment building.

She saw someone's figure recede between the buildings. From the straight and arrogant slope of his shoulders to his casual swagger, she knew exactly who it was. She crept to the opening of the alley and watched him sidle up to the bricks.

He put a hand through his hair, and sang out.

This time the tune was different, filled with joy. The notes flew up and around each other, and little fingers reached out and poked her, begging her to get closer to their source.

She locked her knees back. *Stay right there,* she thought, *or he'll see you.*

The music swelled, celebrated. His song divided itself into two, three, four melodies that braided into each other like a rope and reached through an open window overhead.

Someone heard the singing and shuffled to the broken door in footie pyjamas. That someone pushed the broken door open and made his way down the front steps, over the soaked front lawn, and around the side, to the alley.

At the sight of him, the young man knelt and held out his hand.

Tyler stuck a finger into his mouth and tugged his bottom lip down, interrupting the smile on his thirsty lips. The young man rolled his wrist, urging the boy to come forward. Tyler followed the hand, the music. He folded himself against the chest of the young man, who scooped him up and turned to go, back through the split in the universe.

Whatever world he belonged to, wherever it was, it was better than here, better than now.

When his back was turned, and before it sealed behind him, Adoni ran towards the light, took a deep breath, said a quick goodbye, and broke on through.

The air surrounding her bent and melted. The alley wavered back and forth. Her ears rang and popped. She floated up, rushed forward, grappled a wave of nausea and wrestled it back down in her guts.

There was a sonic boom, then static and noise, then a slam against the ground. Each element kicked the rest of her world away and welcomed her to somewhere else.

Somewhere in between.

Chapter Four

She blinked hard and looked around. Four cedar pillars, over twelve feet high, with faces and bodies and intricate knots carved into their oily wood, surrounded her in what she now could tell was a clearing in the middle of a thick forest. A roaring fire topped each pillar and served as a giant torch, casting light onto the snow-covered ground. A giant ivory moon hung full in the night sky, and beyond its pale light hung tapestries of stars—millions of them twinkling and dancing, and not a single cloud there to spoil the view. The smell in the air was of cedar and pine trees, sulphur, and melting wax.

All around the clearing were rows of tiny log cabins, each a perfect little dwelling for one or two people, a sanctuary straight from an old-fashioned Christmas greeting card. They each had a pointed roof and a stone chimney puffing out curls of sweet-smelling smoke. Blankets of snow settled thick on their shingles, and rows of icicles served as shimmering gables above their doors and windows. Orange light fell from their glass panes and pooled on the ground beneath the window ledges. Each log cabin bore a plaque with a brass numeral, hammered to the left of the door, lit by a small gas flame that flickered in the breeze. A second plaque, fixed above every door, displayed a word Adoni couldn't quite make out.

A large chalet of wood and stone stood at the furthest end of the clearing, away from the cabins. Two storeys high and decorated with a trellised balcony running beneath the top row of windows, it too looked like something out of a holiday fantasy. Piles of chopped kindling, an axe leaning against the logs, and empty barrels flanked the chalet walls, and in the centre of the clearing a bucket hung on a muddy rope above the gaping mouth of a well.

Adoni sat on her haunches and hugged her knees, staring at the cabins, at the chalet. She had expected the tear in the universe to lead her somewhere else, of course; she saw the young man disappear and knew she would too, if she followed him. But she hadn't expected a place of such disarming beauty as this. Places like this were reserved for the well-off kids who went to Whistler or Switzerland for winter break. They were for kids who could afford expensive skiing and snowboarding equipment. She wrapped her arms around herself and squeezed as hard as she could, hoping the strain of her muscles would prove she was actually there, smelling it, tasting it, taking it all in. She wanted to knock on the chalet door and ask whoever lived there if she could stay forever.

She coughed and turned towards it.

The young man stood in her path, holding Tyler in his arms, his angry face bearing down on her. He looked older than she was. His eyebrows pinched together, and he frowned.

"You've got to be kidding me!" His rasp—tone upon tone, like the rings in a tree sawed in half—raised the hairs on the back of her neck. "What are you doing here? Get out of here!"

He freed an arm and waved it over his head. The crack in the air reappeared behind her. She got to her feet and leapt away from it.

"I mean it!" he said.

"No."

He took a step towards her. She matched it with one step back.

"I'm not in the mood for this!" He hiked Tyler up in his arms and tried to get around her, to put her close enough to the portal to push her through. She sidestepped him, crossed her arms, and shook her head. "This is ridiculous!" he huffed.

Tyler stuck his thumb in his mouth. Apparently the young man didn't see anything wrong with kidnapping a little boy. Adoni snapped back at him. "Why do you have my neighbour?"

"What business is it of yours?"

"You need to *explain* this."

"If I explain it to you, will you go away?"

"No."

"*No?*"

"Where the hell are we?"

"We're in the In-Between world," he said. "At the northern colony, The Welcome."

"The what?"

"*The Welcome.* In the In-Between. I've no desire to enlighten you, darling. Go home!"

"Are we in Canada still?"

"Sort of."

Adoni gawked at him. He cleared his throat. "Fine. Look there." He pointed at the trees.

Adoni squinted. At first she saw nothing but the needles and branches of the forest, the occasional highlight of snow beneath the full moon. But shadows moved between them like ghosts, and the more attention she paid to them, the more she saw a city beyond—a layer of life beneath the one she stood in—like an image on twice-exposed film.

Through the murk she could make out a concrete pathway, a lamp post with ragged paper flyers taped around it, wrought-iron railings and puddles of melted snow. Something caught her eye, a flash of movement deeper in the fabric: a woman bolting down a set of stairs and over a muddy lawn. The woman's face was pale and hysterical, her eyes as large as kitchen sinks. Her lips twisted and her mouth opened. Adoni couldn't hear her but knew she was shouting.

She recognized the tightly curled hair, the hands.

It was Toronto. It was home. And Tyler's mom was looking for him.

"Holy *shit*!"

"You see it?"

She nodded. "We're still here? What's going on?"

"Why should I explain it to you?" he grumbled. "You're not supposed to be here in the first place. It's not my problem if you can't be bothered to figure out where you're going before you get there."

"You said north. How can we be north and still be here?"

"I don't have time to give you a geography lesson, darling!"

She bent over and grabbed her knees.

He sighed. "The In-Between lies beneath your world, like a shadow. Which is why you can't simply hang around because you feel like it."

She shivered, unable to tell if it was from the cold, or from the realization that even in this forest, she still lingered just underneath the city. She knew Toronto like the back of her hand, knew the names of most of the streets, could find any landmark just by picturing the subway line and knowing which way was north, which was south, east and west. Her sense of direction abandoned her, and her head swam.

"I'm gonna puke."

She turned and stumbled towards the well. He shouted after her.

"Don't you spew in that water you filthy thing!"

She put her hands on the well and pressed her cheek against the cold stone until her breathing steadied and her stomach stopped lurching. After a moment's peace she straightened up and peered into the deep. It was a long way down, but she could still see the moon on the surface of the water.

"That was Tyler's mom," she said weakly.

"Who?"

"Tyler, the kid you swiped. That was his mom." She pointed at where she saw the stain of Tyler's mother stumbling around in the dark.

He watched the woman for a moment, his anger softening into something more closely resembling pity. His sympathy didn't last. "All right," he muttered, "you've not soiled anything. Now will you leave?"

"No!"

"All right missus, listen up!" he said. "There's no place for you here, and I'm not about to let Steppe find out you've followed me through the agate, do you understand? Now take yourself and your attitude back to where you came from, and have a good night's sleep in your own bed."

Adoni sniggered. "I love how you talk like I know what the hell you mean."

He was about to tell her off when, out of the darkness, another voice interrupted him.

"Ritter?"

It was a voice cut from the same woven texture, only more stoic, more serious. The young man, Ritter, shot Adoni a look of warning.

The new member of the conversation—a man of Ritter's height, with longer, darker hair and a pair of light blue eyes set in an angled, lupine face—bent forward and came towards them. The same wide clothes were draped across his shoulders and hips, and he wore a leather belt studded with polished black stones and fur trim on his boots. He stopped a few paces away from the two of them and peered at Adoni through a thick shag of bangs. "Who's this?"

"I have no idea, Steppe," Ritter grumbled. "But apparently she's not leaving."

"Did you bring her here?"

"She followed me through the agate."

Steppe glared at Ritter. "You let her follow you?"

"I was *occupied*, if you haven't noticed," Ritter said, hiking Tyler up again under his nose.

"You were only supposed to make contact with the boy."

"You told him to kidnap my neighbour?" Adoni asked.

The blue eyes locked onto her. "Kidnapped? Why do you say that?"

"What else do you call it when someone takes you away in the middle of the night?"

"Yes, Steppe," Ritter said with a smirk. "What else would you call it?"

"Take the boy to his cabin, Ritter," Steppe said, his voice laced with thunder. "I'm not discussing this with you until morning."

"Fine by me," Ritter said. "Good luck, darling." He left on the percussion of his boot soles pressing tracks into the snow.

"The boy heard the call of a piper," Steppe said when they were alone. A rumble twisted the ends of his words, the sound of boulders falling off a cliff. "When a child hears a piper's song, he or she has chosen to go with them."

Adoni frowned. "What's a piper?"

"The sworn immortal protector of children. We appear to children in need and remove them from harm's way. The children are taken through the agate to the In-Between world and remain until they're eighteen years old. This is the northern colony, The Welcome."

"What do you mean protector? Who're you protecting?"

"That boy, for one. And others like him."

"Why's he need protecting? Who's gonna get him?" He scowled, and didn't answer her. She changed the subject. "You're a piper?"

"Yes."

"Him too?"

He sighed. "Yes, him too."

"So you guys are magic?" She knew the answer already but needed to hear it said. His reply, however, was cold and terse.

"Somewhat."

It wasn't enough to curb her curiosity. "But he waved his hand and this portal just appeared and…"

"That's the agate. The agate's everywhere in the In-Between. Watch."

He raised a finger, traced a line in the sky, and the light broke through. She stepped away from it and stood behind his shoulder. The forest scene dripped back into place.

He gazed at her. "You're very calm for someone who has no idea what's going on."

Adoni was relieved she had him fooled. "So?" she said.

"So. What's your name?"

"Adoni."

"And why are you here?"

"Because."

"Because why?"

"Because I don't want to go home."

"Why not?"

Her shoulders went rigid. "Because I don't want to!"

"All right," he said. "All right. You seem to be set on staying. I'll have to find some place to put you. You shouldn't be living with the pipers, mind you. But you can stay with Theresa tonight. Follow me." He turned and headed towards the chalet.

"Is that guy gonna get in trouble?"

"Ritter?"

"And your name's Steppe?"

"It's Istvan, actually."

"Why do they call you Steppe?"

"It's a nickname Ritter gave me a long time ago. Something he pulled from a book that stuck." He stood on the porch and kicked the side of the chalet to knock the snow free from his boots. "You're welcome here, Adoni," he said. "Come on in." She followed him over the threshold.

The chalet was everything it had appeared to be from outside: warm rooms, comforting smells—a refuge in the middle of a dark and stunning wilderness. She smelled cedar logs burning, fire smoke, candle wax, and musty rugs. The tiny blue wicks of oil lamps hanging on the walls kept the main hall dimly lit. A grand staircase stood before them, and off to the right, a sitting room murmured and buzzed with life. A crackling fire danced away in a grand stone fireplace at one end of the room.

It's perfect, Adoni thought. *Just like a holiday.*

Two women, twins, with shiny black hair hanging in two perfect braids on either side of their heads, sat facing each other on a couch strewn with animal hides and a broad, colourful quilt. They were dressed in red and black knitted robes that fastened at the neck with white bone hooks and flowed down to their ankles. Every shade of laughter imaginable made up their conversation—giggles, chuckles, whoops, and cheers. A man was curled up under a blanket made of brushed hide and stone. He bowed his head, crowned with white-blonde hair, over the pages of a book in his lap.

Adoni followed Steppe to a narrow kitchen ripe with the heady scent of a bubbling stew. Another woman, with dark hair braided and looped high on the back of her head, stood at the stove. A trail of black feathers kissed the brown skin on the nape of her neck and fell down the back of her robe. She wore a sash of copper and polished stone diagonally over the curve of her chest and hip. She stood on a braided rug, her feet bare.

Steppe cleared his throat. The woman glanced over her shoulder at him. Dark eyes, a trail of freckles over a short, round nose, and full lips brought curious life to her face. "Theresa," Steppe said, "this is Adoni. She'll be staying the night. At least."

Theresa briefly considered Adoni before turning back to the stove. "And?"

"I'm wondering if you have any space for her."

"The cabins are all booked," she said. "You know that."

"She's not a resident. She's a tenant."

"She's a *tenant*?" Theresa turned back to them, her hands folded into each other.

"Yes, a tenant."

"Nobody sang her away?"

"No. She's here of her own accord."

"How'd she get through the agate?"

"Courtesy of Ritter."

Theresa shook her head. "You're not going to report…"

"I don't have any place to put her tonight."

She shrugged. "What do you want me to do about it?"

"I thought maybe she could stay with you."

Theresa glared at him. "And you thought about that out loud and right in front of her, eh?"

"I thought…"

She waved at him, dismissing his excuse. "She can stay in my room, no worries."

"Can you make her some…?"

"Hot chocolate, yeah."

"Thank you, Theresa."

He brushed his hands down the front of his coat. "Theresa is den mother to us pipers," he said to Adoni. "And she's very highly respected."

"Especially by Steppe," Theresa said, without looking at him.

"I'll leave you two. Have a good night. I'll see you both in the morning." No one acknowledged him. He disappeared through the kitchen door.

Theresa took her spoon out of the pot and laid it in a bowl next to the stove. When she looked at Adoni again she was smiling; warmth flooded her face between the upturned corners of her mouth. "I make hot chocolate with chilli peppers, I hope you don't mind. Come have a seat."

A bundle of dried flowers hung upside down between a collection of copper pots and pans, frozen in time above a round table and four mismatched chairs. Adoni pulled out one of the chairs and sat down. Theresa set a double boiler on the stove and got to work shaving off whorls of chocolate from a block she took from the cupboard. She blended the chocolate with cream and pepper, whisked them both into a silky drink, and poured the drink into two earthenware mugs. She joined Adoni at the table, curling her legs up beneath her robes. "Careful, it's hot."

"Are you pissed off I'm staying in your room?" Adoni asked.

"I'm pissed off at *him*, not at you."

"Why?"

Theresa took a long whiff of the chocolate before putting her lips to the cup and drinking. "It would've been nice if he'd asked me first when you weren't there. What am I going to do, say no when you're standing right in front of me?"

Her voice was low, the sound of hot peppers mixed with honey and orchids, but without the texture of Steppe or Ritter's voice.

"I could sleep on a couch," Adoni offered.

"No, no, it's fine. I've got plenty of room."

Adoni tilted the mug and let the chocolate spread over her tongue. Theresa watched her until her face grew hot.

"So why are you here?" Theresa finally asked.

"I don't wanna go home."

"Ah. That sounds familiar."

"Yeah, why?"

"That's how I got here." She took another sip. "Do your parents drink?" Adoni looked away and didn't answer. "A lot of the kids here have parents who drink. My dad drank. He was a mean drunk too. He'd smash anything he got his hands on. He got his hands on mom's face a lot."

"Mom does."

"That's tough."

"So you came here?"

"Yeah. That was a long time ago. Steppe found me, actually. Behind a school in my neighbourhood, when I was about your age. I used to go there at night and sit on the swings until it was safe to go back home. Dad had just lost his job and came home blind drunk when there were dishes in the sink. It was my turn to do them but I hadn't gotten to them. He figured he'd teach me a lesson, I guess. Cleanliness is next to godliness. I'm glad mom wasn't there to see it." Theresa's smile was sweet, wry, and her eyes sparkled in spite of her story.

"He's not gonna kick me out, is he? Steppe?"

"No, he wouldn't do that. Though you really shouldn't be here if you haven't heard a piper's song."

"I heard him singing. He just wasn't singing to me."

"Really? You're not supposed to hear it if it isn't intended for you. Only marked kids are supposed to hear the call."

Adoni wrinkled her nose. "I don't get it."

Theresa put a hand on the table and drummed her fingers on the wood. "Didn't Steppe tell you what a piper is?"

"Not much. Just that they protect kids who need it."

"Man of few words," she grumbled. "I don't know why he's keeping it a big secret. Pipers are... sort of like sirens. Mermaids, you know? Only they walk on land, and instead of leading you to harm they take you away from it. They can suck up sounds and add them to their voices to make them richer and more appealing, more unique. Things like instruments, that's an easy one, or sounds from nature, like falling rain or fire or birdsong. And when you hear it… when you hear a song sung just for you… when you can hear yourself in it…" She smiled. "You can't help but follow it to the end of the world."

"Where do they come from?"

"They used to be people," Theresa said. "Just regular people like you and me. But to become a piper, you have to be given a piper's voice. Meaning a dying piper has to send their voice into yours. Sort of like swallowing a magic spell. The rumour is they only pass their voices down to the person they love most in the world." She shrugged. "Nobody knows how true that is. It's a romantic idea, though."

"Steppe sang a song just for you?"

"He sure did."

"How could you tell?"

"Just a feeling that came over me. I can't explain it… They only sing in piper language so you can't tell what the words are, but somehow… you can just tell they're singing about you. I still remember the tune, too. Every time I think about it, it brings me back to that night. One minute I felt like I was trapped forever and the next minute he was there and… I had a way out. And he hasn't changed in, oh, going on fifteen years."

"You ran away when you guys were kids?"

"I was still a kid. He's older than I am."

"He looks your age."

"He's eighty-five."

Adoni set her mug down on the table with a hard knock.

"Pipers don't age," Theresa said. "Ansgar's magic keeps them young forever."

"Who's Ansgar?"

Theresa ran her hand over her shoulder and squeezed. "Ansgar's the Creator of the In-Between world. She rules over the five colonies. There are five colonies laid out across the In-Between. You've got Ocean's Wake in the west, Long-and-Gold, Accueil-Silencieux, and Seventeen Bay. The Welcome's just the northern colony."

"Have you ever seen her?"

"Nope, not me. Steppe has come close. She asks for reports from the colonies and he has to make the trip up to her fortress in the mountains. Every piper in the In-Between is bound to obey her decree." She pointed to a scroll that was hanging on the wall, black ink scrawled across its yellowed surface.

Ansgar's Code

A piper sings his song and brings away the child who hears him.
No child shall be harboured who has not heard a piper's song,
Nor shall a piper interfere with those he has borne away.
A piper sings his songs to Ansgar in the morning. He thanks Ansgar for Her benevolence.
A piper speaks to Ansgar of his transgressions and admits his failures, for She is his Mistress and to Her he owes his voice.
A piper sings his songs to the child in the evening. He gathers with his piper brethren and sings his song at dusk.
No piper shall leave another piper behind. No piper shall forsake his brethren, nor give them up for destruction.
No piper shall forsake his duties, nor default on his debt to Ansgar.
This is what Ansgar decrees. This is what will always be.

"She's the one who created the power that gives a piper his voice," Theresa said. "So they're all indebted to her. They owe her their lives."

Adoni caught a hint of melancholy in her voice. She changed the subject. "How old's the other guy?"

"Ritter? Ritter won't tell anyone how old he is. We just know he's old. Really old."

"He freaked me out when I first saw him. He was yelling at me and then he's all, 'don't sing that song.' Do you know what he's talking about?"

"I have no idea. Ritter's got a lot of secrets. No one ever really knows what he's up to."

They sat for a long while, sipping their drinks and listening to the clock on the wall. Adoni stared into her cup. "Mom's gonna kick my ass when she sees me. She's probably shitfaced right now. You won't make me go back, will you?"

"No. No one'll make you do anything here. Trust me."

"Why do all the other kids have to be here? Why aren't they at home?"

Theresa stood and stretched her arms over her head. "You don't think you can figure that out on your own?"

Adoni wouldn't look at her. "How does she know which kid to take?"

"They say she crosses the In-Between and looks for them. When she finds one, she sends out a summons to the head of the colony and assigns the song."

"But how does she decide who goes and who stays?"

"I wish I knew." She tilted her head towards the kitchen door. "Ready for bed?"

"One more question."

"Go for it."

"Steppe said you're only supposed to be here until you're eighteen. How come you're still here?"

Theresa laughed lightly. "Sometimes I wonder."

Adoni slipped off the chair and pushed it back against the table. Theresa led the way out of the kitchen and down the hall to the main staircase. Her train of feathers shone black and blue in the lamp light, and the stones in her sash caught the flickers of fire on their polished surfaces. The folds of her robe swayed back and forth as she mounted the steps.

Six rooms were spread out on the second floor landing, each with a name carved into the door. Adoni recognized Ritter's name first, and the others followed; *Aniuk, Paj, Finnur, Roxanne, Istvan.*

Theresa opened the door to the room at the top of the staircase and drifted into the darkness. "Hang on," she said. Adoni heard wood and metal grinding together and sliding apart, the slips of bare feet over a dozen steps, and the swipe of a match. The glow of an oil lamp pooled at the base of a set of stairs leading up to an attic. Theresa poked her head through the opening in the ceiling. "Okay, come on up."

Adoni climbed into the attic just as Theresa lit the fourth candle standing on a tiny vanity in the corner, next to a quartered oval window. Like the kitchen, the attic was long and narrow, the space above their heads cinched by a sharply angled roof and pronounced rafters. The double bed was low and dressed as the couch in the living room was, with a quilt, animal hides, and wide, flat stones. The floor was cozy beneath an overlapping pile of braided rugs, and the air was spiced with amber, patchouli, and a whisper of Theresa's skin.

Theresa pointed at the bed. "Make yourself comfy. I'll find some pyjamas for you."

She picked through the wardrobe that was tucked in the opposite corner of the room, let out a happy whoop, and emerged with an orange shirt and baggy grey pants. "Here, these are great." She handed them to Adoni and turned her back to find her own clothes.

The pyjamas smelled faintly of lavender and vanilla bean. Adoni pulled off her musty uniform, put the pyjamas on, held them close around her like a new second skin. Theresa slipped out of her sash and robe and feathers, the golden light softening the curve of her shoulders, hips, and thighs, caressing her skin with an orange blush. She chose a creamy cotton nightgown with a splash of red at the hem and let it tumble over her, down to her ankles. She set about unravelling her hair from its braid. It fell to the top of her rump, a rippling chocolate spill threaded with silver.

She smiled at her spellbound guest. "Comfy?" Adoni nodded. "Good. So this is my room. The room we went through to get here is the music room. That's where all the pipers meet for morning songs."

"What do they do all day long?"

Theresa took a brush from the top drawer of the vanity and put the bristles through her hair. "They sing," she said, drawing her arm down each thick lock.

"Or they play instruments. They write songs about the children. Ballads about who they are and why they sang them away, in piper language, that kind of thing."

"But what do they do with the kids once they get here?"

Theresa turned away from the girl. "Do you mind if we just call it a night?"

Adoni shrugged. There were too many questions to ask, too many knots to unravel, and her heavy eyelids were ready to rest.

She slid beneath the quilts and hides. The brushed suede smoothed over her skin, and the weight of the stones kept out the draft. She turned her face into the pillow and caught a hint of cedar on the linen. Theresa blew out the candles and carried the oil lamp to the other side of the bed. She settled down next to Adoni before fully extinguishing the flame.

Adoni lay there in the dark and listened to Theresa's breathing grow long and languid, until it was clear she was asleep. She rolled onto her side and took another deep whiff of the linen, pulled the sheets closer around herself. For the first time in weeks her stomach wasn't churning acid, her ears weren't filled with useless noise. For the first time in weeks, there were no late-night demands, no need for vigilance.

Ida could keep her booze, if she wanted and loved it so badly. If it was a choice between her dingy apartment and the beautiful chalet of The Welcome, it was an easy one to make.

Adoni decided she was never going back.

She drifted off to sleep with Ritter's lonely melody weaving in and out of her thoughts.

Chapter Five

The western colony, Ocean's Wake, lay nestled between a lake and two mountains. Its sheer beauty was a treat for those who lived there, especially the residents, who dwelt in spacious, rounded huts with thatched roofs and doorways made of embroidered leather. It was subject to cruel weather sometimes—torrential rain, or fog, or lightning storms—but its summers were warm and bright. The residents hiked or swam, or, when the snow fell, tobogganed down the steepest slopes they could find. The pipers of Ocean's Wake had pristine reputations throughout the In-Between, and being assigned to the western colony was an honour many pipers only dreamed of. They sang their morning songs exquisitely, their voices composed of sounds from the deepest depths of the ocean, and each one played at least three instruments.

Next was Long-and-Gold, the prairie colony covered in fields of beautiful yellow wheat and wild flowers, where the air was thick with the smell of sweet grass. Mornings began with pink and golden sunrises, and the days ended with a horizon bathed in brown and black. Long-and-Gold was a quiet and unassuming place, with nine wooden longhouses standing in a dry, sometimes oppressive heat. The residents of Long-and-Gold lived in groups of eight, which seemed to work out well and gave the entire place the feel of a summer camp. There were epic games of hide-and-seek and plenty of hollow tree trunks to stash treasures in. The pipers lit the fires at 11:00 every night, and someone many years ago started the tradition of roasting marshmallows and telling ghost stories on Saturday nights. The pipers of Long-and-Gold weren't especially impressive; the sounds of scythes through grass and the harvesting of wheat rolled through their thin voices. No one could deny, however, that their residents were the happiest in all of the In-Between.

Accueil-Silencieux was built in the shape of a square, around an angel oak tree whose heavy, moss-covered branches dipped and sagged and spread out over a wide cobblestone courtyard. The building was a marvellous structure made of wood and brick, with pointed roofs and stained glass windows. Each resident had his or her own bedroom with a window facing the countryside. The pipers lived in the furthest end of the structure, where the ceilings were higher and skylights kept their dwelling bright behind two heavy oak doors. The doors were chained shut to keep the residents out. Accueil-Silencieux had its share of unfortunate incidents; sobs at night, fights in the courtyard, frequent threats. None of these registered with the pipers behind their high walls; every piper at Accueil-Silencieux was deaf. The residents frequently tried to run away, hedging their bets against whatever might be lurking out of doors. This was why, at night, the pipers opened their windows wide to sing their evening songs. No resident, shuddering alone in the dark somewhere, could resist the lure of their magnificent voices. They sang in pairs, in trios, in a full choir, and the many layers of sound made anyone within earshot long to return to their rooms, to their beds.

The fourth colony, a coastal spread known as Seventeen Bay, existed in the furthest eastern corner of the In-Between. It was the smallest of all the colonies, with room for only ten residents in tiny cottages dotting a great sloping hill. Six rowdy, spirited pipers presided over it at any given time, stashed away in a three-storey cottage made of aluminum siding painted eggshell blue. They sang and played their instruments from sunrise to sunset, pausing only to suck back as much food as they could pack into their furious bellies. Evening songs took the form of raucous parties lasting well into the night and made every resident feel as though they were trespassing on someone else's good time. The residents never spoke to each other, never looked at each other, and never knew each other's names.

The Welcome was the last of the five piper colonies. None of the other colonies spoke of The Welcome, or of its leader; the pipers who dared to do so first turned around to see who might be listening. Mentioning The Welcome's name was like telling a cruel joke. Even the northern sun seemed willing to forsake it, taking its time breaking the horizon, then hanging in the sky for just a few hours before dipping into the west and leaving the pipers who lived there in evening shades of green. Every piper in the In-Between knew The Welcome was home to the very desperate, the very broken, residents and pipers alike.

And unlike Ocean's Wake, whose pipers garnered the utmost respect whenever their names were mentioned, The Welcome's pipers were notorious.

There was Finnur, easily seven feet tall, who loomed over everyone he met and wouldn't speak to anyone for months upon arriving at the colony. Paj and Aniuk, the twins, refused to be separated; when they were assigned to opposite ends of the In-Between they abandoned their posts and walked for days to find each other again at The Welcome's doorstep. Roxanne was missing her left hand when she showed up in the north, and for weeks her vivid nightmares caused her to shriek like a banshee in her sleep. There was Ritter, all attitude and innuendo. And over them all, charged with their care, was stoic, sombre Steppe.

Adoni knew none of this when she went to bed that night. But after fifteen years, Theresa certainly did.

Theresa waited until the dawn's fingertips could just touch the wardrobe on the far side of the room before slipping out of bed and throwing her nightgown over the open door. She stood naked before the full length mirror, her dimples and curves bathed in smoky shadow, and gazed at herself until the corners of her eyes wrinkled with pride. She took a porcelain pitcher off the top of the wardrobe, poured some still water into a bowl on the vanity, splashed her face, armpits, feet, and nethers clean. Drops of water fell like little bells all around her. She dressed in blue and olive robes, set her hair back in its braid, dressed the end with two white feathers, and climbed down the staircase to the second floor. The pipers wouldn't be up for morning songs for at least an hour, but Theresa slid the stairs back into place to be sure they wouldn't wake Adoni up.

She lit the fire in the music room first, with an old bellows and scraps of parchment paper, then moved on to the living room. The kitchen was last, where she set one final fire to work in a potbellied stove before sweeping the previous day's dust and dirt out the back door.

When the floors were clean and the room was warm, she found her sharpest knife and put it through the starchy flesh of a russet potato, slicing and chopping it into a pile of pearly cubes. She dressed them with salt and laid them out on baking sheets. She wanted them plump and golden, the way she liked them, the way the pipers liked them, crowned with sprigs of rosemary, served in her favourite red tureens. She wiped her forehead with the back of the hand that held her knife so expertly.

Ansgar's name was pressed into the tiny copper plate soldered to the knife's handle. The name appeared on every pot and pan in the kitchen, above every resident's door on the cabins outside.

She held the knife up. The light caught it in just the right way, with just the right mood. She put the point of the blade to her thumb and slid it methodically through the pad, underneath the print.

No pain. No urge to scream. No blood. She pulled it out again.

Her skin knitted itself back together.

She shuddered and tossed the knife into the sink.

She browned the onions in a cast iron pan seasoned with salt and oil, lost herself at the sight of them turning a lovely shade of caramel, the sweet smell of them wafting up from the stove top, and started to daydream about the place in the forest where the maple trees grew, where she collected the buckets of sap from the nails in the trunks.

"Reese?"

Steppe stood in the middle of the kitchen, holding a branch of witch hazel dusted with ice. He glanced at the pan, and at the spoon in her fist. "Hash browns?"

"They're for omelettes," she muttered.

"I love your omelettes."

He put the branch down on the table and waited for her to speak to him. She didn't. "You're angry."

"Yeah."

"You have every right to be."

"I know."

"I would have found a better way to ask you, Reese," he said. "Really. But she'd just come through the agate and I hadn't planned on…"

"You were thoughtless."

"Yes."

She held up the spoon, now decorated with sweet and sticky bits. "You should've considered my comfort. All right? I understand you wanted to make her feel welcome. But my space is my space. I may be cook and *den mother*," she said with a curled lip, "but I still have a right to privacy."

"My choice of words?"

She lowered the spoon. "I wish you wouldn't call me that."

"I meant it as a compliment."

"Right."

"You make everyone feel at home," he said. "Special."

"That doesn't mean they get to cross my borders."

"No, it doesn't."

His fingers curled around the branch, and he picked it up gingerly. "They're still blooming," he said. "It must be thirty below outside."

Theresa slid the skillet off the burner and joined him at the table, a reluctant grin forming on her lips. "Resilient little suckers, aren't they?"

"I love these flowers," he said, stealing a quick glance at her. "I love their colour. That yellow can... melt... it's so intense. I love their crimped petals."

Theresa ran her hands over his arms in a gentle, sweeping arc. He leaned his forehead against hers. "They call it snapping hazel too, sometimes," he said.

"Why's that?" Her palms folded his fingers over each other.

"I can't tell you. It's too suggestive."

"I can always look it up, you know."

They stood together for a moment, braced by the silence, in the most highly coveted part of the day. It wouldn't be long before the pipers woke up and started singing their songs, playing their instruments, eating their meals and having their arguments.

"I love when you bring me flowers," she said.

He leaned forward and kissed her softly.

This was how she liked him best; despite the piercing eyes, the unforgiving voice, he couldn't hide what a helpless romantic he was at heart.

"Almost time for morning songs," he murmured against her lips.

She smirked. "Way to ruin a moment."

"I'm hoping to speak to Ritter before we start."

"Assuming he's going to show up at all. He hasn't been keen on morning or evening songs in a few weeks. Not that he was keen on them before, but at least he showed up."

"I'll speak to him in his room."

"Oh, you mean Shangri-La upstairs? He's gonna *love* that."

"*No piper shall forsake his brethren, nor give them up for destruction,*" he said, quoting the code with lyrical precision.

"I know. I just wish he felt the same way."

"So do I."

He kissed her again, left her standing there with the branch of witch hazel between her palms. She looked at one of the cupboards and thought of a ball of twine. A moment later she pulled back the door and found it at the ready.

She used it to tie the branch up over the kitchen table. The glistening onions waited for her in the pan. No matter how long she took, they wouldn't burn.

Steppe hesitated before knocking on Ritter's bedroom door. It was one thing to catch him off-guard after morning songs—the music room was the perfect venue for lecturing, for demanding—but since Ritter's attendance at morning songs was no longer a guarantee, Steppe had no choice but to breach his fellow piper's sacred space.

Ritter's room had been a forbidden corner of the chalet for decades, a place he made clear to the other pipers was strictly off-limits. He was so fiercely private about the space he even avoided opening the door too wide, lest someone catch a glimpse of anything inside. He was especially annoyed when someone came knocking while he was listening to or writing music. Steppe frowned when, standing behind the door with knuckles raised, he heard the bleat of Ritter's saxophone. He sighed; best to get it over with and get on with the day.

He knocked.

The saxophone's melody continued its sashay across the landing, making Ritter's point clear.

Steppe knocked again, more insistently.

Ritter answered. "What?"

Steppe opened the door.

Ritter's walls were lined with shelves stocked end to end with CDs, records, cassette tapes, and 8-tracks. A bean bag chair and narrow bed took up much of the remaining space. Everything was lit by a small fire roaring away at the end of the room.

It looked exactly as it had the last time Steppe saw it, almost thirty years ago.

Ritter was sitting in the bean bag chair, thumbing the keys of his saxophone and glaring at Steppe. "Yes?"

"We need to discuss your actions yesterday," Steppe said flatly.

"I was halfway through the damn thing when she showed up," Ritter replied. "And I don't have eyes in the back of my head. How was I supposed to know she was there?"

"Do I really need to tell you how to sing a child away? You wait until the dead of night when no one is around. You take *precautions*..."

"Oh, *spare me*."

Steppe closed the door behind him. "When I include this latest item in the list of ways you've violated code..."

Ritter rolled his eyes. "*Violated*. What a stupid word."

"I'm not here to argue semantics with you," Steppe said. "I'm here because your carelessness has brought an outsider to the In-Between."

"And I've told you it wasn't my intention. It's not my problem if I don't look sorry enough for you."

"You refuse to sing morning songs and evening songs, you've been overheard talking to the residents..."

"So what?"

"I'll *tell you* so what!" Steppe barked.

The floorboards shuddered beneath them. Ritter stopped fidgeting with his saxophone and sat up straight.

Steppe took a deep breath. "I have to report this to Ansgar."

Ritter's face went pale. "Why?" he asked.

"It's code. Harbouring the girl goes against it."

Ritter put the saxophone aside and stood up. "Does Ansgar have to know about this? How long will she be here, really? One or two nights? A week at the most?"

"I'm not sure. But her stealing through the agate isn't a good sign."

"Maybe you can convince her to leave on her own accord."

"I spoke to her yesterday. She's not in a hurry to go."

Ritter ran his hands over his thighs.

Steppe stood in the grip of the fire, clenching and unclenching his fingers, his way of getting on top of his anger and forcing it down again. Losing his temper with Ritter would be bad, especially if he was on the cusp of another trip to Ansgar's fortress. He took stock of his day to calm himself down, thought of morning songs, practice sessions at his piano, evening songs, Theresa's hearty meals, her rosy smell, and dark hair.

She'd be waiting for him up in the attic at the end of the day, and would appreciate him, love him, just as he was.

"Istvan."

Steppe looked up.

Ritter's eyes were cloudy with despair.

"Please don't tell Ansgar," he said softly. "Please."

Steppe shoved his hands in his pockets. The sun grew brighter and highlighted the flecks of dust floating through the air. They hadn't shared such a moment—so heavy, so still—in eons.

"Ritter…"

He stopped when he heard the other bedroom doors open. Finnur, Roxanne, Paj and Aniuk were making their way to the music room for morning songs, shuffling in their robes and masks.

Steppe remembered himself, and his role.

"Are you coming?" he asked Ritter coldly.

Ritter shook his head. "Sorry darling. I've got other places to be."

Steppe left him standing there without a parting glance.

Chapter Six

Adoni sat up and peered around the empty attic. The daylight revealed the deep grooves and chips in the floor boards. She slid out of bed to take a look at herself in the vanity mirror. Black spots of age were splattered over one corner of the glass, the bolts holding the wood together speckled with rust. She sat down on the chair, its fibres worn smooth from frequent use, and squinted at herself. There were no dark bags under her eyes, and her plump cheeks were smooth and almost rosy. She hadn't seen such health or rest on her face for weeks. Her hair, however, still mussed from sleeping, sat in a tangled heap on her head.

She pulled the top drawer of the vanity open, searching for the hairbrush Theresa had used the night before, revealing a collection of tin bottles and wooden boxes stuffed with silk scarves and silver hair clips. The next drawer was filled with dried flowers and ribbons that let a sweet puff of past summertimes into the air. The last drawer held only a heavy pewter jewellery box with a heart-shaped lock, and a key at the end of a purple ribbon.

She lifted the box out of the drawer and set it down in front of the mirror. An image was pressed into the metal, a face with a wide, flat nose, a tongue poking out past thick, grimacing lips. She smoothed her palm over the lid, brushing away a layer of dust on its surface, and quickly glanced at the stairs to make sure they were back in place. She ran through how long it might take someone to pull the stairs down to the second floor and climb to the top. One quick calculation later, the key was in the lock and turning.

Purple velvet lined the inside of the box where a stack of photos had come loose from a length of twine. One image was of a woman standing next to one of the burning pillars in the clearing. Wind swept long black strands of hair across her forehead and cheeks, sent the ends in all directions. She held a cape closed at her elegant throat. Her eyes, deep as galaxies, sparkled black and diamond in an oval, sunburned face. The next photo had her sitting in the kitchen with a bowl of gooseberries in her lap. Someone behind the lens was making her laugh so heartily she tilted her head back, revealing a horseshoe of polished teeth.

Adoni flipped through the photographs absently, but stopped when she recognized Steppe's image. He was stretched out on one of the sitting room couches—a book, pages down, on his chest. Another picture showed him wearing a mask composed of strips of brass, two lying flat against his forehead and chin, and one forming a point over his nose and jutting out past the tip. A third was of him sitting at a piano with his fingers spread over the keys.

The last photograph was a picture of Ritter.

Lying on his back with a pillow beneath his head, his hair cut in shag and sideburns, he looked straight into the camera's lens.

Adoni stared at the photo, at Ritter's melancholic expression, until her face flushed and she tucked the pictures back into the box.

She wrapped herself in one of Theresa's skirts—a billowing thing that stopped at her ankles—and a shirt with sleeves that trumpeted at the wrists. With her hair still tangled, she lowered the attic steps and climbed down to the second floor. The dwindling fire light in the empty music room fell on a dishevelled collection of mismatched chairs and musical instruments. There was the piano from the photograph, with years more experience on its varnished wood and keys. Violins, French horns, a cello, and a flute formed a semi-circle in the middle of the room. Adoni found the time on the face of a grandfather clock standing near the wide windows, its pendulum slicing out an impressive *tick tock*. It was almost noon. Theresa had let her sleep in.

She bounced down the stairs to make a dash for the kitchen when she heard a soft knock on the front door. No one was around. She answered it herself.

The man on the porch wore a curiously old-fashioned suit, bowler hat, and round, rose-tinted sunglasses. He tilted his head sharply when he caught sight of her, and a smile came to his waxy face when some invisible hook first pulled one corner of his mouth up, and then the other. He unsheathed a set of perfect teeth at her. "Hello," he said. His voice was soft, creepy, like a spider. "I'm here to see Steppe."

Adoni held the door open and stepped aside. The man didn't budge.

"You must be new here," he said. "I haven't had the pleasure. What's your name?"

"Adoni."

"Adoni." The invisible hooks pulled his smile wider. "What a pretty name." He took off his hat, revealing a head of messy brown hair, and held it in front of him.

Adoni shrugged. "Are you gonna come in?"

"Oh yes," he said. "Eventually." He stared at her until she blushed. "You must be a new resident," he said at last.

"No, I just followed Ritter."

He perked up. "Ritter," he repeated, as if savouring its taste on his tongue. He took his glasses off and fixed her with a stare. There was something curiously lifeless, almost doll-like, about his eyes. "Is he here?" he asked, too sweetly.

Adoni heard someone stumbling down the staircase. Steppe made his way to the door. "Thank you Adoni," he said, fixing an electric stare on the visitor. "You're welcome here, Sylvester."

Sylvester's feet came loose from the porch. He gracefully crossed the threshold and put his glasses back on his nose. "Hello Steppe."

Steppe bristled. "I hope you didn't have any trouble getting here."

"No." Sylvester shook his head slowly. "No trouble."

"Good. Good." He put a shaky hand through his hair. "The music room's available now."

Adoni heard Theresa's weight and bare feet on the floorboards as she rounded the corner to the front foyer. "Oh good, I'm so glad you're dressed. I was going to tell you to help yourself to anything in the wardrobe…"

She caught sight of the visitor and froze, her lip curling with a hint of disgust.

"Hello Theresa," Sylvester said, with the same sickly sweetness as before.

"Theresa, would you…?" Steppe began.

"No," she growled, stepping up to Adoni and seizing her by the wrist. She pulled her away from Sylvester and stepped between them. Sylvester smiled away like a jack in the box.

"You look nice today, Theresa."

"Let's go on upstairs," Steppe said, standing aside. Sylvester nodded at Theresa and headed up the staircase.

When she could no longer see Sylvester's face, she turned to Steppe. "You've got a lotta nerve," she hissed. "Don't you ever ask me to get anything for him." She pulled Adoni along behind as she made her way back to the kitchen.

"Who's that guy?" Adoni whispered when they were alone. "Who's that guy, Reese?"

Theresa slammed a frying pan down onto the stove, splashed some oil into it, and set about beating a pair of eggs in a bowl with a fork. "That's Sylvester."

Adoni recognized the name as Theresa tossed the fork into the sink. "That guy Ritter said something about Sylvester the other day."

Theresa poured the eggs into the heated frying pan, tossed in the leftover potatoes and onions from breakfast, and sprinkled a layer of cheese on top. "Sylvester's a changeling. He's the leader of the changelings, actually. He's the only one of them that can talk."

Adoni sat down on a crooked chair, her stomach growling at the smell of the omelette. "What's a changeling?"

"A shell without a soul," Theresa said. "Just fake meat and plastic skin and black blood thrown together to make something that looks like a person but isn't." She lifted the edges of the omelette. "Creepy things."

Adoni fingered her earlobe and tried to picture what Theresa described. "What do you mean *without a soul?*"

"I mean they're like dolls," Theresa said. "Like puppets. They even look like puppets, if you get close enough to one of them."

"Where do they come from?"

"From Ansgar. But she hasn't made changelings in a long time. They're useless now."

"What're they made of?"

Theresa smirked. "Frogs and snails and puppy dog tails."

"I'm serious."

"Only Ansgar knows. They're not flawless, mind you. You saw Sylvester. Ansgar can make something look human, but she can't make it truly be human. You always know a changeling when you see one. Their eyes give them away. Their eyes are empty."

"Why'd she make them in the first place?"

Theresa flipped the omelette. "Pipers used to leave changelings behind when they sang children away. That was part of Ansgar's original decree, a long time ago. They were ordered to switch the child for the changeling in the middle of the night, so nobody would know the real child was missing. It was supposed to keep the existence of the In-Between a secret."

"They left them behind?"

"Yeah. Not that they knew what was going on. Changelings don't have any emotions of their own, they just pretend. They watch how people react and over time they learn how to fake it."

Adoni shifted in her seat. If changelings were still left behind, and if she'd heard Ritter's song and followed him to the In-Between and some poor thing was left in her place, she knew what it would have to deal with. She wouldn't wish it on anyone. *At least they didn't feel anything, really,* she thought. "Where do they live?"

"On a colony somewhere deep in the woods, north of here, past the river. Not a colony like The Welcome, though. They've made it pretty clear they don't want anything to do with the piper way of life. Their colony is some mess of shacks hidden away where the thickest trees grow. Pipers haven't left changelings behind for a few hundred years now. Rumour has it Ritter was behind the decision, but he's never admitted it. And now Sylvester's reignited the whole mess. He says he's the changeling leader, not that anyone can check that out with the rest of them. He comes here at least once a week to 'negotiate'. Steppe doesn't like to talk about it, but it's got something to do with the changelings keeping their distance in exchange for favours. I don't think Sylvester deserves five minutes of anyone's time."

"Why?"

Theresa still remembered that day in the forest near the maple trees, remembered the way Sylvester slithered between the trunks and into her view. She'd never seen something as false, as surreal, as a changeling before; a thing that moved with such carefully prepared steps, a thing that smiled with unnatural precision. She remembered how Sylvester asked to speak with Steppe, in a voice as chilly and detached then as it was now, so many years later. She could tell, even then, he was dangerous.

She took the pan off the heat. "You can't trust something that doesn't have a soul," she said at last.

She put the omelette on a plate and served it to Adoni with a basket of freshly baked bread. Adoni picked up a fork, severed a piece, and stuffed it in her mouth. "Isn't anyone afraid he'll snap and hurt someone while he's here?"

Theresa snorted. "He wouldn't try anything in the chalet. Not with Steppe around."

"If he did you could mess him up outside."

"No you couldn't. You can't cut a changeling. Once they return to the In-Between their skin—whatever it's made of—it just sews itself back together when it's wounded. There's only one piper alive who can kill a changeling. And he's trying everything he can think of to keep from having to do it."

"Steppe?"

"Yeah."

Adoni snorted. "He's badass?"

"He can be."

"He's so calm. I can't imagine him killing anyone."

"Neither can Sylvester. But he can. And Sylvester knows it too."

Adoni shivered. "How come Sylvester can talk and the others can't?"

"I have no idea."

Adoni polished off her dish as Theresa bustled around the kitchen. How could anyone leave a creature, human or otherwise, behind like that, so cruelly, so carelessly? Did any of the pipers of The Welcome perform such a heartless act before it was abandoned from Ansgar's decree?

What kind of ruler could make up such a merciless decree in the first place?

A heavy cloud of steam leaked out from underneath the lid of one of Theresa's pots. "That pot's been boiling for a while," Adoni said.

"Oh, don't worry about that." Theresa took a pan down from its hook on the wall and held it out. "Ansgar sends supplies to the colonies and makes enchanted products for us to use. Anything that's got an Ansgar logo on it is enchanted." She held the pan up as if modelling it for a television commercial. "*Ansgar. Everything enchanted.*"

"So your pot's magic?"

"Basically, yeah. It'll only empty when everyone's been fed, it'll never burn the food, it'll always be the right temperature, all of that. If you see the name on a bottle of shampoo, it'll make your hair come out exactly the way you want it to. If you see it on a cupboard, your cupboard will never be empty. If you see it on a wooden log, it means you can set fire to it and it won't burn out until you're finished with it. If you see it on a cabin, it means no one can come in unless they're welcome. And nothing can hurt you while you're inside."

"Nothing?"

"Nope."

Adoni smiled. Not a hairbrush, not a slap, not a kick, not a punch. *Nothing*. She stifled a belch and reached for a thick slice of bread with butter. "This is really tasty," she said. "Is that because of you or the pan?"

"That's all me, kiddo," Theresa said. "I'm a hell of a cook. So what are you going to do today?" Adoni pushed her plate away and bit off a chunk of bread before shrugging. "You should go introduce yourself to the other residents. Make a couple of new friends."

"Sure," Adoni said.

"It'll be good for you to hang out with some kids your own age. Maybe meet a cute boy, eh?"

"I don't want a boyfriend." She finished off the piece of bread.

Theresa sighed. "Okay, well, there's an extra pair of boots in the front hall closet, and you can wear my jacket, it's the red one with the big pockets. The residents are usually hanging around the colony, but some of them might have gone off tobogganing. If you need a sled there's one hanging off the west side of the house."

Adoni glanced at her. "Thanks. You make good bread too."

"Thanks, kiddo."

Adoni found the boots—a pair of mukluks dressed with fur and bright blue stones—and Theresa's wide jacket in the front closet. She stepped into the mukluks and pulled the coat over her shoulders, but stopped abruptly and sucked in her bottom lip. The sharpest, most critical eyes in the world belonged to kids her age. Residents would be no exception; they'd probably start gossiping as soon as they saw her. But she couldn't think of a good enough reason to stay hidden in the chalet, so she buttoned her coat and put her hand on the doorknob, expecting to be proven right the second she stepped onto the porch. Rejection was a dish best served hot.

Before she could open the door, a clear, unspoiled tune drifted down from one of the bedrooms, sung with crystal on top, with rich, dark earth underneath. One of the pipers was spinning a song that danced around Adoni's ankles and splashed up like raindrops in a puddle. She stood at the door and listened. The song dipped down at times, and then looped back and forth onto itself like a snake coiled in the desert sun. The piper stopped singing, and left the song quivering in the air on a ledge of hope.

It was enough, to fall in love.

Adoni slumped down the porch steps and crossed the clearing. She'd have an advantage over the residents if she kept her distance, so she crept along on short steps and kept her eyes open, to see if one of them might be worth approaching.

The first few cabins were empty; no sign of fires burning or lights in their windows. The residents who lived in these cabins were probably younger and out playing somewhere. Other windows were covered with heavy curtains, and Adoni smelled marijuana burning when she passed. She kept going until she reached the last row, where one cabin's curtains were shamelessly open. She sidled up to the wall and peered inside.

Tyler was sitting on the floor, playing with dolls.

His cabin walls were decorated with dowdy tapestries woven in bright shades of orange, green, yellow, and red. His bed, buried under a rumpled quilt, stood in the far corner, next to a chest of drawers. A braided rug lay across the centre of the room before a rumbling fire, as well as an open hope chest and a pile of dolls with limbs entwined. Tyler's fist closed tightly around one of the dolls, and he spun it around as if it were flying over mountains, oceans, volcanoes, and pits of alligators.

Outside the cabin the wind picked up and stung Adoni's cheeks. She raised a hand to knock her knuckles against the window pane. She caught a glimpse of Tyler's face through the window and stopped.

He was smiling.

Why should I mess it up? she thought.

She turned her back against the wind and pulled the hood on Theresa's coat over her head. Just raising it past her ears was enough to keep out the cold. She found the Ansgar name threaded on the inside of a sleeve.

She walked between the first few trees surrounding the clearing, running her hands over their bark as she passed. Their naked branches stretched like veins across the sky. They grew further apart from each other the deeper into the woods she walked, until they were far enough apart for her to catch sight of a swatch of bright blue between the trunks.

It was the blue of a jacket and toque—regular winter clothes, not draped robes and shirts and pants—worn by another girl, who sat cross-legged on a high shelf of densely packed snow and stared at a tree a few inches away from her nose.

Adoni stepped into the little clearing and looked around. A block of snow the same size as Theresa's vanity, with sharp corners and a wide, flat surface, stood off to the right, next to a small pedestal of snow acting as a stool. Lines of stones ran along the left side of the clearing and formed a rectangle. Other stones formed Xs, as if marking where treasure lay buried beneath the surface. The girl continued to stare at the tree, until Adoni cleared her throat, turned, and scraped the bottom of her boot against a tree trunk.

The girl whipped her head around towards the noise. Adoni saw vibrant purple bangs poking out from under her toque. She had glossy pink lips that were twisted into a scowl. "What?" she asked.

"Why're you just sitting here?"

The girl leaned forward and looked ready to pounce. "Is it your business?"

Adoni's shoulders went rigid. "You're sitting in the snow alone like a loser."

"Are you even allowed to talk to us?" the girl asked. "What if your piper buddies hear you?"

Adoni tossed her head. "Yeah, I'm a piper," she said.

"You're not?"

"No, I'm a kid."

"Why do you get to wear their clothes?"

"Because my school uniform sucks ass."

"Whatever, you're in my room, so get lost."

"You live in the woods?" Adoni let out a nasty laugh. The girl shrivelled and turned around.

"Leave me alone."

Adoni ambled around the perimeter of the clearing, examining the footprints in the snow. "Seriously, why're you just sitting here?"

The girl didn't bother to turn around. "How long have you been here? You still can't see it?"

"See what?"

The girl raised a hand and twirled her finger in a circle. "You can't see the city from here?"

Adoni looked long and hard. It took a moment before she could see it: the outline and pastel smudges of a bedroom lying just beyond the wintry surface. A guitar lay on the floor, its outline marked by shiny black stones. The block of snow stood in for the dresser, and the ledge where the girl was perched was a cold, solid version of a double bed. Adoni looked past the girl's shoulder, into the tree that was holding her attention.

She could make out two people, a man and a woman, arguing with each other, their fingers stabbing at the air. The girl watched them, her expression as dull and grey as a slab of concrete.

"Those are your parents, eh?" Adoni asked.

"Yeah."

"They always fight, eh?"

"Yeah."

"They ever kick your ass?"

"No."

Their eyes met, and they took each other in.

"Do yours?" the girl asked.

"My mom does. I only live with my mom."

The girl nodded. "I'm Natalie."

"Nice."

"What's your name?"

"Adoni."

"That's a bible name for a boy."

"I don't know. My mom wanted to name me Jennifer."

Natalie wrinkled her nose. "You don't look like a Jennifer."

"So you come here every day?"

"Yeah." She moved over to one end of her snowy bed. Adoni stepped over an X marking a pile of magazines and sat down. She smelled lilac coming from Natalie's clothes and drew her knees up close to her chest.

Natalie's parents continued to scream at each other, their fury playing in dumb show, until Natalie's mother put her hands over her face and bent forward, sobbing. Natalie's father slammed a fist against the door frame and left her there, alone.

The trees faded back into place.

"You stopped watching, eh?" Natalie asked after a time.

"Sorry."

"Don't worry about it. I stopped too." Natalie grabbed a handful of her bed and pressed it into an icy lump in her fist. "They fight all the time, but they fight more now that I'm gone." She let the skin of her palm flush red before flinging the ice lump at the tree. "I was mad before because I thought you were one of the other kids who live here. They don't respect anybody's privacy."

Adoni's stomach flipped, her ears strained to catch the cruel snap of a twig, or the nasty laugh of a gang of kids coming from behind a tree.

"There's no place to knock, eh?" she said, when she was sure no one else was around.

"What?"

"Like, I would've knocked." She tucked her hair behind her ears and peeked past the red hood, put her thumb to her bottom lip and gnawed on her fingernail.

"Yeah, you're gonna knock," Natalie said, showing her crooked teeth as she smiled. "Bruise your knuckles up against a tree."

Adoni wanted her to keep talking. She thought of a thousand questions to ask, and picked the most difficult one first.

"Why're you here?"

Natalie grabbed another handful of snow and closed her fingers over it.

"My mom doesn't believe me."

"About what?"

The ice nugget disappeared in Natalie's mouth. She sucked on it for a minute before shoving it against the inside of her cheek with her tongue. "About anything."

Starling song braided across the blanket of snow, rose from the ground, and circled the girls in the eye of its tune. Each note skittered over the Xs and makeshift furniture, shivered against their temples. Natalie's sombre face lit up. She turned and sat cross-legged in the middle of her bed.

Adoni recognized him even before he stepped through the trees.

Ritter caught sight of her first and stopped in his tracks. His lips turned up and, twinkling, he turned his attention to Natalie. "Natty, Natty, Natty," he said. "Talking to strangers now, are you?"

"You got any smokes on you?" she asked.

"Of course not. Filthy habit. I'm surprised at you Natty, I thought my good influence was finally rubbing off on you."

"Who said you're a good influence?" Natalie slipped off the bed and playfully knocked her knuckles against his head. Ritter stretched his back high enough to keep out of her reach.

"I'm the paramour of good influences," he said. "They swing by whenever the spirit moves them. As they do with everyone, I suppose." He sat on the stool in front of Natalie's dresser and held Adoni, gently and firmly, in his sight.

"Ritter's the only cool piper," Natalie said to her in a hush. "He's the only one who talks to any of us. All your other friends are too good for us, eh?"

He smiled and didn't answer her. His silence didn't affect Natalie, who bent and scooped up a handful of snow, passing it between her hands until it formed a perfect sphere. "What are you doing out here anyway?" she asked him. "I thought you didn't like the cold."

"Just enjoying the day," he said. "And avoiding. Procrastinating."

"Who are you avoiding?"

"Natty, darling, who am I *not* avoiding these days?" His smile widened. "You're more beguiling than I'd originally thought," he said to Adoni. "I'm impressed. No offence to my darling Natty here, but it takes quite the snake charmer to be allowed into her sanctuary."

"She's not a snake!" Adoni snapped.

He raised his eyebrows.

"She asked nicely," Natalie said. "Not like the other kids."

"Yes," he said. "She must have asked in quite the tone of voice."

He kept Adoni in the same peculiar sight for another moment before standing and stretching. "Well then, I'll be off," he said. "Pardon the interruption. It seems as though you're up to quite a bit out here today."

"Wanna hang out later?" Natalie asked.

"Sorry darling, my dance card's full. Another time."

"You can't go yet!" She held up the snowball. "I haven't even thrown this at you!"

"Make it quick, sunshine. I've got places to be."

It landed with an elegant thump against his chest, and pieces of ice slid down the front of his coat. He put his hand over his heart. "Cupid's arrow," he said with a sigh. "Or maybe a bride's bouquet. Who knows?" He turned to leave.

"What time is it?" Natalie asked.

"Almost three," he said on his way through the trees.

"Shit," she said when he had gone. "It's so late. It's gonna get dark soon. Wanna go hang out in my cabin?"

"Yes," Adoni replied. "Yeah. Yeah, okay."

By the time the girls reached the clearing, the older residents were standing out on their porches and talking amongst themselves. Eight girls and five boys, all around Adoni's age, wearing regular winter clothes, lowered their voices as she and Natalie approached. Their combined conversations buzzed like an electric fence as Natalie stepped up to her front door and pulled it open. "You're welcome," she said. Adoni followed her inside and stood in the corner until the door was shut.

Natalie's floors were covered with a braided rug, as they were in the chalet and in Tyler's room, but the walls were decorated only with brown polish on the surface of the wood. A wrought-iron chandelier with seven candle settings hovered above the bed. Natalie took off her jacket and boots and retrieved a lighter from the hope chest at the end of her bed. She reached up and set to work lighting the candle wicks.

"I'm so glad you're wearing those clothes," Natalie said. "The other kids probably think you're a piper too." She sat on her bed and leaned against the headboard. "You can sit here if you want."

Adoni crept up to the bed and sat down on the very end. Natalie put the lighter back into the chest, then pulled out a tin of chocolate cream cookies.

"Where do you get cookies around here?" Adoni asked.

"The chests. We all have them. If you want something you just think about it and then you open the chest and there it is."

Adoni peered at the unassuming hope chest and wondered what else it could conjure up. "I smelled weed before. They can get it from the chests too?"

"Yeah," Natalie said. "That's where we get it." She smiled. "So now you get to tell me why you're here."

Adoni recounted her story of jumping through the agate, after Ritter, away from Ida. Once she found Natalie hanging on her every word, she went on about what she had left behind—Assumption's dirty halls and disgusting gravy, Shabnam's unreliable friendship, the bills Ida couldn't pay and the threat of having to move again. By the end of her story the sky was black, and a bible's worth of Adoni's life spilled between the cabin walls. Natalie stayed with her every step of the way, with her head tilted dreamily to one side and her fingers twisting the ends of her purple hair. "So you're staying in the chalet, eh?" she asked.

"I guess so."

"You can stay here tonight if you want. But you don't have to."

Adoni blushed. "No, I should go back. I should give Reese back her coat."

Natalie stood. "You can come by tomorrow if you're not doing anything."

Adoni eased off of Natalie's bed and fumbled back into her coat and boots. "Okay. I'll see you tomorrow, okay?"

Natalie nodded and opened her cabin door. Before long, Adoni was standing alone on Natalie's stoop, in a heavy silence.

Clusters of snowflakes caught the light of the four burning pillars and sparkled as they fell to the ground. Adoni swallowed hard. She wanted to sit on Natalie's bed and listen to her talk all night. There was no real reason to leave; Theresa wanted her room to herself, after all, and was only sharing it because Steppe had guilted her into it. But the memory of failed sleepovers with Shabnam, always ending in screaming matches, kept Adoni from turning around. She looked across to the next row of cabins.

An older boy was peering out of his cabin window.

He was tall, his silhouette filling the glass, with black hair, a large nose, and spangled eyes she could see even across the way. His lips were a wide, solid line across his face, and he stared at her.

She froze, a thick crease forming between her eyebrows.

He let the curtains fall back across the window.

She had nearly reached the front door of the chalet when it slowly opened and Sylvester stepped out onto the porch. He straightened his hat, and slipped on a pair of fingerless gloves.

"Hello," he said in his spider's voice. "Have you enjoyed your day? I've enjoyed mine. It was very productive."

She waited for him to elaborate, but he was too completely charmed by his hand filling with a whisper of snowflakes to do so. She headed up the steps.

"I have a question for you," he said.

She froze.

"If a wrong had been committed against you," he said, "a heinous wrong… an unspeakable trespass… wouldn't you want that wrong to be righted?"

Adoni stared at him.

"Don't answer me," he said as he stepped down from the porch. "And don't fear me."

She turned and knocked on the chalet door, stood stiffly and stared at the grain of the wood. Sylvester's footsteps retreated across the clearing and into the forest beyond.

She cinched her collar tight in her fist. There was something about the way Sylvester held his hand out to catch the snowflakes, something sweet and almost endearing about the way he admired their beauty as they fell into his waiting palm. Then it hit her: despite being a changeling, despite being, as Theresa had put it, an empty thing without a soul, he truly, genuinely, *adored* snowflakes. Just as anyone would.

The door opened, and Theresa welcomed her inside.

Chapter Seven

"Hope you're hungry," Theresa said as Adoni stepped over the threshold. "I left enough of everything for you." After an entire day of cooking, she smelled of spiced lamb with raisins, mint salad, a stew of chicken and wine, tagliatelle dripping with cream and butter.

Adoni slipped out of the red coat and delivered it to Theresa's grip, nodding at the promise of food despite her part in devouring an entire tin of cookies.

"Did you meet any kids?" Theresa asked.

"I met this girl Natalie. She's cool."

The grandfather clock in the front room chimed ten, heralding a landslide of piper voices. Adoni looked up to the second floor landing, where a splash of firelight spread across the chalet's ceiling. The voices split into millions of shards that hung in the air like bits of broken glass. Hundreds of melodies twirled around the chalet. Theresa hung up the coat. "You should go up and listen," she said. "It's pretty amazing. Go on. I'll bring your dinner up to you."

Adoni climbed the stairs and peered into the music room. Each piper was part of a semi-circle facing the bellowing fireplace. Each wore a mask made from a combination of hammered brass, copper, stone, and feathers. Steppe's mask lay snugly across his angular face. Paj's and Aniuk's left cheeks were covered by a polished, sculpted stone; Paj's as black as a bottomless pit, Aniuk's a vibrant turquoise. A beard of copper studded with tiger eyes hung on Finnur's jaw. A brass band, cut and hammered into the shape of a widow's peak and flanked by black feathers, lay against Roxanne's forehead, with her hair, as red and unruly as a comet's tail, curled around it. Ritter's green eyes pierced the dim light from behind a mask of copper and onyx.

The pipers fell silent when Adoni appeared in the doorway. Ritter glared at her and shook his head, but Steppe held a hand out to her. "Hello Adoni. Feel free to join us. Everyone, this is Adoni. She'll be staying with us for the next little while."

The pipers gawked at her like goldfish in a bowl.

"Adoni is a tenant, not a resident," Steppe continued. "She came here of her own accord. We're free to speak to her." He raised an arm and began his introductions with the first of the twins. "This is Paj, her sister Aniuk, Finnur, and Roxanne. Of course you've already met Ritter," he said flatly. "This is when we sing our evening songs, so just get comfortable. You can sit at the piano if you like."

Adoni straddled the piano bench and tucked her arms in front of her. Steppe waved Paj to her feet. The little brown woman stood up and faced the fire, put her hands together, and released a melody spiced with peppercorns and alive with millions of fingers and toes. Next came crystals and fistfuls of soil, and as the music burrowed into Adoni's ears and drove into her nerves and muscles, she recognized it from earlier in the day, and in it, thin fingers, pink lips, and a straight back against a room furnished with ice and snow.

She had met Natalie, long before she had actually met Natalie.

Natalie's essence swam in every note, back-flipped over every lyric, melted against Adoni's skin and fused with her DNA. Piper song was blood and oxygen calling its listener home, branding hieroglyphs on the back of the mind. Language was irrelevant; the tiny piper sang about a girl with a volcanic temper, a wily intelligence, a loneliness that broke into an unquenchable mean streak, a longing to dance and a reaching out for laughter, for solace. There were tenors and bows sawing on thick strings and bears growling before an attack. The song wrapped itself around Adoni, and she could almost feel Natalie's breath on her cheek and smell the lilac oil behind her ears. The ledge of hope Paj left her lying on earlier, the twinkle of promise, it turned out, was indeed the last phrase she had written. But the song had so bred itself into their bones, everyone in the room could hear what it might have sounded like if it continued. It branched out and came to an end on both a thunderous, joyful crescendo and a devastating whimper of hopelessness.

"Beautiful," Steppe said. "Really Paj, it's beautiful. It's a wonderful tribute."

"That's Natalie, eh?" Adoni said.

The pipers grinned and cooed at the question.

"You can tell it's her?" Steppe asked.

"Yeah, I met her today."

"Do you think Paj's interpretation is apt?"

"Huh?"

"Does it sound like Natalie?"

"Yeah. How come it's got two endings?"

Ritter snapped to attention and leaned forward. Adoni witnessed his sudden intensity and shrank in her clothes.

Steppe tilted his head. "We never know what will happen to the residents once they leave," he said. "There are always two endings. Sometimes there are more."

"She can hear it!" Paj said happily, her voice ringing with laughter. "I'm *good*, aren't I?"

"Very good!" her sister agreed. "High five!" She held up a hand, and Paj dealt it a celebratory slap.

"Where did you come from?" Finnur purred. "This girl, where does she come from? She seems to have a head for music." He blushed before speaking to her. "Do you have a head for music?"

"Yeah?" she replied, as if she were asking for permission.

"She does," Ritter said from across the semi-circle. "She remembers tunes. Can pick them out of the air and sing them, even if she's only heard them once. Go ahead girl. Sing Natalie's song back to us."

Adoni looked at their eager faces and wished the floor would crack and drop her down into the kitchen. "I can't sing."

"Sure you can, I've heard you. Show us what you've got. Our esteemed leader has asked you to join the circle, after all, so you've been invited to share your talent with us."

Steppe glared at him. "If she's uncomfortable..." he began.

Ritter chuckled. "Comfort? Since when is that a priority? Go on, darling, don't be shy. It's a tribute, remember? A tribute to a girl who sits in a snowy room day after day, watching her life as it passes her by."

Adoni dropped her chin and sang Natalie's tune softly. The more it took over her throat, the greater her desire to go back to Natalie's cabin became. The notes settled her stomach and strengthened her nerves. She forgot all about the pipers around her, forgot about the exchange she'd had with Sylvester at the front door, and sang the song out, bar after bar, until she couldn't remember which way it continued and it trickled to a stop.

Even Steppe watched her with a distant respect.

"Lovely," he said. "Like a bell in an empty sky."

"Like a call for a toast," Finnur added. "*Ting ting ting*, with a fork on a glass."

"Like icicles falling to the ground," said Roxanne, her voice buzzing with chainsaws and electric eels.

"Like a promise," Ritter murmured. "Like a hint of perfection. Marvellous."

Theresa came into the music room with Adoni's supper laid out on a wooden tray. "I bet Beethoven had his dinners at the piano too," she said with a wink. Adoni gave Theresa a small smile, reached for the fork, and stuffed her mouth full of buttery pasta.

Aniuk sang next. She chose a simple melody, dedicated to a boy whose pride hissed and popped under a bluish tune. Finnur's song swung between the rafters and bounced the image of another boy around in their heads. Roxanne's rusty motor of a voice was perfect for a girl who constantly ran away, from everything and everyone, until the only thing left of her was a shadow, a cloud of black exhaust.

Finally, Steppe turned to Ritter. "Do you have anything prepared?" he asked.

Ritter put the back of his hand to his forehead and swooned. "Not tonight, darling, I have a splitting headache."

The rest of the pipers grumbled and clucked. Ritter crossed his arms, an arrogant smile on his face.

Steppe took in a breath. "All right. That leaves me."

He opened his mouth and unleashed a melody so intense the walls around them shuddered and the instruments vibrated.

It was finally clear to Adoni why Steppe commanded the pipers, why he was the one who gave orders and conducted negotiations. Millions of voices, in harmony and in dissonance, shook the very fabric of the air around them with such strong hands that the agate bled into view like a splash of wine on a tablecloth. Steppe's song paid homage to every resident who ever passed through The Welcome, celebrated their successes, wept for their failures. Adoni felt every note thunder in her veins and fizzle across her nerves. Steppe, who had been so calm in the hours leading up to that moment, bared his teeth and sent one last bolt of music towards the ceiling, rattling the wood and sending streams of dust fluttering down onto their shoulders.

"My," said Ritter when the floorboards stopped shaking. "What an opus. *Belinda* would have *loved* it."

The pipers looked from Ritter to Steppe, and then to each other, stuttering and whispering between themselves.

Adoni frowned; she couldn't remember seeing the name on any of the bedroom doors, and Theresa hadn't mentioned it earlier. She caught herself holding her breath.

Steppe turned his back to them.

"Goodnight, everyone."

Ritter was the first on his feet. He tore his mask off and tossed it onto the piano, where it slid to a stop next to the wooden tray. He winked at Adoni and stooped as he passed by.

"Marvellous," he whispered.

The rest of the pipers followed, one by one, until only Adoni, Steppe, and Theresa remained in the room.

Adoni looked at Theresa. Her hands were folded together and resting on the slight bulge of her stomach. Her eyes went starry as she watched Steppe straighten up the chairs and return the instruments to their stands. When everything was put back in its rightful place he turned to her. "I'm really glad you decided to listen tonight," he said, a quiver in his breath as he exhaled.

Theresa glanced down at Adoni and wrinkled her nose. "Any chance you can find another place to sleep?" she asked.

Adoni's answer stuck in her throat for a moment, but came free as Natalie's tune floated back into her head.

"Uh-huh."

She turned around and left them standing there, alone.

Chapter Eight

Theresa leaned against the piano and crossed her arms. Steppe let his eyes wander over her body until a tiny smile formed on his lips. She grinned. "Do I have to come over there?"

"Yes."

She threw her arms around him and kissed him hard, felt him wrap her up tightly in his embrace. She put her nose against his neck and drew his musky scent deep into her lungs.

"Have you forgiven me?" he whispered into her ear.

"Not so fast," she said, pulling away. "Why'd you ask me to run you an errand for him?"

He ran his hand over her shining black braid and took the feathers at the end between his fingers.

"Because I'm a heartless bastard and I wasn't thinking," he said, kindly, sadly. "It just… slipped out." He ran a fingernail over the feather's edge, between the tendrils. "I'm sorry. I know it's a problem."

"You know, you can keep apologizing for this kind of stuff, or you can just stop doing it. I figure the second choice is better."

"You're right, it is."

He took a seat at the piano and patted the empty space next to him. "This is a song I like to call *Theresa's Revenge*."

"Oh man," she said, shaking her head. "What's it about?"

"About a woman I know, who'll one day have her revenge on my thoughtlessness."

"How's she gonna do that?"

"I don't know," he said. "But it won't be pretty."

The black and white piano keys had long since turned brown and yellow with age. Steppe ran his palms over them, pressed each one softly against its respective string.

The song began with an apology; a lullaby that kept its head low and shifted back and forth on childish legs. It crept into the room, ashamed it had caused so much panic, regretting its actions. In the first movement, Steppe said all he had to say and stole away again without waiting for a response. The second movement was quick to take its place. There was Theresa, raging in all directions, millions of notes played in millions of sequences, in billions of layers, all at once. Each note was a filament, a silkworm's thread, and each note clung to the next, weaving the story into a fabric. The third movement roared its displeasure, swore an oath to have its day, and devoured the second movement from the bottom up, until it obliterated the very memory of it, reached into their hearts and ripped it, screaming, out of their chests.

Then Steppe stopped playing, and try as she might, Theresa couldn't remember what they had been talking about before the song began.

"What did you say to Sylvester?" she asked.

He reached up and rubbed his eyes. "The usual. I told him holding a grudge against the pipers for so long is pointless. I told him Ansgar wouldn't tolerate his talk of rebellion. Everything he already knows."

Theresa sighed. "But he still wants Ritter."

"He still wants Ritter." He struck a key; the note was tinny and flat. "There I go. I've made him sound like a punch line."

They slouched together on the piano bench. She held her hand out, and after the briefest pause, found his palm, calloused and warm, against hers. "It's hundreds of years ago," she said. "It's a completely different time and place. Anyway, his real problem's with Ansgar and her original decree, not with Ritter."

"Oh, you should have heard him today," said Steppe. "With all of his pleasantry nonsense. Small talk about the weather and how healthy I'm looking these days. Empty *pleases* and *thank-yous*. That's all I ever get from him. It's sickening." He ran his hand through his hair and tugged at the strands.

"Why do you let him in, if it's always the same thing?"

"Because Ansgar told me to take care of the situation. I'm responsible for every soul on this colony. If I disobey Ansgar's decree she'll cut us off. We'll starve to death. Unless the changelings get us first."

"Or..?"

"Or..." He sighed. "I can't give Ritter over to them. It's against the piper code. *No piper shall forsake his brethren, nor give them up for destruction.*"

"And you can't ignore the code."

He cocked an eyebrow at her. "Are you suggesting I do?"

Her fingers reached for the lone key he had struck earlier. It made the same pathetic sound. "I like Ritter," she said. "I do. But he's the one who should be talking to Sylvester, not you. He should be fighting his own battle."

"Sylvester will tear him apart."

"I know." She closed her eyes. "Does he ever threaten you?"

"In his darker moments, yes, but never directly. He'll tell me he can't be held responsible for any horror that might befall me. Or he'll tell me he'll miss me when I'm gone, he'll miss our conversations when they come to an end. He used to say I was protecting Ritter. Now he says I'm *colluding* with him. As if Ritter and I were behind the entire plot to leave the changelings behind. He speaks so simply. Someone who speaks so simply about such things... you can't reason with them. Something's missing." He rubbed the back of his neck. "Not speaking for Ritter is the same thing as turning my back on him," he said. "As a piper, it's against what I'm supposed to believe in."

Theresa put her hand on his lap. "What you're *supposed* to believe, eh?"

"I tried to live without the code. I tried to rescue children on my own, without the rules. It only made things worse. I'm not strong enough to live without it. When you don't... when you can't... you can do a lot of damage." Slowly, he shook his head. "I still think about the boy. Sometimes I can see him on our residents' faces."

"It was *years* ago, Steppe. You have to forgive yourself."

"It was a betrayal. I should have known better."

Theresa bit her lip. Though Steppe had mentioned the boy before, he'd never revealed what exactly happened between them, and she couldn't bring herself to ask.

He closed the fall over the keys. "Ansgar's chosen this battle for us—for me—to fight. Of all the ways we can express our devotion to her for the gift, why is this one of them? She hasn't asked us to put aside our differences and forgive what happened in the past. She hasn't asked the changelings to back down. She hasn't asked the pipers to make reparations. I don't understand. If it's about loyalty..."

The word stuck in his throat.

"Maybe Sylvester knows something I don't," he said. "I can't tell if he thinks he's got me fooled."

"So you're not fooled?"

"I hope not."

He took her hand and led her to the door.

Chapter Nine

Adoni pulled Theresa's hood as far forward as she could, hiding her face from the residents. They got quiet as Adoni approached Natalie's cabin. Someone chuckled. She heard whispering, and a nasty hiss came from an older boy with a square, damaged face.

"Dyke."

"Dyke dyke dyke…"

Adoni was about to knock when the front door of the chalet opened. She leaned out over the porch railing to get a better view.

Aniuk and Paj stepped out of the chalet and walked arm in arm towards the last row of cabins, the stones on their cheeks glinting in the firelight. They moved with straight backs and formal steps, bereft of the levity they had shared in the music room. Adoni and the other residents watched as Aniuk stepped up to one of the cabins and knocked.

A tall boy with braided hair answered, looking as though he had just woken up, with rumpled clothes and bare feet. He scowled at the twins and shrugged. Aniuk curled a finger at him, urging him forward. He disappeared for a moment, and reappeared wearing a long winter coat and boots. Aniuk took her sister's arm, and together they returned the way they came, with the boy following behind. He gave the residents he passed a quizzical look. They shook their heads.

Adoni followed the three of them back to the clearing. Aniuk turned and faced the boy again.

"What?" he asked, his voice cracking.

She reached out and opened the agate before him.

The boy shook his head. "You're kicking me out?"

The twins stood still and said nothing.

"Why're you kicking me out?" he demanded. "I was just sitting in my room. What did I do?"

Aniuk shook her head and pointed at the agate.

The boy looked from one twin to the other. "Where am I supposed to go?" he asked them.

Aniuk turned her head and left her finger pointing at the agate.

"I don't wanna go," he said softly. "I don't wanna go back. I've got no place to stay. Let me stay here. I won't piss anybody off, I swear."

They didn't speak.

"You can't send me back," he said, his voice trembling even as he fought to keep it still. "You can't just kick me out."

Aniuk caught his eye and shrugged weakly. Paj stepped up next to her sister and pointed at the agate.

"Let me get some things," he said. "I need to get some things from my room."

Paj shook her head, her finger insisting at the agate.

The boy's face twisted the closer he drew to tears. "I've been here for five years. I can't go back home. What am I supposed to do?"

Paj took Aniuk's hand, and together, they turned their backs on him.

"Answer me!" he yelled. "Answer me!"

They didn't.

His shoulders shook, and he sniffled loudly. Then he took a step back to strengthen his stance, and spat at their heels.

"Fuck you!"

His eyes darted between the silent pipers and the residents who stood staring at him on their porches. He ran a shaky hand over his head and stomped through the agate as if he had never meant to hesitate at all.

"*Bitches*," one of the residents muttered.

Adoni looked up to see which of them had spoken. She caught sight of the boy from earlier; the boy with the black hair and the sombre expression on his face. He was back in his window. Adoni slowly raised her hand to wave at him. He disappeared as unceremoniously as he had before.

Paj put her arm around her sister, who shrank against her and whimpered.

"I hate when they cry," she said.

Paj brought her back to the chalet.

"Oh man, what did you do?" Natalie asked when she opened her door and found Adoni standing on her porch. "Did they kick you out?"

Adoni shook her head and pulled Theresa's coat closer around her. "I think Reese wants to hit it tonight. Can I stay with you?"

"You're welcome." Adoni crossed the threshold. "Who's she gonna hit it with? I bet Ritter, he's a skank."

"Ritter's a skank?"

"Yeah, totally!"

"No, she likes Steppe."

"*Really*!" Natalie reached out and yanked on the coat's red sleeve. Adoni took her cue and slid out of it. It was promptly and dramatically tossed over the foot board. Natalie leaned against it and crossed her arms. "Why Steppe?" she asked.

Adoni eyed Natalie's mattress and dishevelled bed sheets. "He was singing just now and she was blown away and then she's all 'find someplace else to sleep tonight' so I figure they're into each other. Were you sleeping just now?"

"No, just hanging out. She better watch it. Steppe's *dangerous*." She flounced down onto her bed and stretched her legs, folded her arms behind her head to cradle it against the head board, and crossed one ankle over the other with a glib flourish. "Ritter told me Steppe messed a kid up once," she said. "The kid pissed him off and he tore his face up. You've heard him sing, he can rip a tree out of the ground with a voice like that. Ritter didn't say, but I bet Steppe killed him."

Adoni snorted. "I talked to the guy and he's a pussy." She glanced down at her skirt and hastily brushed the dust from the music room rafters away.

But he could, if he wanted to, she thought. *If he got mad enough.*

Natalie smirked. "When you're pissed off you'll do some freaky stuff. I can understand that. Have you ever been in a fight?"

Adoni sat on the end of the bed. "No. Have you?"

"Yeah," she said. "And back home I've been in fights. You know what you do? Poke their eyes with your fingers. They can't hit back if they can't see you."

As Natalie dispensed her tips for fighting dirty, Adoni's mind went back to the boy with the braided hair. She pictured him returning to the world he'd left behind and standing stiffly until he decided which way to turn. She thought of him first heading back to whatever home he'd lived in, and then losing his nerve and stopping in his tracks. Boys who were furious enough to spit wouldn't dream of returning to a place they weren't welcome. Boys like that would find a street corner, and an empty coffee cup, and a flap of cardboard, and a magic marker, and start asking passersby for change. *That's what I'd do,* she thought. *I'd rather live on the street than live…*

Before she let herself picture the kind of home the boy had come from, a thought occurred to her. *Reese turned eighteen and she got to stay. How come she gets to stay?*

Natalie waved at Adoni. "Hey, are you listening?" Adoni nodded. "So anyway…"

Adoni tried to hear Paj's tribute behind Natalie's thick bravado, but was instead reminded of a song she heard on the radio once—an upbeat pop tune that hit the street with a grinding of guitars and a relentless melody sung by two girls in unison, their voices so perfectly matched, they mimicked the piper split Adoni detected the first time she heard Ritter sing. The song's confidence flooded her thoughts; she wanted to feel the afternoon sun on her face, and to smell jerk chicken wafting on the breeze. She wanted the colour and vigour of Kensington Market, the bulletin boards decorated with fliers, the free newspapers. She wanted to spend the day with Natalie, browsing the vintage clothing shops, flipping through old vinyl record albums.

Natalie's talk mellowed to light banter. "You look really tired," she said as Adoni stifled a yawn. She leaned over the edge of the bed, retrieved a long t-shirt from the hope chest. "Wear this. You can sleep next to me."

Natalie pulled off her sweater and jeans. Her skin was dotted with freckles and tiny pimples. Adoni found comfort in the little flecks of brown and red crisscrossing her shoulders; the imperfections eased her nervousness when she compared them to her own. She folded Theresa's clothes and hung them over the foot of the bed before settling into the soft fabric of Natalie's t-shirt.

Natalie smiled, stood on her bed, and blew out the candles. She dropped to her knees, slid under the covers next to Adoni, and buried her face from view in one of two fluffy white pillows. "G'night."

Adoni lay on her back, her eyes itching from the smoke of the extinguished candles. It didn't take long for Natalie to fall asleep. Adoni put her hands on her belly, forced herself to breathe slowly, deeply. After lying there for a time, listening to Natalie's breath, counting the beats, the world faded to static and Adoni was sound asleep.

She woke a few hours later, found herself curled on her side with her face deep in her pillow, felt someone watching her.

She made Natalie's silhouette out in the residual glow from the burning pillars. Her fingers were woven lazily through her hair, and there was a smile on her face. She pressed her lips against Adoni's temple. "I'm really sorry I yelled at you," she said softly.

She cupped Adoni's cheek, her thumb stroking the skin there.

Adoni rolled over, reached for her, pulled her down, and kissed her.

Natalie's song crashed through and flooded every crevice as their fingers wove together and they wrapped their arms around each other tightly. Paj had sung everything about Natalie with such precision, laced her song with such aching verity. Adoni lay in a puff of lilac and musk, her chest rising and falling—crescendo, diminuendo—her fingers strumming Natalie's hair like the strings of a harp—pizzicato, pianissimo—her mouth laying delicate kisses on Natalie's, the way a flautist brings out a tune by barely touching it with her lips.

Nothing felt the way Natalie felt, curled next to her under the blankets while the pillars burned away outside; nothing was as sweet, as strong, as painfully beautiful as she was.

They stopped for just a minute to look at each other, to catch their breath.

Adoni reached for her again.

Chapter Ten

In the morning Adoni woke to find Natalie curled up next to her, with her arms folded over her chest and her jaw loose behind closed lips. Adoni stared dreamily at the pattern of light the sun left across the bed. This was what sleepovers were meant to be like; mornings filled with promise, not with the dread of returning to a shabby apartment, empty cupboards, and a mom who may or may not be coherent. There weren't supposed to be interruptions, demands for the door to be left open, endless rounds of hallway gossip or petty arguments.

The last time Adoni had slept over at Shabnam's place they ended up sniping at each other until eleven, when Adoni packed up her overnight bag and stormed out of the place. It took an hour to walk back home, but she didn't have enough subway fare on her and had to take the old-fashioned Ankle Express. When she got home Ida was half gone, and they ended up knocking back a few and badmouthing her so-called friend. "I can't stand that kid anyway," Ida drawled. "What the hell does she want with you?"

For a time she thought Shabnam wanted the same thing she wanted—to spend time with her, to be best friends.

But Natalie wanted to spend time with her for different reasons, which made the morning all the more glorious.

Natalie opened her eyes. "How long've you been awake?" she said, slurring her words.

"Just a bit."

Natalie reached out and draped an arm over Adoni's waist. "So tired."

"What time is it?"

"I dunno."

"Wanna get up?"

Natalie shook her head. "Comfy."

"Maybe Reese'll make us breakfast."

"No, you want something *really* good?" Natalie slid out from under her quilt and stooped over the hope chest for a moment before throwing back the lid. She straightened up with a white bowl and spoon in each hand. She handed one of the bowls over. "Try this."

Adoni leaned over and smelled it. "It's maple syrup and what?"

"Eggs. It's *soo* good, try it."

Adoni dipped her spoon in and swallowed a fluffy mouthful. Of course it was sweet, with a ribbon of golden yolk running through it, but there was something else on her palate—something homey, something nostalgic that Natalie specifically wanted the chest to imitate. Natalie emptied half her bowl before she spoke again. "My mom used to make this all the time. It's my favourite." She turned away to finish her breakfast in silence.

Adoni kept eating. The dish was almost painfully sweet. It was meant to be a treat, meant to make someone feel special. She stole a glance at Natalie, whose face had gone dark.

If it was my favourite and mom stopped making it for me, she decided, *I'd be pissed.*

She clasped her hands together. "Maybe we can go for a walk," she said.

Natalie shrugged. "Okay."

They dressed, and Natalie pulled a fresh pack of cigarettes and a lighter out of the chest before they left the cabin. Adoni was thirsty; she hadn't had anything to drink for hours, and the maple syrup and eggs had left her tongue feeling dry and puckered. Natalie leaned over the railing and looked down the path between the cabins. None of the older residents were out yet. "Let's go this way," she said, pointing to the forest.

Adoni thought they would find a quiet corner and pick up where they left off the night before. Soon, however, she realized the forest was full of youthful voices calling out to one another. The younger residents were running back and forth, playing a spirited game of hide and seek. Adoni almost tripped over a little boy who was crouched behind a fallen tree trunk, a skinny, rascally-looking thing with shaggy orange hair. He held his finger to his lips, wrapped his arms around his legs and ducked lower.

Adoni looked at Natalie, who stared at the ground and chipped away at the snow with the toe of her boot.

The residents found a little girl a short distance away, and Adoni heard a high-pitched squeal and the sound of several pairs of boots pounding their way back to home base. "They're having so much fun," she said.

"Yeah," Natalie snorted. "Wait'll they get older."

She drew a cigarette from the pack and put it to her lips. Adoni reached for one herself.

How long had Natalie had been at The Welcome? At first Adoni suspected it had only been a couple of months, based on the faraway look on Natalie's face when she had first met her in her bedroom in the snow. But who knew exactly when the residents felt homesick, if they felt homesick at all?

"How long have you been here?" she asked.

"A year last week." Natalie pulled a long drag off the cigarette. Another little boy sped past them, searching for rivals behind a large boulder.

"Were you happy?"

"To be here? At first, I guess."

"You're not happy still?"

Natalie shrugged. "It's all right most of the time. I just hate the kids my age."

Adoni nodded, remembering the residents she had already encountered, and the kids she left behind at Assumption. If she had been a popular girl, maybe, or at least the kind of girl who could fake giggles and demureness at appropriate moments, it would have been easier to make friends. She wanted to hold Natalie's hand and fold her fingers between the soft webbing of her skin, but lost her nerve as two other little girls found the orange-haired boy behind the tree trunk and went whooping back to home base as he stumbled along behind them.

She saw a tiny figure tucked under a wide swoop of spruce tree branches and squinted to get a better look.

Tyler peeked out from his hiding place with a satisfied grin on his chubby face.

"Wait here," Adoni said before dashing over to him and stuffing herself under the evergreen canopy.

"Hey Tyler," she whispered. "Are you hiding?" Tyler smiled at her and didn't answer. It was good to see him this way—smiling, engaged, excited even—and she gave him a thumbs-up of approval. He reached over and scooped up a fistful of snow, which he promptly shoved into his mouth. Adoni chuckled; snow was a delicacy she used to indulge in long ago, on her way home from school, after a fresh quilt had fallen from an overcast sky. Still thirsty, she grabbed her own handful and did the same. It was cold, clean, and cut through her thirst perfectly. She winked at him.

They heard footsteps. Natalie's boots stopped a few inches away from their noses. "I'm not looking down so they can't tell where you are," she said, "but are you gonna stay here?"

"No, I'm coming." Adoni looked at Tyler and put her finger to her lips before pulling herself out from beneath the tree.

Natalie glanced back as they headed on their way. "You know that kid?"

"He's the kid I told you about, the one who lives in my building."

"I guess he's having fun too," she said, folding her arms and bending forward in the cold.

Adoni would have asked her what was wrong, if Theresa hadn't emerged from a corner of the wood and stepped up to one of the maple trees growing a short distance away. She wore a simple black dress and a dusty blue cloak that she must have borrowed from one of the pipers.

"There's Reese," Adoni said, drifting away from Natalie's side.

"Hey kiddo," Theresa said as Adoni drew near. She lifted the lid off of the bucket attached to the tree, checking the sap level. It only reached halfway up the galvanized steel. She put the lid down and decided to leave it. "Where'd you get the smoke from?"

"Want one?"

"Nope."

"I got it from Natalie," she said as Natalie caught up with them.

Natalie wrinkled her nose and eyed Theresa with a glimmer of mistrust.

Theresa put the empty sap bucket down on the ground and straightened her fingerless gloves. "You guys shouldn't smoke, you know. It makes your breath stink."

"We can make gum," said Adoni.

"Uh-huh. What're you up to?"

"Just walking."

Theresa looked off into the distance, where Tyler was finally found by the intrepid group of girls and dragged out from under the tree. "Good," she said. "Don't get too far though. If you hit the river, turn around and come back."

"How come you don't just get maple syrup from a chest?"

Theresa glanced at the bucket. "I like to make my own."

"Where's Steppe?" Natalie asked her with an insolent smirk.

Theresa crossed her arms over her chest and tongued the corner of her mouth. "Inside," she said, tilting her head towards the chalet. "Why?"

"Just wondering." She giggled, cutting her eye at Theresa.

"You should make maple fudge," Adoni said. "That stuff's tasty."

"I'll keep that in mind," Theresa said.

Adoni shuffled her feet in the snow. "We're gonna go," she said finally.

"Remember, if you hit the river turn back, okay? Don't go past it."

Natalie snorted, reached for Adoni's hand, and led her away without a word.

Theresa moved on to the next bucket. She could easily have the cupboards give her maple syrup, it was true, but she loved the process of making it herself—the collecting and boiling, the smelling and tasting along the way. Besides, there was always something slightly off about Ansgar food, something the pipers and residents couldn't detect or had learned to ignore over time; an artificial tang, as if it had been grown in a test tube. Theresa's syrup, on the other hand, was golden, sweet, and gave off the bouquet of a crisp winter morning. Nothing could imitate its organic flavour, or replace it.

The walk in the woods was wonderful on freezing, sunny days like this, but it also gave her an opportunity to check on the residents as she went from tree to tree. She'd decided long ago that, since pipers couldn't interfere with the lives of those they sang away, she would make sure they were okay as they went about their games or their gossipy strolls. Every resident on the colony could tell she wasn't a piper—she aged, for one thing, and when she spoke her voice was as regular as a glass of water—and on most days she could ignore the squints and glares they threw at her when she engaged them or passed by.

She couldn't blame them for it; so many of them had made friends with kids who were unceremoniously thrown out of their cabins once they reached their eighteenth birthdays. She didn't have to suffer that indignity.

She tried not to let it get to her, but that morning, when she compared Adoni's gentle conversation to Natalie's sullenness, she found herself shaking—the way anyone would shake if they'd been called out for telling a terrible lie.

She moved to the next tree and checked the bucket. It may have been a little too early to collect the sap, but she was eager to set it boiling on the large stove she kept just outside the kitchen door. The moist smell in the air made it clear it would snow, which meant a blank canvas for her to pour the syrup out for maple taffy pops. The pipers would be grateful for them and eat them quickly. Only Steppe would take his time and savour their richness, their gently burnt flavour. She wanted to make at least one, for him, as a thank-you for the witch hazel hanging over her kitchen table. She knew she would find him in the music room, sitting at his piano and dreaming up some opus or other. She would pull him over to one of the dusty arm chairs in front of the fireplace, hand him her sweet gift, and watch it melt over his tongue.

She headed towards the thickest tree on her rounds, a massive maple she couldn't close her arms around. The bucket she had placed there the day before had fallen off its spout and lay empty at the base of the trunk. She kissed her teeth at the sight of the wasted sap and stomped over to retrieve the bucket and hang it up again. The plastic spout was no longer attached to the trunk, but snapped in two and lying on the ground. She crouched down and picked it up to examine it. It had been used to hold a lot of weight at one point during the night, but the bucket itself couldn't have broken it this way. It looked as though it had been stepped on.

She held both pieces up to the light to get a better view, and saw a curve of something dark gently drift into view from the other side of the tree. She heard a sick, dry twist of rope as it turned in the wind, and a crescent of leather became two crescents, heavy with thick soles, with laces. Her eyes drifted up.

A pair of socks. A pair of ankles.

She covered her mouth, held her breath.

It must have happened in the night, when no one was watching, and nobody cared.

Chapter Eleven

Steppe was in the music room, playing his piano. The notes moseyed along on three and four note chords, bounced as leisurely as any Sunday picnic, matching the thoughts in his head. He loved these solitary afternoons, when all the pipers were out, when Theresa was busy with one of her hobbies, and he had all the time in the world to write and play his music; afternoons when he could pretend he wasn't a piper, and his only obligation was to himself.

That changed when Theresa burst into the room.

Steppe looked up at her from behind the keys, gave her a small grin. "Any requests?" he asked lightly.

His expression went ashen as the tears came to her eyes.

"There's a boy," she croaked. "There's a boy, in the forest…"

She shook her head, looked up at the ceiling.

Steppe closed the fall over the keyboard and leaned his elbows on it, tenting his fingers. He pressed his forehead to them and closed his eyes.

She didn't have to finish. It had happened so many times before; he knew the boy was dead.

"Which one?" he asked her gently.

"I don't know." Her chest heaved. "I don't know their names."

He left the piano and went to her, put his arms around her, and held her close. They heard footsteps on the landing. Finnur and Roxanne stopped at the mouth of the music room when they saw Theresa in Steppe's arms.

"What's happened?" Roxanne asked.

Steppe let Theresa go, and chose his words carefully.

"We've lost another resident," he said. "I'll get my things."

He started toward his room. Theresa followed behind.

"You don't have to go now," she said sharply. "Ansgar can wait."

"It'll be worse if I wait."

"What about the others? What are you going to say to them?"

"What do you want me to say?"

She rolled her wet eyes and shrugged. "I don't know. Something kind. As a friend."

"I'm a leader first, Reese, before I'm anyone's friend."

She frowned as they got to his bedroom. "What about Adoni?"

He reached under his bed and grabbed a canvas satchel that had seen several trips north of The Welcome. "What about her?"

"Are you going to report her too?"

"I have to, and I'm making the trip. Wouldn't you?"

"Honestly? No. I wouldn't."

"I have to report her. It's code."

Paj and Aniuk poked their heads out from behind Aniuk's bedroom door. He shot them a look that made it clear they should mind their own business and made his way down to the kitchen.

"I don't think it's a good idea," Theresa said as she followed him. "At least wait until the kid figures out what she wants to do."

"Sylvester knows she's here. He may have already said something to Ansgar. If he has, she'll be expecting me to say something. If I don't she'll come down harder."

He stuffed a couple of biscuits into his satchel and pulled a flask, already filled with water, out of a cupboard.

Theresa put her hands on the back of a chair and leaned forward. "You know what happens every time you report something like this."

"I won't mention Ritter. It wasn't his fault, anyway. We've all been careless at some point."

"You know what I'm talking about."

He buckled the satchel and faced her.

"Every time you come back, you come back older," she said, her voice quivering. "You don't think I notice, but I do."

He set his lips tight and said nothing.

"What does she do to you?" she asked. "Why do you let her?"

He slipped the strap over his shoulder. "There are fifty souls on this colony, Reese," he said. "I'm responsible for each and every one." He kissed her cheek. "I won't be long."

Ritter was next to the front door, leaning against the wall, his arms and ankles crossed and unforgiving. Steppe paid him no mind as he reached into the closet for his boots and a long winter coat. He tried to leave the chalet without another glance, but at the very moment he left the doorjamb, he caught Ritter staring gloomily at him.

It wasn't enough to make him stay.

The journey to Ansgar was an hour's trek north of The Welcome. There was no fast way to travel in the In-Between; the agate led only to the world beyond. Getting to the fortress was a gruelling affair. The ground was uneven, the snowstorms frequent, and a wrong turn might not be detected for hours. It was particularly difficult for the leaders of Ocean's Wake and Seventeen Bay, who were the furthest away. The leaders of Long-and-Gold and Accueil-Silencieux had a better time of it, though they, like the others, were never fully prepared for the sharp drop in temperature. After years of making the journeys on their own, they decided to travel in pairs to ward off the possible danger, to ward off the loneliness.

The Welcome was the closest colony to Ansgar's fortress. Its leader always made the trip alone.

The fortress stood far in the north, past the river, the forest, and up through a narrow path between two craggy cliff sides. It was built into the side of a mountain, its hallways carved out of million-year-old rock, its thin, glassless windows chiselled high and on angles to keep the frigid weather out. There were dried-out vines and patches of lichen growing in the sheltered nooks in the stone. The only way into the fortress was through a pair of enormous steel doors, splattered with rust and baring Ansgar's name, which squealed on their hinges whenever they parted to let someone in or out. Standing before Ansgar's fortress, easily a few miles in height, was enough to make anyone feel insignificant. The ground before the fortress was always covered in snow, regardless of the season. It was nestled too deep in the rock to ever see enough sunlight to melt.

Past the front doors was a vast foyer, with floors made of polished stone that bounced back the light from four bonfires, burning all around the room, in fireplaces as wide and large as three-storey houses. A pool of silvery water rippled in the centre of the room and gave off the faintly sweet smell of cut grass and dirt. A narrow staircase wound its way around the room like the coils of a screw until it disappeared in the thick gloom hanging above. The mountain gave off a subtle buzz, as if it existed between a pair of hands that squeezed it, blocking out the din of the outside world. Beyond the foyer were several gaping hallways burrowed deep into the mountainside. Only one hallway was ever used; the hallway leading to Ansgar's quarters.

Accueil-Silencieux's leader, a piper named Edith, crouched by the pool and swirled the water around with her fingertips. She bent low, parted her lips, and drew the delicate tinkling into her throat, where it threaded with flutes and harps and the cries of mourning doves and became a part of her. A piper Steppe hadn't met before, a new colony leader named Ichabod, stood a little way off. His black hair hung over his eyes, and his face was red from days spent journeying underneath a blazing sun. The two leaders had finished meeting with Ansgar and were resting in the foyer until the time came for them to return to their colonies. Ichabod looked rattled from his first visit with the In-Between's Creator. He wove his thick fingers together and stared at the stone floor.

Steppe tore one of the heavy doors open. Edith leapt to her feet and swooped out of his way as he crossed to the pool and knelt down for a drink. His black coat was covered in snowflakes and pellets of ice, and he smelled of sweat and the elements outside. He didn't look at either of them as he quenched his thirst. He seemed not to notice them at all.

"All right?" Ichabod asked with a glassy stare.

Steppe wiped his hands on his coat and straightened up. His face was as sombre as any church. "Yes."

Ichabod attempted a friendly smile and held out his hand. "I'm the new leader of Seventeen Bay. My name's Ichabod."

"Istvan," Steppe said, with his hands firmly down at his sides.

Ichabod dropped his arm. "You're from The Welcome, eh?"

"Yes."

"Must be nice, eh, not having to go so far to get here?"

Steppe paused. Ichabod shifted his weight, put his hands on his hips, and nodded.

"I suppose so," Steppe said at last.

Edith called to Steppe with a delicate lilt, moving her hands in time with her words. "What are you reporting?" she asked.

It was an innocent question, meant only for small talk. But The Welcome was never an appropriate topic for small talk, its plight never one to be made light of, never to be washed over. Steppe got close to her, so she could read his lips in the firelight. He stared at her for a moment before deciding on an answer.

"The usual," he said.

She shrank from his piercing stare.

He made his way to the end of the hall that led to Ansgar's quarters, where he pushed another tall and narrow door open to step inside. The room was dark, save for a fire burning away in a pit several feet wide. The darkness surrounding the fire pit made it impossible to tell how large the room was. A single chair stood before the flames; this was where piper leaders were expected to sit.

Steppe closed the door behind him, moved towards the light with as confident an air as he could muster, and sat down on the chair. He always took a moment to guess where in the dark Ansgar might be sitting. There was no way of ever knowing; when she spoke, if she chose to speak, her voice came in the form of a whisper, deep in his ears, as if she lived inside his head, beneath his skin.

First Sylvester, then Ritter, then the boy, then the girl, he thought. *It'll be easier that way.*

"Sylvester and I continue our negotiations," he said. "He seems better these days. The threats are fewer and farther between. There was a chance he would extend his vendetta to include the pipers on the other colonies, but I feel that's less likely to happen now, based on my recent conversations with him. Of course he still harbours an extreme resentment for Ritter, but he hasn't changed his scope at all. The other colonies are safe, so far.

"Ritter's becoming more and more openly defiant of the code. He hasn't sung away any new souls for a while. I've given him a list of souls that he hasn't gotten through yet. It's been six months and he's only managed one of four. Now he's refusing to sing evening songs in addition to morning songs. I've attempted to engage him on a number of levels… reinforced the importance of piper songs as tributes to our residents… stressed the beauty of the tradition and what it means for us and for our ways. He's still… obstinate. Of course I'm open to any guidance you have to offer."

She didn't respond. He couldn't see her, couldn't hear her, but he knew she was listening.

He cleared the tickle in his throat.

"Unfortunately The Welcome has… recently lost another resident. A boy." The blackness closed in on him. The fire's ochre burn was little comfort. "It's the boys who go through with it," he said, his voice softening as the weight of the day's events started to come down on him. "The girls try too, but the boys… tend to succeed more often. From my understanding he didn't have many friends on the colony. Kept to himself. Stayed indoors, mostly. No one knew what he was up to. I took a look at his cabin before I came to report. His room was empty. I think he took the time… to put everything he had back in the hope chest. He must have chopped it all up and put it back in the chest, piece by piece. Until there was nothing left. He must have asked for it all to be taken away. I've never heard of a resident using the chest like that. He wanted it all to disappear completely." He swallowed hard. "I take full responsibility for this failure. I'll write a tribute for him, to sing at evening songs."

Then, because he'd been safe so far, because he wasn't thinking, he said, "Sometimes I wonder… if we'd had the chance to get to know him… to talk to him… maybe it wouldn't have come to this. If we'd had the chance to talk…"

And he felt it—a kind of light fogginess seeping into his thoughts, an ethereal sensation in his limbs. The darkness faded to grey. Bursts of golden light flashed around the edges of his vision. He felt the weight of the In-Between tumble away from him, felt as though he could fly. He opened his mouth and sucked in a quick, ecstatic breath.

It was always so pleasant, at first.

He felt an iron grip around his heart and knew it was only a ruse, a trick for his submission.

He gripped his knees, inventoried the changes overtaking his body. He needed to stay calm, to not struggle for breath.

Skin, wrinkling around the eyes. Hair, drying out, turning grey. Veins shrinking. Joints throbbing. Chest caving in. Suffocating.

Suffocating.

He slumped down in the chair and fought to keep his eyes open, to keep them aimed straight ahead at the darkness, where he assumed she sat watching him.

How many years would she force him ahead this time? One or two? Five? Or would she let him suffer until his entire body was made up of every single one of his eighty-five years?

A tiny croak eked out of his bruised torso, and he thought, for certain, this time she would kill him.

He held on, for the residents, the pipers, the colonies, for Ritter, and for Theresa.

Ansgar put him back under her spell, and let him breathe again.

He recovered and pressed his back against the chair, as composed as he could be after looking death in the face for the hundredth time.

He heard her voice, right in his ear; a part of him.

"No."

And he thought, *Don't say another word.*

Don't say another word, or she'll destroy you.

Ichabod and Edith were sitting at the pool, filling their flasks with water for the journey home, when Steppe returned to the foyer. Ichabod put his hand on Edith's arm. They rose, straightened their robes, and scuttled past him towards the door.

They gasped when they made out Steppe's features in the light of the bonfires.

Steppe unscrewed his own flask and knelt by the pool. He caught his reflection on the surface of the water.

More grey hair at his temples. More fine lines around his eyes. He pulled his collar away from his neck and noticed how much thinner it was, how much more pronounced the tendons were. His cheekbones were sharper than ever, his skin paler. He looked older.

He was older.

He tucked the flask into the wide pocket of his cloak and turned.

Ichabod and Edith were looking at him, their eyes vacant, their arms hanging feebly at their sides.

Edith put her right hand to her lips, extended her palm to him. She mouthed the words *be careful*, before the two of them stole away from the fortress.

Chapter Twelve

Adoni and Natalie returned from the frozen bedroom in the woods, their lips raw from kissing, wind chapped from the breeze. Adoni was anxious to return to Natalie's cabin before the sun set, to hunker down beneath the quilt, eat cookies, and whisper to her. She wanted to break into Natalie's sorrow and cheer her up again. The older residents grew quiet as the girls approached.

Natalie stopped a story she had been telling mid-sentence, let go of Adoni's hand, and shoved her own into her pockets.

Adoni pursed her lips.

Two girls, each with cigarettes between their fingers, watched Natalie and Adoni walk up the path. Adoni glanced at one of them, a short and frumpy girl with gold-rimmed glasses. To her surprise, the girl addressed her. "You know what happened?"

Adoni shook her head.

"What?" Natalie asked.

"You know the guy who lives there?" She pointed at one of the cabins. "He killed himself."

They stopped walking.

Natalie shook her head. "Which one? The tall guy?"

"The one who used to live there," the girl repeated. "He was like seventeen or something. He had a really big nose. Maybe you didn't see him. He didn't go out a lot."

"How'd he do it?" Natalie said.

Adoni glanced at her quickly.

"Hung himself in the forest."

"How do you know?"

"We saw that woman go running past into the big house and, like, a minute later that blonde guy goes into the woods, and when he comes back he's holding something like this." She held her arms out as if cradling someone. "We all saw what it was."

"I wonder why…" Adoni muttered.

"He was gonna be eighteen and probably he didn't wanna go back," the other girl said.

Adoni stared at the boy's cabin. It seemed different somehow, heavier and darker, its foundations running deeper into the ground than the other cabins. Its windows were bereft of light, its smokeless chimney a black square against the dusky green sky.

"Okay," Natalie said. And she moved on.

Adoni was beside herself. She couldn't understand how the girls could seem so unaffected. She couldn't believe they had spoken so facetiously in the first place. It seemed the girl with the glasses was elated at being the one to break it to them, desperate to be the centre of attention for a brief moment. And Natalie spoke as if the death of residents was a regular occurrence. Worse, she spoke as if she didn't care at all.

Adoni followed Natalie back to her cabin. Natalie leaned into her hope chest for another box of cookies and sat on her bed.

"But he wasn't eighteen yet," Adoni said.

"Huh?"

"He wasn't even eighteen yet. He didn't have to go. Why'd he do it?"

Natalie looked at her pityingly. "The kids here are messed up."

"Has it happened before since you've been here?" Natalie nodded. "Who?"

"I dunno. Some other kid. Another guy."

"Did you know him?"

"No."

"Did he have any friends?"

"No one I hung around with."

"I don't get it," Adoni said. "You've got your own place, anything you want, don't have to go to school, don't have to listen to anyone. Why wouldn't you just stay? Why wouldn't you stay for as long as you can?"

Natalie shrugged. "Because you're a coward," she said, too easily. "Only cowards kill themselves."

Adoni looked down at her boots.

Ida got the news from a hospital late one evening, when Adoni was ten years old. They were calling to notify Ida, as next of kin. Adoni eavesdropped on the entire conversation, pieced what had happened together based on Ida's terse responses. She never forgot the way her mother kept the phone gripped in an unshakeable fist, or the way she stared at the floor and didn't blink as the nurse on the other end of the line explained the situation, or the way she stumbled to her bedroom and clumsily slammed the door closed behind her. Adoni heard her mother sobbing and cursing into her pillow, heard the old mattress creak under her weight, and knew her grandmother was gone. There was no booze in the apartment—Ida was on the wagon at the time—and the fridge was empty, the cupboards barren.

She sat on the couch in the living room and listened to her mother weep for hours. Through it all, her own eyes stayed dry.

Ida came out of her bedroom at midnight, when one of the late night talk shows was on TV. She sat in her favourite corner of the lumpy couch and lifted her arm to cuddle Adoni in the crook. She said, "You have to hate yourself so much, to do it the way she did."

She described what had happened, without any fuss, without embellishment, without breaking down again, as plainly as she would to a room full of strangers. Adoni bristled. The end of that day couldn't come quickly enough.

Adoni took a cookie from the box and let it soften on her tongue before swallowing it down. It tasted funny, with a plastic tang she hadn't noticed before.

She knew the dead boy even less than she did her grandmother, but he was there on the colony with the rest of them, and someone had to honour him, for whatever it was worth.

She took off her mukluks, stood on Natalie's bed, took a candle from the chandelier, and hopped back onto the floor.

"What're you doing?" Natalie asked.

"Going out."

The sky had slipped into a cloudless darkness. Adoni drew a frosty gulp of air into her lungs and made her way to the boy's abandoned cabin. The steps were covered in a light snow that she brushed away with the sleeve of her coat. She sat down on the top step, tucked her knees up, and watched the candle's flame flicker in the gentle winter breeze.

Several residents noticed her sitting there and the whispering started up again. For once, she wasn't worried about what words were said. All that mattered was the little slip of flame between her hands. Someone had to make the point: a person had been there a day before, living and breathing, alone. And now he wasn't.

She lost herself in the candle's glow and didn't hear Ritter coming up the path. He approached her slowly. "You heard," he said with a frown.

"Nobody's doing anything," she mumbled.

"You can't expect them to." He sat down next to her and held his hand up to the little flame.

"What do pipers do when kids die?"

"Sing their final homage, and bury them in the wood, without a marker."

"How come no marker?"

"They're easier to forget that way." She threw him a sour look. "I know it doesn't sound fair," he said. "And it isn't. But that's the way things are in the In-Between. No markers, no trace of every failure to face each day."

"We're not failures, we're kids."

"I know."

The northern lights of the In-Between danced above their heads.

"What about Steppe?"

"Steppe is… not okay, I should think," said Ritter. "He's reported it to Ansgar by now."

"What if he doesn't report it? I mean, how's she gonna find out? Is she everywhere?"

"Oh she'll find out," he chortled miserably. "She's got a very reliable source for everything that goes on at The Welcome. He's here every other day, poking about, making us sing for our supper."

Adoni shrugged. "She's gonna listen to Sylvester?"

"Absolutely. Who better to get the unfettered truth from than him? He has everything to gain if Steppe fails to please her."

Adoni was suddenly aware of the bird-like stares of the older residents. They weren't focused on her at all. Instead all eyes were on Ritter, as a piper, as a guardian of the colony, as the only one who stayed still long enough for them to memorize. Ritter scratched the skin behind one of his ears.

"I spoke to him a few times when he first came here. He was a lumbering fellow. Acne all over his cheeks. Enjoyed his fair share of hockey games. Talented artist. Another one of those gentle sailors on a sea of loneliness. Ishmael, always on someone else's course. I remember him sitting here some nights, just as we're doing now, looking up at the lights as though he wanted to break through the atmosphere. Who doesn't understand a lust for wings or the power of flight?" His voice tender, he broke into a smile.

"Why do we have to leave?" she asked.

Ritter cocked an eyebrow at her. "Why wouldn't you want to?"

"Because we've got everything we need here. Why doesn't she just let us stay?"

"You've got everything you need?" He shook his head.

"She brings kids here, doesn't even see them, doesn't let the pipers talk to them or anything. So how come they can't just stay here forever, like Reese? They're not bothering anybody. It's not like Ansgar's running out of space."

"Think about that for a moment," he said to her. "Is this place really all anyone would need?"

She looked around. It was perfect; mountains of snow bathed in pale green northern light, glittering icicles hanging from the roofs of adorable log cabins, a wishing well, thousands of trees. Maybe The Welcome was an entirely different place in the summertime. Maybe under all that snow, the grass was as green as any football field. Maybe the air grew as warm and smelled as sweet in July as it did on the strawberry farms she loved back home. Maybe the echo of piper music was enough to sustain her, inspire her.

But then there were no coffee shops, no movie theatres, no music stores. No opportunities to travel.

Everything she wanted—provided it could fit inside a hope chest.

She wanted it to be perfect. But she knew, deep down, it wasn't.

"Sing something," she said. "You know you should."

He chuckled and looked down the path; the tawny light in the chalet's windows beamed across the snow.

An evening song, on his own terms, when there was no one around to praise him for it.

He started to sing.

There was the boy, taken on his way home after a night in the ravine, drinking cheap beer and coolers with his friends. There he was, standing on the broken corner of an industrial street, in the glow of a shabby convenience store's fluorescent sign. There was Finnur, standing against the wall, hidden from the boy's view, his black clothes clinging to the shadows, his hair about to catch the shine off a pale full moon. And there was the boy, led away by Finnur's atonal promise that he'd never be lonely again.

The melody, made up of wind and brass and echoes bouncing off of ice, brought the residents down from their porches and around Ritter's feet. They stood together like a broken picket fence and listened as the phrases rose up all around them. Adoni soon found a second candle next to hers, held by a boy as chubby as she was. Now other residents went back to their cabins and returned with candles of their own, and soon a brim of firelight skirted around the dead boy's porch steps and lit it up like the memorial it should have been. There were trombones and trumpets and baritones and tubas walking arm in arm with quiet nobility, on their way to a great beyond.

A single, robust tenor pushed the instruments forward and sent them on their way. It was Ritter's voice, without its piper split of harmonies; Ritter's true voice, without enchantment. He sang the final line unaccompanied, with unfettered honesty.

He rose and the residents parted to let him down the stairs. He glanced at Adoni, gave her the slightest of nods, and walked back to the chalet.

Adoni watched him move from six feet tall to a tiny smudge and disappear behind the chalet door. Something in his nod welcomed her closer to him, made her part of him. She wanted to be by his side and wrap herself in all his layers of sound. She always wanted the things around her to be sacred—time, space, words, feelings—and he was the first person she had met who seemed to want to hold these things as dearly as she did.

She got to her feet to follow him back, and noticed Natalie standing on her porch, gazing at the scene.

She pouted, turned her back, and went inside.

"What was the guy's name?" Adoni heard someone ask.

"Gordon," Adoni replied. "He just said it now."

"I didn't hear him say a name," another kid muttered, and they tried to remember hearing it within the piper lyrics.

"I did," Adoni said.

Chapter Thirteen

She went back to Natalie's cabin and knocked. Natalie opened her door, muttered a welcome, and quickly turned away. She sat on her bed and lit up a cigarette.

"Can I have one too?" Adoni asked.

Natalie tossed the pack onto the edge of the bed, where Adoni helped herself and lit the end with her candle.

She sat on the hope chest and stared at Natalie. "You look mad," she said finally.

"You could've told me what you wanted my candle for."

"I just thought someone should've done something."

"You didn't even ask me if I wanted to come too."

"I didn't think you did. You didn't seem to care before."

"*I don't care*," she snapped. "Why should I? It's not like anyone knew him. He hardly ever left his cabin. He didn't care about any of us to be friends with or anything. All of a sudden I've gotta care about him?"

"Maybe he was nice. You're nice and you don't go out and talk to people or anything."

"Those kids out there are assholes," Natalie said. "Don't let this make you think anything different. Just because they feel bad about it doesn't mean they give a shit about you or me. You haven't been here long enough to know what they say about people like us. Okay? Wait until you're here for a week or a month or whatever. You won't always be the kid with the candle that one time."

Adoni looked at her helplessly. She didn't have the many months of experience on the colony to know whether or not she could trust the kids around her. Natalie had spent more than a year learning the ropes, testing the climate, building her armour, hardening her shell. Maybe it was true, and Adoni *was* naïve about their intentions.

She went to the window and saw several flames still flickering on the porch steps across the way. There were arms around waists and shoulders and a few easy smiles, a few laughs. She didn't know what to think.

"You know how you said your mom doesn't believe you about anything?" she asked.

"Yeah."

"What do you mean?"

"Just what I said."

"I guess it was your dad, eh?" Adoni leaned against the wall and slid down to the floor, where she crossed her legs at the ankles and folded her hands in her lap. Natalie eyed her suspiciously.

"Why do you wanna talk about it?"

"I just wanna understand. I just wanna know why."

Natalie took a long drag off her cigarette and stared at her quilt. "I told mom," she said. "She told me I watched too much TV. Or someone at school planted it in my head. She said that's what they teach you now, right? She said before it never used to be like that. Now it's all about overreacting and making parents feel like they have no rights anymore. She blamed my friends for making me lie. She said girls get into groups and they do these kinds of things now, like they all plan to get pregnant at the same time or they all lie to get some teacher fired or something. He grounded me the week before I told her. Then she said that's why I was doing it. 'I've been with him for fifteen years, no way am I taking your word over his.' Bitch. Stupid fucking bitch." She finished off her cigarette and ground the burning end into the headboard. "She used all the times I was grounded against me. Every time I was bad, she used it like it was proof. He stopped after that. Maybe she told him about it and he didn't want her to keep an eye on him. So after, I just had to sit there, and he got to tell us what to do all the time like always. Because he's my dad and I'm just a spoiled little liar. The kids know about stuff like that here. That's why you don't tell anybody anything about yourself. They find out all about you and then rumours go around. Then they wait until you do something they don't like, and it's proof you're garbage. It's proof you're not worth them being your friend. If they like you, they tell you it wasn't your fault. If they don't, they tell you it was."

She swept her finger tips under her damp eyes.

Adoni sat on the edge of Natalie's bed. Natalie eventually lit another cigarette. "So now you've got dirt on me," she muttered.

"Don't even say that. It's not dirt. I just want to know you better."

"Okay, so now you do. And I know you too."

Adoni prickled. "You really think I'd go tell everyone your business?"

"You could if you wanted to, right?"

"I'm not like that."

"Not now."

Adoni reached over and put her hand on Natalie's knee. "I'm not like that ever," she said. "I don't go tell people's business just to make friends. Why should I care about that?" Natalie shrugged. "Would you do it to me?" she asked.

"No."

"So?"

Natalie stuffed the last cookie into her mouth and rolled over onto her side with her arms, cradling her head, tucked under her pillow.

Adoni pictured what it would be like, to have every resident know she was the daughter of an alcoholic, if they knew she liked to drink herself if it meant staying on Ida's good side. It didn't matter so much until it was used against her, just as Natalie said. Just as it didn't matter that Shabnam knew about Ida, until they had one of their worse fights, when Shabnam smelled the beer on her breath and hissed at her, "You're a drunk piece of shit, and your mom's a drunk piece of shit too."

She curled up behind Natalie and put her arm around her. For a while she stayed propped up on an elbow, tracing Natalie's ear with her fingertip. She leaned over and kissed her temple but got no response. "I just wanna know why, so I can make you feel better," she said.

Natalie pulled her covers back and got underneath them. Adoni she sat up and waited to be welcomed in. Natalie rolled onto her back and fixed her grey eyes on her face. "You already make me feel better," she said, "you're not like anyone else here."

Adoni leaned over and kissed her. And kissed her again. She lay down next to her and they settled against each other, grateful the night was at an end.

And outside the window came a crash, a howl, and the thunder of a thousand feet stampeding across the frozen ground.

Chapter Fourteen

Adoni jumped up and threw the curtains open. Beyond the window pane were hundreds of creatures running between the cabins in a twisted mass. Their feet relentlessly beat the ground as they swarmed the colony. Some of them even climbed over the low-slung roofs, heaving and hissing.

Adoni squinted. They were people—teenagers, it seemed, judging by their waxen faces and how tall they were—wearing the same old fashioned clothes Sylvester wore. Their jackets, shirts, pants, and skirts caught the wind as they sprang forward from the forest. Natalie gripped Adoni's shoulder and pulled her from the glass. "Get away from there!"

"They're attacking the cabins."

Adoni stared as the mob set to work pounding away at the wood and windows of a dwelling nearby. The mass of them spread like spilled ink and split off into clusters, each of which chose another cabin and rattled its walls with their feet and fists. One of the more rabid packs charged at Natalie's cabin. Plastic faces pressed against the windows and glared with slashes of rage for eyes, with thin lips curling away from broken teeth. Clouds of heated, angry breath fogged the glass. They sneered and snarled, their loaded wheezing loud enough to permeate the otherwise silent night. No screams, no yelps, no catcalls or derision; their attackers simply breathed, hoarsely and heavily, as they ran the palms of their sticky hands over the windows. Shivers raced across Adoni's neck and shoulders.

"Those are changelings," Adoni said.

Natalie twisted the end of her t-shirt. "How do you know?"

"Reese told me. They can't talk. Listen."

Adoni stared at them. They used to be children once, she remembered, left behind while their human counterparts were taken away to live at The Welcome. Children who grew up drowning in sickness and neglect, while those they replaced had everything they hoped for neatly delivered to them by the chests at the foot of their beds. Adoni tried to find the smallest scrap of reason still lurking in their malicious stares. She couldn't find any.

The younger children started screaming.

Adoni snapped out of her sympathetic daydream. "What are we gonna do?"

"They can't get in," Natalie said. "Maybe they'll get tired and go away."

The changelings battered away at Natalie's cabin with unwavering fury when something caught their attention and pulled their chins up towards the gables. They threw themselves against the front door with renewed vigour. Adoni leaned her cheek against the window. Fingers, fists, and teeth pried at the plaque above the doorway—the plaque bearing the name of The Welcome's benefactor, Ansgar.

She sucked back her breath as the nimble fingers worked to loosen the wood from the wall. "They're going after the plaque," she said. "They're trying to break in." She grabbed Natalie's hand and pulled her to the window.

"Oh shit!"

"We need to fight them off."

"We can't fight them off! There's a million of them!"

"They're gonna tear it off and come in here. We have to do something."

She looked around for anything sharp enough, cruel enough, to scare them away. She looked at the chest by the foot of Natalie's bed.

An image came into her head, and she dove for the box and threw the lid open. Empty. "How do I get this thing to gimme an axe?"

Natalie balked. Crouched and silent, Adoni waited for an answer.

"It'll only make what I want it to make," said Natalie.

"Tell it to make me an axe."

"I don't want you going out there!"

"Yes you do."

"You'll get hurt!"

"*Not if I have an axe.*"

"No!"

She glared at Natalie. "I *don't* want them to get you."

Natalie bit her lip. Her eyes, in a fleeting glimpse, cast themselves on the lid of the chest.

"Don't go past the doorway," she said.

"I won't." Adoni threw back the lid and seized the axe with both hands.

The door knocked against the jamb as the hissing outside grew louder. Adoni gave herself the briefest moment to steel her nerves and settle her weight.

With her weapon poised above her head, she slammed her hand down on the knob and yanked the door open.

An eerie stillness greeted her as, one by one, each member of the changeling mob backed down from Ansgar's plaque. Adoni swallowed. Theresa was right; they looked like puppets—vicious, soulless puppets. They weren't quite alive, weren't quite *real.*

She heard a sniffle. Natalie whimpered. "Donny... I'm scared..."

Adoni gripped the axe tightly in her fists and raised it higher.

A hand struck out at her, though it couldn't cross the threshold. And then a second, and a third. One of the changelings wheezed a sound as close to a laugh as it could, and soon the entire crowd rollicked.

Adoni sneered and swung the axe down.

The changelings easily bent out of her way. She struck again with the same result. Each useless swing amused them more and more, until Adoni heaved a frustrated grunt and brought the axe down with all of her might. Inadvertently, she stepped over the threshold.

They seized her shoulders and tore her from the cabin.

Natalie screamed as Adoni landed on her back at the foot of the steps. A changeling broke from the middle of the mob and pounced on her. She held the axe across her body as firmly as she could, its thick handle her only leverage, and furiously kicked out with both legs. She heard the whizz and thump of dozens of fists landing all around her, pinning her hair and her clothes to the icy ground. One of them pulled the axe from her sweaty hands.

She saw the blade rise and snapped her eyes shut for what she thought would be the final time—when a shriek, so loud and so terrible it trembled all the way to the centre of the earth, slammed against her attackers and blew them away like a handful of snowflakes.

Steppe stalked towards the changelings with chin thrust forward and teeth exposed. He took a breath and shrieked again.

Adoni felt her heart and lungs quake in her chest.

Steppe's face was as electric and cruel as his changeling enemies. He hurled a barrage of the most feral and relentless screams she had ever heard. The changelings sucked their breath back and churned with fright as they retreated. He pursued them all the way to the edge of the forest, driving them into the first of the looming trees.

When the last cringing changeling was about to make its escape, Steppe's hand shot out and grabbed it by the throat.

"Listen to me carefully," he growled. "You tell Sylvester…" The changeling hissed. Steppe wrung its neck tighter. "You tell Sylvester I want to see him tomorrow at midnight. You tell him he comes alone, or it's war. You understand me?"

He hurled the changeling to the ground and watched it disappear into the forest. The residents stared at him.

Adoni hopped up Natalie's steps and poked her head into the cabin. Natalie was curled up in the middle of her bed, shivering, her face wet with tears.

"I'm gonna see what's going on and then I'm coming back, okay?" She left without waiting for a response, and followed Steppe back to the chalet.

"Are you all right?" he asked. His voice was low, calm, but he glanced back and forth across the clearing, searching for any lingering threats. She was about to answer when the door to the chalet opened.

Ritter slouched in the doorway, looking as exhausted and hopeless as the residents.

He stepped aside as Steppe stormed past him. Then he muttered, "You're welcome," to let Adoni inside.

Steppe grabbed Ritter by the collar and slammed him back against the wood. "*Coward!*" he hissed, an inch from Ritter's face.

They glared at each other.

Steppe shoved him again, stormed up the stairs, and disappeared behind the slam of his bedroom door.

Adoni looked at Ritter. "Dude…"

"Not now darling," he said softly.

A moment later, she was alone.

Chapter Fifteen

Ritter lumbered back to his bedroom, untangled himself from his shirt and tossed it into the corner. He reached for an oversized pair of headphones lying on the carpet and put them on his ears. His fingers walked across the CDs and settled on a broken jewel case. He put the disc into the CD player, dropped into the chair, and let the beans cradle each of his limbs.

It was his favourite album of late—synthesizers and drum tracks punctuated by guitars and two voices, one male, one female, folding into each other and spiralling towards the centre of the universe. His voice was fine enough, if somewhat distant, somewhat unreliable. But hers—hers was a treasure, a sultry alto that licked the eardrums. The first song began as a tease—just a single guitar string, plucked from behind a black veil on an empty stage. A bed of synth held it up for a couple of bars, a bass drum beat out the promise of life as the guitar repeated its phrase. The drums came in stronger when the guitar let itself break with tradition. The voices picked up the melody of the guitar and soared through the darkness. It was a passionate, honest tune, perfect for erasing bad memories.

Each song took him further away from the colony, further from responsibility. He remembered the streets he loved so much, and the neon lights washing over them, the smell of perfume and cologne from party-goers, the sound of human laughter. He remembered standing in line in the rain to get into some dive in some crumbling building, to see three bands no one else cared about for five bucks a ticket, his arm around some pretty young thing. He pressed his lips to hers between sets, and while she fixed her makeup in the shoddy bathroom mirror, his heels beat down the pavement as he walked away into the night. Every jolt of the bass, every turn of phrase, brought him back to his nights on the town, when he was free.

When Ansgar didn't know where to find him.

Hundreds of years crisscrossing the earth on his own terms—the memory of freedom still brought a chuckle to his throat, a smile to his lips. He had finished another incredible night at the El Mo, where he listened to The Cockroaches and April Wine and made out with a girl who called herself Duchess and smelled like Chantilly. Her hair was long, her pink skirt was short, and her black boots went up to her knees. He and Duchess stumbled back to his apartment with their ears still pounding, speaking in tongues along the way. They fell asleep in each other's arms across the mattress he had dropped in the middle of the floor.

When he opened his eyes her hair, her skirt, her boots were gone, and he came face to face with the man who was to be his fine, fearless leader.

Steppe's hair had been longer then, his features without the familiar razor's edge. "Hello," he said quietly. "I'm Istvan."

"Yeah."

"I'm the new head of The Welcome, the northern colony."

Ritter jammed the back of his wrist against his temple. "Where's Duchess?"

Steppe glanced over his shoulder. "My entrance was rather abrupt."

Ritter sat up. "You didn't open the agate *right here*, did you?"

"I thought you'd be alone."

"Well, I wasn't!" He got to the window just as she reached the corner. "Duchess, baby, don't be like that!" he called, but she disappeared in a blur behind a building, and his heart sank.

"Ansgar sent me."

Ritter leaned forward and gripped the window sill until his knuckles turned white. "I know."

It figured time would catch up with him and drag him back.

Every moment Ritter spent behind the front door at The Welcome felt like a thousand years. Every time he brought another unfortunate soul back to the colony he was a traitor, singing children away from harm so they could fade to obscurity in the middle of nowhere. Temperatures in their dwellings were always perfect, constant. They slept when they wanted, ate when they wanted, drank what they wanted, smoked what they wanted, learned what they wanted, said what they wanted. Food and clothing came from the hope chests at the foot of their beds.

"Ansgar's vision for The Welcome is that it becomes a utopia for the souls we sing away," Steppe told him once. "A safe place, where there's nothing to fear."

If he only knew, Ritter thought.

He closed his eyes.

He heard a knock at his door and sighed. "What?"

"Can I come in?" It was Adoni.

He hardly felt like entertaining anyone—there was music to listen to, and landscapes to revisit on the back of hooks and refrains—let alone her, but the stillness that followed her request made her intentions clear: she wanted to be let in on the secret, a secret only he could spill. He went to his closet for a fresh shirt and slipped it over his head. "If you must."

She stepped into the room and closed the door behind her. "What's Steppe's problem?" she asked, without a moment's grace.

Ritter smirked. "He's angry at me for not coming to your rescue, I assume."

"Oh, because you're a superhero?"

"You'd think, given his reaction." He flopped back down on the bean bag chair.

"Is that your job?"

He yawned. "No, of course not. But I suspect the changeling attack has something to do with me. Any threat from Sylvester involves me in one way or another."

"Okay."

She leaned forward on the balls of her feet and waited.

Ritter stared at her the way he had in Natalie's wintry bedroom. He weighed her interest carefully, turned her intensity over in his thoughts. She wanted answers, he could tell. She wanted to know why the changelings would spring on them so suddenly, without warning. But the truth could earn him either friend or foe.

Undaunted, she held her ground.

He waved an arm towards his bed. "Sit down," he said. "You know what changelings are, yes?" She nodded. "Sylvester's story is one of the worst in the whole sordid piper history. Ansgar created him... oh, just over three hundred years ago now. He was placed with some belligerent drunk on a farm, to work in the fields and sleep with the dogs and bear the crack of a whip whenever the spirit moved the old man. What we pipers didn't know, what we *fools* didn't know, was the old man had another son. A twin. And a child can always tell the difference between a brother or sister and a hollow creature with a doomed soul.

"Sylvester's brother tormented him just as much as the old man did. He demanded to know where his real brother was. And the poor devil couldn't answer him. Of course the boy's accusations sent his father into hysterics on more than one occasion. Until one day, when the old man had had enough, chased the boy into the field, and ran him down with his horse."

Ritter's eyes met hers.

"Sylvester saw what he'd look like the moment his short life reached its pointless, violent end. That's where his rage comes from. His rage is every changeling's rage." He sighed. "And I don't blame them for having it."

Adoni frowned. "So what's their business gotta do with you?"

"I'm Ansgar's chosen messenger. A relic of the old days and old ways."

She picked up one of the polished stones on his bed and passed it back and forth between her palms. "If you're a chosen messenger how come Steppe's in charge?"

"Because, my dear, I'm a lousy leader. I don't believe in any of this piper code nonsense. And I can't muster the strength of character it would take to follow Ansgar's code to the letter. But I'm stuck here, because that's what Ansgar wants. So here I am." He folded his arms across his chest. "Besides, Steppe's infinitely more powerful than I am. We're supposed to listen and suck up sounds to add to our voices to make them richer and stronger. Steppe was your age when Ansgar's music made a piper out of him. Over the years he's added every sound known to man to that voice of his. Swallowed everything from the tingle of a bell to a nuclear explosion. Nature herself lives in his throat and vibrates when he calls."

"But you're older than he is. Don't you have more sounds than him?"

"No. I'm missing one." He curled a finger at her. She slid off the bed and stood in front of him. "I've been lucky, wandering this great big world of ours," he said. "I can see trouble coming from a mile away and I'm almost always able to steer clear of it. My wits are sharp and they've saved me more times than I care to count. But Steppe wasn't so fortunate in his early days. Misery stalked him with a vengeance and found him when he was fourteen and ripe for the picking. So when he stood in misery's presence, faced it down, and won, he took away the most devastating sound of all as a prize. The sound of *death*. The sound of *death itself*."

Adoni's hands shuddered as she gripped the stone. "Is that what he did just now?"

Ritter laughed. "No, darling. That was *nothing*."

She reached up and dug her fingers into her aching shoulders. "Why doesn't Ansgar get rid of the changelings?"

"That's another story for another day."

He stood and changed the CD in the player to something more esoteric, something throbbing with strings and hurdy-gurdies and angel voices whizzing up the sides of mountains. Adoni's expression went languid, appreciative.

Her ease with the music stirred something inside him, and the impish grin reappeared. "On to something brighter now, yes?"

"Whatever."

"You should learn how to sing," he said, like a single note out of the blue.

She crossed her arms. "What do you know?"

"You're talented. Your voice impressed every one of my esteemed colleagues, including the head of this sorry little place himself. And I know someone with talent like that shouldn't keep quiet and let it go to waste. You should be standing on a stage somewhere, bathing in limelight, sharing yourself with the world."

"Uh-huh."

"I could teach you, you know."

"Sure."

"I'm serious."

"Okay."

He stretched his arms and legs until he found the perfect position. "All right. We'll start tomorrow. You can bunk with me tonight. I'll take the chair."

He dropped into the bean bag chair and shifted around until he was comfortable, his enthusiasm dancing in the corners of his lips. She grinned and stretched out on his bed.

Chapter Sixteen

It had been snowing all day; by the time night fell, the thatched roof, the fence, the barn were swathed in white. It was silent, long after everyone had gone to bed. The only sound was of snowflakes landing on shoulders and slipping to the ground, and the occasional low from a cow. The candle in the farmhouse window was just bright enough to light the distance from the agate, as it split open in the frigid air, to the short path leading to the front door.

Ritter held a hand over his eyes to shield them from the snow and peered at the landscape before him. The farmstead was alone in this corner of the country, the closest neighbour more than a mile's walk from the edge of the field. He listened carefully for the sound of footsteps in the snow but heard nothing.

It was best to make the switch this late at night, when there was no chance of being discovered.

His nose wrinkled. *Disgusting,* he thought. *Farms always smell of shit.*

Ansgar's order—direct from her lips, not filtered through a colony leader—was clear: go to the farm, find the boy, sing him away, and leave the changeling in his place. She'd called him to her fortress hours before and delivered the changeling straight to his reluctant arms. There was no room for bargaining, no room for charming. Ritter wasn't to return to the In-Between until the task had been carried out. This time he had no choice but to obey. She was running out of patience. He didn't want to know what would happen if she lost it completely.

He looked down at his side. The changeling stared straight ahead with glassy eyes. Ritter took the tiny hand in his and together they trudged up to the front door. It was a short distance, but their stockings and shoes were nonetheless soaked when they reached their destination. He swept the snowflakes from his coat and hair before kneeling in front of the changeling to do the same. He couldn't have it climb into bed with wet hair and clothes; someone was bound to suspect something. He brushed his hand over its oversized nightshirt and dark hair, and fixed his green eyes on its vacant gaze, its lifeless face. At first it barely registered Ritter's presence.

He was about to go about Ansgar's business, to complete the task he was there to complete.

The changeling looked at him.

One corner of its mouth lifted up, and then the other, and it smiled; a hollow smile, but no less endearing than any other smile Ritter had ever seen before.

Ritter's skin began to tingle. Changelings weren't supposed to smile until exposed to a smile, weren't supposed to frown until face to face with one. They weren't supposed to harbour emotions, until they saw them first play out in front of them and knew exactly what to mimic.

What's Ansgar playing at?

He cupped its cheek. "What's this?"

It didn't answer.

"Do you know where you are?"

"I'm home sweet home," it said. Its voice was bright and synthetic.

"Who told you that?"

"Mother."

He sighed. "Did she now?" He sniggered miserably. "Do you know what's about to happen?"

"I'm going home sweet home, to live on a farm."

Ritter gritted his teeth.

The least she could have done was tell the thing the truth, he thought. *There's no need to be cruel.* "You're here to replace a real boy," he said, as plainly and sternly as he could.

The changeling tilted his head, confused. "I am a real boy."

"No, darling, you're not."

It stared unflinchingly at him.

Ritter put his other hand on its cheek and stroked its artificial skin with his thumbs. "Listen to me. We're brothers, you and I. Forget this night, for your own sake. Forget we ever spoke like this."

It didn't reply.

He shook his head. "Poor devils." He stood and held his hand out, commanding the changeling to stay where it was. It watched him conjure a tune from his deepest depths, something soft, and sad, and achingly beautiful, something filled with lark song and violins, something so gentle a gust of wind could blow it out like a candle's flame.

The farmhouse door opened.

The boy, Sylvester, stepped over the threshold, into the snow.

He looked at the changeling, his lips hanging loosely. Ritter strengthened his song, and the boy obediently followed it until the piper's arms closed around him and he was swept off his feet.

The changeling's smile didn't falter.

"I'm your brother," it said.

Ritter held it briefly in his sight.

Take it.

Take it and run.

She'll never suspect. You can take the child back to the In-Between, leave him with The Welcome, and come back before it knows you were ever gone. What's one more changeling to her, anyway? She'll never miss it.

You can't leave it here.

You can't.

But he knew Ansgar would track him down, wherever he went, and drag him back to the In-Between.

If she found a changeling with him, she'd kill it too.

"I'm your brother," it said happily.

Ritter turned, and opened the agate.

The changeling looked around, its head tilting up and down. It didn't know how to open the door, didn't know where to find warmth, to find clothes, to find food. It didn't understand the sounds coming from the barn, didn't recognize the smell in the air. Its feet were cold. It started to shake.

The truth finally revealed itself.

Ritter heard one last call before the portal closed behind him.

"Can I come with you?"

Chapter Seventeen

Theresa watched the changeling attack unfold from her bedroom window. She saw Adoni nearly lose her head to the blow of an axe. She heard her lover's retaliation pierce the fabric of the air, and saw their enemies cower and scatter back beyond the edge of the forest. But the moment she heard Steppe's door slam shut, she looked around at her room, at her rumpled bed, and knew she'd be spending the rest of the night alone.

She opened the bottom drawer of the vanity, pulled out the pewter jewellery box she hadn't looked at for weeks, and unlocked it.

Memories of who Steppe used to be stepped out of the photographs and made their way to her heart. He rarely smiled in pictures, and when he did it was never with teeth. Still, he was handsome enough that he didn't need a smile to invite anyone's gaze.

She sat on her bed and held up a picture of him standing in the kitchen doorway. He looked exactly as he had the night of her eighteenth birthday—his face as blank as a sheet, but his eyes blazing, wary.

It was November. The few friends she'd managed to make over the years were gone by then, having all been born in the spring and summer months.

They'd been summoned from their cabins and marched to the clearing as though on their way to the gallows.

She had been dreading her birthday all week, and had spent what she thought were her last few days at The Welcome locked in her cabin as she tried to figure out what she would do with herself when she was thrown out. Every tiny sound, every creak and whistle of wind, made her shudder and jump, made her think it was that last knock on the door, the knock that would signal it was time to go, and she'd finally be shucked out of her cabin and into the unknown. She waited, and waited, until her eyelids drooped and she rested her head against the wall to allow herself what she thought would be a brief nap.

When morning came she woke and found herself still in her cabin, in the same clothes she had been wearing the day before.

She looked around, her jaw hanging slack, her mouth pasty and dry. She knelt down before her hope chest and wished for a calendar, opened the lid and took a long, hard look. She hadn't miscalculated, hadn't skipped a day. It was the first of December, the day after her birthday, and no one had forced her to go.

She opened her cabin door and stood on the porch. Steppe was leaning against the well in the clearing. He lifted his head and turned around, caught her wide eyes watching him.

The expression in the photograph; this was the same expression on his face at that moment.

And then, without a word, he moved on.

Theresa put the memory aside and went back to rifling through the pictures. Another one caught her attention; she took it out of the box. There was the woman with the gooseberries, smiling and laughing at the kitchen table. She remembered Belinda only faintly, but knew she was more than just a piper who had vanished from the colony long ago. Theresa had caught sight of her kissing Steppe against the chalet wall dozens of times when she was younger. She remembered running across The Welcome's grounds and seeing his fingers threaded in Belinda's long black hair. The ghost of her presence still lingered, behind every tree in the forest, and in every corner of the chalet.

"What was she like?" Theresa asked Steppe once, on one of their darker nights together.

"She was kind," he said as he stroked her hair. "And she *hated* when I kissed and told." He bent forward to nibble her shoulder. She giggled.

"Seriously."

"She loved being a piper. She sang everything with conviction and dedication. She was incredibly loyal."

"What did her voice sound like?"

"Like birds with wings of fire and a shattering sea."

Theresa stood and looked at herself in the mirror, admiring her mussed hair and clothes. "What do you think I'd sound like if I was a piper?"

He scowled.

"I think I'd sound like a simmering stew," she said as she ran her hands over her belly. "And bacon frying in a cast iron pan. Maybe with a couple of biscuits thrown in. What do you think?"

"Are we going to do this now?"

"Yeah."

"We were having such a nice time…" He sat up. "You don't want to be a piper, Reese."

"Don't tell me what I want, Steppe."

"It's a lonely existence."

"You're lonely?"

He grinned. "Not at the moment."

She let him fold her up in his arms and felt the beating of his heart beneath her palm. He tucked her hair behind her ear and whispered to her. "You'd have to follow all of Ansgar's orders. Is that what you want?

To sing children away so they can languish on a colony? To be indebted to her forever?"

She ran the tip of her pinkie down one of his cheeks; it was another precious moment, when his honesty unfurled like a map across her Captain's table.

"You can change all that."

"I don't have the power to change it."

"So she loved it. Maybe I'd love it too."

"Slavery doesn't become you."

She watched his face darken. "Don't go," she said, cupping his cheek.

"You know this conversation depresses me."

"I wish you could see it my way."

He kissed her forehead; let his lips linger against her skin.

"Strong words," she said after a time.

"Hrmm?"

"Languish. Slavery."

He smiled. "You're right. Dramatic. Ritter must be rubbing off on me."

"Are they the right words to use?"

"Yes."

"And you don't ever wonder *why*?"

He sat up. The covers fell away from his chest, the stones clacking as they tumbled against each other. He leaned his arms against his bent knees.

"Why does she demand we bring her broken young souls and make us spit them out again when they're older and no better off than they were before? What the purpose of this place is?" He dug his fingers into his arms and dragged them down, streaking his pale skin red. "Every day. I wonder every single day. And I'm no closer to an answer now than I was when I first got here. My guess is Ansgar didn't make the In-Between. She just exists in it, like a shadow behind the light. And I guess she chooses broken souls because out of all the other souls she could keep for herself, the broken ones are the ones who want to stay."

Theresa reached up, put her hand on his back, felt his warmth. They didn't speak for the rest of the evening.

When morning broke Theresa set about doing what she did every day; lighting fires, sweeping ashes, cooking breakfast, and listening for footsteps on the staircase. By nine o'clock she still hadn't heard a sound, not even the usual din of morning songs. She left the kitchen and went looking for Steppe.

She found him in the music room with the other pipers, looking as if he hadn't slept in months.

"I'm not sure what caused it," he was saying as she opened the door. "Yesterday's meeting went well. He didn't seem more distracted than he usually does. I don't want to undermine the shock or the severity of this attack, but I've invited him back here at midnight to try and work things out between both sides. I'll let him know we respect where he's come from, but we won't tolerate a strike against our residents. Especially not our residents."

The pipers exchanged fleeting glimpses at the walls, at the dust, at the instruments around them.

"I think it's best to show him the same courtesy we always do while he's here," he continued. "No accusations. He has to feel as though he's welcome. Keeping him at arm's length will alienate him further. He should know we still have a handle on this. We need to demonstrate a sense of diplomacy." He rubbed the skin beneath his lip with the back of his forefinger. "Are there any questions?"

Aniuk leaned her head on Paj's shoulder. Paj put her arm around her sister and stared at Steppe's feet. Roxanne raked her hand through her tangled hair and clucked when her ring got caught in the locks. She tore it loose and muttered something under her breath. Finnur held onto a listless expression, curled his fingers to his palm, and got to know his cuticles more intimately.

Steppe cleared his throat. "I'll speak to Ritter later."

He waved a dismissal at them.

"Why wasn't I invited to this?" Theresa asked when they all had gone.

He turned his back to her and straightened the chairs. "I didn't think you needed to hear it."

"How do you figure?"

He shot her a look and sat down at the piano. "You saw what happened just now. The entire meeting went that way. They just sat there and stared and I told them exactly what they already knew." He pinched the bridge of his nose. "I thought I'd spare you the trouble."

"They didn't say anything because they're afraid of you."

"Of course," he scoffed. "They're so afraid they ignore my order to meet and stay in their rooms, sulking."

"Ritter's a lost cause. The rest of them can't say 'boo' to you without wondering what will set you off."

"Have I ever raised my voice at a single one of them?"

"You don't have to, Steppe. They know what you're capable of, they're not stupid. They got a taste of it last night. You can be terrifying."

"Fine. So I terrify them into blind obedience. That's just the kind of leader The Welcome needs."

He bent over the piano and struck the keys quickly and lightly, whipping them into a frantic melody as if making his escape. Theresa put her hands on her hips. "Why didn't you ask me to join you?"

"I thought I made that clear a minute ago."

"Bullshit."

"Lovely, Theresa."

Her hand shot out and grabbed the piano fall. He had just enough time to pull his fingers out of the way before the heavy wood crashed down and the strings hummed with a violent refrain. "Sylvester's not messing around anymore," she said. "He doesn't want to negotiate. He wants to destroy us. And the rest of the team won't say anything to you because you're a shitty listener. But if you'd invited me, you all would've heard something you don't already know. *We're in over our heads*."

She glared at him until he shrank in his seat.

"What do I do?" he asked.

"You need to petition Ansgar for help."

He chuckled. It came out too fast, spilled into the room like a broken vase. He shook his head. "Ansgar isn't going to help us."

"You're sure?"

"A bloodless battle isn't going to suddenly get her interest, Reese."

"What happens when there's blood?"

"If there's blood…"

"I said 'when'."

He leaned against the piano and took her in. "There'll *have* to be blood. That's what I'm saying."

She gave him a moment to change his mind, to admit his morbidity and agree it didn't serve anyone any good. He lifted the fall off the piano keys. "I can play you something."

"I'm only Theresa when you want to put me in my place."

"That's not true."

"Really."

He coaxed a melody up from the strings and ancient wood, something light and airy and deceitful. "They don't respect me, Reese," he said. "They fear me, they don't respect me."

She sat down on the other end of the bench and let the song turn her around. She found herself alone again, crouched in the gravel and the pulp of fallen leaves, in the concrete school yard, with a knife in her hand.

That night he sang her a song, lifted up her tear-soaked face and brought her safely to his arms.

His music always changed the subject. She choked as the piano spun its lies.

Chapter Eighteen

Adoni felt the warmth of a beam of morning sunlight on her cheek. She sat up and looked across the room at Ritter's bean bag chair and saw she was alone. She yawned and stretched her arms over her head, then remembered her promise—now broken—to return to Natalie's cabin.

She leaped out of bed and stabbed her arms and legs through Theresa's clothes. Hair tangled, face unwashed, she bounded down the main staircase and dug a cloak and a pair of mukluks out of the front closet. The mukluks were too large for her feet and almost slipped off a number of times as she trudged and panted her way across the clearing.

There were only two residents out on one of the porches when Adoni stepped up to Natalie's front door. She cringed when the boy with the square jaw and rough, pockmarked cheeks shouted at her.

"Hey! Hey! Lemme ask you something!" She turned and looked at him. "Seriously, you're a dyke, eh?" he said.

Aniuk's melody for this boy drifted underneath his bravado. She had woven a thread of sensitivity throughout her tribute; Adoni wondered if the piper had ever actually met the boy before composing such a gorgeous melody. Pinned by his vulgarity, she stared at him with red cheeks and a sour frown.

"Yeah, you're a dyke," he said. "Lookat'er face!"

The other boy had stringy blonde hair hanging over his eyes. He nudged his friend's arm and smirked.

"So, okay," the ringleader continued, "you're gonna eat your girlfriend out now, eh?" He slurped and smacked his lips together.

Adoni turned away and struck Natalie's door.

"They shoulda cut her head off," the other boy said. "*Pig.*"

Natalie opened the door.

"I fell asleep," Adoni said.

"You're a jerk!" Natalie snapped.

"I went to figure out what was going on and I fell asleep inside. I'm sorry. But I know what's happening now."

"Natalie, she's gonna do you like this!" the boy called to her. He repeated the noises, shot them between two cigarette-stained fingers. His friend's smile twisted into a delighted sneer.

Natalie leaned out of the doorway. "Just like your uncle did to you, eh David? Just the way you like it."

David pushed his friend out of the way and lunged for Natalie's cabin.

"You're welcome," Natalie said to Adoni before yanking her across the threshold and tucking her safely behind her back. David dove for Natalie's front door and cursed when it shoved him back onto the veranda. He spat at her; it hit the invisible barrier and trickled down to the floor.

"Dyke bitch!"

Natalie smirked and flapped her fingers open and closed. "Just like your auntie, right David? That's why your uncle…"

David slammed his fist against the open doorway. His friend joined him on the veranda and pointed at her.

"I'm gonna beat the shit outta you! You come outta there once and I'll shove my…"

"Shut up, Gareth, nobody gives a shit about you," Natalie said. "That's why you're here."

Adoni put her hand on Natalie's shoulder. "Close the door," she said.

Natalie tossed a brutal laugh at her aggressors. She slammed the door in their faces and leaned her head against the wood, listening to their insults and threats with a serene grin on her face. When she heard the sound of their footsteps receding, she turned to Adoni.

"What?"

Adoni shrugged, silent.

Natalie crossed the floor and sat on her bed. "So what did you find out?"

Adoni recounted Sylvester's story and Ritter's suggestion the attack might have something to do with him. Natalie leaned over the foot of her bed and opened the chest. "Can you get those?" Adoni retrieved a box of chocolate cream cookies and handed them to her. "Want one?" she asked. Adoni shook her head. "I thought it was gonna kill you," she said. "I told you not to go past the door."

"I'm sorry."

"So what does Ritter think?"

"He says he doesn't blame them."

Natalie laughed. "Right, not until they put an axe to his head instead. What a jerk! Good thing Steppe's around to protect him."

Adoni shifted her weight from one foot to the other. "Ritter said he was gonna teach me how to sing," she said.

Natalie looked as though she'd been slapped in the face. "Why's he teaching you to sing?"

"'Cause he thinks I can sing."

"Can you?"

"No."

Natalie crossed her arms. "Then why's he gonna bother?"

Her words were tipped with venom. Adoni's back straightened, and her fists grew tight. "Maybe it'll be fun, right?"

"Whatever. I don't see why he's gonna do it if you're not into it. Doesn't he have anything better to do?"

"I don't know," she barked. "What's your problem?"

"I always ask him to hang out and he's always too busy doing whatever. But he's got time to give you singing lessons now?"

"It's not my fault."

"He's such a liar!"

Natalie pushed the cookies away from her and dove for the chest again, for a pack of cigarettes and a lighter. She put a smoke to her lips. Adoni watched the end of her cigarette burn away with a bright orange glow.

Natalie held the pack out. "Go ahead."

Adoni grabbed a cigarette and smoked until it was nothing more than a stub between her fingers. "I want to learn," she said, staring at her knees.

"Whatever, go ahead and learn."

"Are you mad at me?"

"I'm mad at you for freaking me out yesterday."

"I'm sorry."

"If something happens to you I'll be alone. I don't have any friends here."

"I'm sorry."

"Don't go running around at night."

"I won't."

Natalie softened. She sat back and slipped her bare feet in Adoni's lap. Adoni wrapped her hands around one of them and warmed the skin. She rubbed harder or softer, depending on how loudly or softly Natalie purred.

"Hey," she said after a while.

"Yeah?"

"How did you get here? Who brought you?"

"One of the twins," she said. "The serious one."

"Paj?"

"I guess."

"How did it happen?"

Natalie's face took on a faraway look. "Mom and I had another fight. She told me I was just starting something because I'm a spoiled brat, like always. So I was like, screw this, and I just left. So she yells down the street and tells me if I leave she's gonna lock me out. And I didn't think she would. So I went downtown and just walked for a while, went to China Town and had some noodles, and when I got back I knocked…"

Her voice tightened.

She swallowed, and a blush spread across her neck and chest.

"She wouldn't open the door. So I was gonna go to a friend's place, but I heard singing… that growly singing they do, you know… and I followed the sound. She was sitting on the steps of the building across the street, and I was just… amazed. It was like a hug, in music." She shook her head. "They bring us here and we think they care about us. And then we find out they don't."

"Ritter cares."

"Sure he does."

Adoni looked at her. Gently, she asked, "Are we going out?"

Natalie leaned back and stretched. "Yeah."

She found the collar of Adoni's shirt, grabbed hold of it with her toes.

Adoni let her pull her down, and spent the rest of the afternoon in a lilac haze.

Adoni's head was full of Natalie—of the sizzle and pop of her questions and the leisurely murmur of her voice—by the time she headed back to the chalet. It was dark by then, and her stomach twitched for something wholesome from Theresa's kitchen. She hummed Natalie's song quietly as she strolled; it pressed against her lungs, wrapped itself up in her arms, tickled her with a lazy finger. She wished she had the guts to sing it out loud, and counted on Ritter's lessons to build her courage.

As she approached, she saw two people standing outside the chalet. She squinted, trying to figure out who they were before she got too close to change direction, but they caught sight of her before she could duck out of view. Halfway across the clearing she recognized them: Steppe and Sylvester, leaning against the chalet wall, taking polite swigs from amber bottles and staring into the distance. Adoni squared her shoulders and headed straight towards them.

Steppe quickly came away from the wall and stood in front of her. "What are you doing out?" he asked.

"I was visiting Na…"

"You should go inside," he said.

Sylvester's voice crept between them. "Oh no, please, let her stay. It's nice to have a young person here with us. Don't you think? Let's say she's… an ambassador. For the residents."

Steppe's eyes flashed her a warning before he spoke. "Of course. Of course. They should have some sort of representation."

Sylvester's joker smile flickered. "Diplomacy, always."

Adoni stood next to Steppe and kept her hands tucked up in her shirt sleeves. They continued to drink in silence, until Steppe finally spoke.

"Why the attack?"

"I've always admired that about you, Steppe. You cut to the chase. No nonsense. Always by the book." He sighed. "I'm tired of this, Steppe. It consumes me. I want an end to the impasse. I want an end to the past."

"I understand."

"You have to realize we suffer because of it. Your failure to make amends is disappointing. Deeply disappointing."

"Your demands aren't *reasonable*, Sylvester. You can't expect us to capitulate, it's completely out of the question."

"Reasonable? One life, instead of countless numbers destroyed? That's all we want. I should think it's quite reasonable, considering how much you have to lose."

"Why can't we just stop this?" Steppe asked. "You know we haven't supported the subjugation of changelings for centuries now."

Sylvester looked up at the night sky. "You and I didn't create this," he said. "I know that. We inherited the sins of the past. Sometimes I want nothing more than to forgive. And then I realize it's simply not possible. Not when I remember what horrors we suffered."

"There has to be something else that can make amends," Steppe said. "You wouldn't be here otherwise."

"I was given a very clear message. My changeling brethren made it quite clear I was to be here. To try to negotiate."

"But you won't."

"No," he said. "I won't."

Steppe pinched the bridge of his nose. "So we should expect another attack? That's how we're going to leave this?"

"I don't see another alternative."

"This is insane, Sylvester."

Sylvester chuckled. "Times are changing, Steppe. I'm interested to see if you will change with them. Very interested."

Steppe shook his head. "We could come to an agreement of some sort. An exchange of services of some kind maybe. There has to be something else you want."

"No," he said, lightly, simply. "Nothing."

Steppe stared ahead for ages. He raised his arm and put the bottle to his lips, took a long sip, stepped up to the chalet porch, and knocked on the door.

Theresa came out first, wrapped in her red coat. She looked Sylvester up and down, on her guard. Finnur and Roxanne were next, dressed in robes and their piper masks, arm in arm. They circled behind Steppe and glared at Sylvester, their backs straight and their chins jutting.

Paj's onyx cheek caught the fire light and sent a glint of light across the clearing. She stepped up to Steppe and gingerly put her hand on his arm.

"I can't find Aniuk," she whispered.

Steppe squinted at her. "What?"

"I can't find Aniuk," she repeated, stealing a glance at Sylvester. "Not since dinner."

"She's probably gone for a walk."

"She walks with me," she said as she put her hand over her heart. "We walk together always."

"Then she's with Ritter," he said. He cocked an eyebrow at Theresa and mouthed, *Ritter?* She shook her head and took up a spot behind him.

"She's not *here*," she said, her hand insisting at her chest. "*Listen.*"

"What have you prepared for me, Steppe?" Sylvester asked.

Steppe gave Paj's back a quick sweep with his hand and faced him. "We've stepped out of the chalet as a gesture of goodwill," he said. "As a sign of our trust in you. We ask you to please stop this war, for the sake of the residents of this colony. Whatever your quarrel with us is, they're innocent. We ask that you don't…"

Sylvester's shoulders heaved, as if he were fighting for breath.

Adoni watched his face peel into the widest, weirdest smile she had ever seen. She heard him wheeze and chuckle. He turned his head and caught Adoni staring at him.

"They speak for you too, it seems," he said. "They call you innocent. I don't *dare* to judge you. That's what makes me different."

He let his chuckle die, until the clearing was quiet and every piper fought to keep from shivering in their boots.

"Ansgar has a chosen messenger," he said, "who left us with shuddering bellies on floors and streets, to spit as we begged, to claw the corners for mercy that was stolen from us nightly, to quake for fleeting ounces of dignity. Who knew he'd thrown us to our knees, just to please his mistress. And who ran like a coward when he realized the stain he left behind would never vanish, no matter the sweat, no matter the tears. I know this. I watched him walk away."

He paused, following the memory for a moment.

"You're wondering when we'll attack again," he said. "You're wondering if it will be the same as last night, or if every time I come to pick apart your fortress I'll bring more of my brethren, more of my hunger and my hatred for you. Maybe you're wondering when this disease will be cured."

His smile split into a cruel gash.

"Or maybe you're wondering where Aniuk is."

He pulled a jar from the inside pocket of his coat, unscrewed the lid, and slowly tipped it over. As the ashes poured from the lip he said, "When the flames rose… you should have heard her scream."

Sickness swelled in Adoni's stomach. She clenched her fists and swallowed the nausea.

When she saw what was left of her sister, falling and whirling away to every corner of the In-Between world, Paj stumbled forward, dropped to her knees, and screamed.

She gasped for breath and reached for her sister with both hands and splayed fingers, screamed her name over and over again, fought for enough breath to do it. The wind whipped up as she tore at her braids and ripped her hair from her head, until the jar was empty and the darkness swallowed her sister's remains.

"There won't be any *agreements*," Sylvester said, over the wails, over the sobs, to Steppe alone. "There will be no other arrangements made. You know what we want. To offer anything else in its stead is nothing more than an insult. We've had enough of your insults."

He calmly finished his drink, and then whipped the empty bottle at Steppe's feet.

"Give him to us," he said. "Or you'll all suffer."

He turned and walked away, back to the forest, back to his army.

And Steppe stood silent, numb, and watched him go.

Chapter Nineteen

Paj rocked back and forth on her knees; eyes squeezed shut too tightly to let the horror break through. Her voice became the grunts and groans of a person being torn apart from the inside out; it called for Aniuk across oceans and tundras, searched for her in every corner of the cosmos. Finnur and Roxanne didn't dare interrupt her. Paj dragged the tears from their eyes until they looked away and buried their faces in each other's robes. Finnur's chest heaved once with a hopeless plea for air, and Roxanne stopped fighting and let herself sob against his neck.

Steppe fixed a cold stare on the well in the centre of the clearing and didn't flinch, no matter how loudly Paj wailed. He held the collar of his coat closed against the wind with one hand, and kept the other firmly in his pocket.

The lights from the cabins spilled into the clearing, and the residents stepped onto their porches. They watched Paj as she yowled to the black night sky, their hands clutching teddy bears and blankets, cigarettes and bottles of beer.

Steppe looked at them, one by one. "We should go inside," he said.

Adoni heard the soft click of the chalet door opening.

Ritter stepped onto the porch, his face soaked and stunned. He kept his head bowed as he slipped down the staircase and slinked towards Paj. His steps quickened the closer he got, until he reached a sprint, leaped forward, and threw his arms around her sagging shoulders. Adoni heard his lips, muffled against her heavy cloak, utter over and over again, "I'm sorry…Paj… I'm sorry…"

The residents leaned over their porch railings. Steppe glanced at them and muttered, "We have to get inside. We don't know when the changelings will return. We can't risk anyone else's life."

Finnur let out a quick, cruel laugh, shook his head and bit his lip until it almost split. He glared at Steppe. "Now we can't risk anyone else's life."

"You've done nothing but risk our lives," said Roxanne. She raised her head off of Finnur's neck. "You let him past the front door. You let him get close to us." She wiped her nose with the back of her hand.

Steppe kept one eye on the residents as he crafted his response. "Inviting Sylvester to The Welcome has kept us safe for years."

"Are you sure of that?" Finnur asked him. "Are you sure it's not because he's left us empty handed every time?"

"Sylvester will always leave us empty handed," he said with a cold, jagged look. "I won't hear another word about that."

"I can't believe this," Roxanne said. "You have the power to put a stop to this whole thing, and you won't." She turned to him. "Finnur and me, and Paj, and Aniuk… We've been here for decades, we've followed your lead, we've followed the piper code to the letter…" Her words caught in her throat. She swallowed, then continued, pointing at Ritter. "He doesn't feel like singing evening songs, you just let him sit there and mock the whole tradition! He refuses to come up and face us when fate finally catches up with him, and you practically apologize for getting in his way!"

"Stop this," Steppe said.

"He's cost us a piper," said Finnur. "A treasured friend. If you won't stop Sylvester yourself, at least give him what he wants so he'll leave the rest of us in peace."

"No!"

Adoni heard the end of a whip crack the air just past Finnur's lips. Finnur tucked his chin close to his chest and out of the way.

Paj got to her feet, her eyelashes heavy with salt and ice.

"I'm going inside," she murmured.

They watched her climb the chalet steps and disappear behind the door.

Steppe looked around the semi-circle of diverted gazes before settling on Ritter. "Do you have anything to say?" he asked.

Ritter sneered. "What do you *want* me to say?"

Something that ached deeply, that hated deeper still, lit up behind Steppe's eyes.

"Thank you," he said, turning to go.

Adoni heard Steppe's words for what they were; a dismissal of Ritter's challenge, an attempt to break away, to leave the clearing and find refuge in his room, in his thoughts.

Ritter only heard what he thought he would hear, what he wanted to hear: Steppe lauding his power over him, as always.

"For what?" he said. "For hiding how much you despise me behind this senseless piper code? For not having the guts to agree with my destruction because of what Ansgar will do to you? For not destroying Sylvester because deep down you'd love to see him succeed?" He laughed bitterly. "I've had enough of your weakness. I've had enough of your shame. You don't have the strength it would take to decide The Welcome's fate, one way or the other. What in the entire In-Between do I have to thank you for?"

Steppe's face flushed.

"Hypocrite!" he said. "You're a hypocrite, and you're a coward! Never forget this, Ritter. We're in this predicament because of you! You and no one else! You've hidden behind these walls for decades, and the thought of making amends has never once entered your head! I've done nothing but stick my neck out for you, and you've never repaid me with anything more than contempt! Aniuk is dead because of you, Ritter, because of your selfishness! We all suffer because of you! And we'll see how weak you think I am when you're hiding behind my back again!"

"You're absolutely right," Ritter said. "I am selfish. I didn't choose this life. I'm trapped in this fate forever. I don't know what I would have done if I'd had the opportunity to make something else out of my life, and I'll never have the chance to know. But it certainly wouldn't have had anything to do with this." He flung his arms out to his sides, and in them he held the pipers, the cabins, the wind and the snow, the burning pillars and the night sky, and the voices, hundreds of voices, frozen and silent. "If I'd had a choice between this and me, I would have chosen myself. It would have been better for everyone involved."

"You have no idea what you've cost me!" Steppe said. "The hours I've spent trying to save your sorry skin!"

"Not to save *me*. To save *face*." He looked at every piper, every person in the clearing. "Because he knows what will happen if he doesn't cling to this code like a second soul. He'll have to face his demon alone. And his demon has a name. It's *Belinda*."

Steppe reared back and snarled.

The force of it threw Ritter back and slammed him against the chalet wall. He crumbled to the ground and coughed as he fought to catch his breath.

Steppe stared at him, shaking with regret. The pipers stood, dumbfounded, as Ritter gasped.

One of the residents let out a nervous chuckle.

Steppe turned on his heel and threw his voice at every one of them. "GET INSIDE!"

They retreated.

When Steppe turned back to his charges, his face was stony. "I want you out," he said, as softly and as steadily as he could. "After evening songs, tomorrow. Go wherever you want. Go to the moon. Just remember who's kept you for all these years. Remember who keeps you still."

Ritter chuckled. "What about the code?"

He heard Steppe's knuckles crack as he drew them into fists.

"Fuck the code, and *fuck you*."

His voice, his body, dripped with menace and wiped the smile off of Ritter's face. He retreated to the chalet, and left them standing in the clearing.

Theresa was the first to follow him. And then Finnur and Roxanne, arm in arm as they were before, climbed the porch steps and receded into the light beyond the threshold.

"That's done it," Ritter said. "I've officially worn out my welcome."

Adoni crossed her arms. "You did it on purpose," she said. "You pissed him off so he'd kick you out and not feel bad about it."

"Just how do you know that, missus?" he asked.

"'Cause I'm listening," she said.

He smirked. "Clever girl."

She reached out to turn him around and get a better look at the wound. "We should go fix your head."

"It's fine," he said as he waved her away. "I've bonked it a hundred times. Bleeds like hell at first, but it stops quickly."

"Are you going tonight?"

"That's the plan."

"You owe me a singing lesson."

"Oh yes," he said. "I forgot my entire life revolves around you now. All right. I suppose I should keep at least one promise before I go. But I want to be alone for the rest of the night. My room, tomorrow morning. In the meantime, you're welcome." He turned and retreated back to the chalet. Adoni waited a moment before going inside.

The air in the chalet was different now; the pine and wax and fires gave off an oppressive reek, and the walls buzzed with accusations.

She turned down the dimly lit hall towards the kitchen, searching for Theresa. She slowed her pace when she caught a low and distant rumble in her ears. The air grew thinner as she crept up to the kitchen door. Someone was crying uncontrollably. She peered around the corner.

Steppe was kneeling at Theresa's feet, his arms around her waist, his face buried in her lap, sobbing so hard his entire body shook.

Chapter Twenty

Ritter sat in the bean bag chair, absently twisting the hair at his temple between two fingers, welcoming the heat of the fire on his bare feet. He cleared his throat, swallowed, and felt a lump twisting its way down.

He couldn't get Paj's voice out of his head; the sound would haunt him forever.

He had watched it all from his bedroom window. Steppe and Sylvester looked so civil, leaning up against the chalet, drinking piper ale, chatting. He knew what the topic of conversation was, of course—there was nothing cordial about it—but from a distance one could have easily mistaken them for friends. They talked for a while, smiled at each other several times, seemed, at one point, to enjoy the other's company. He saw Adoni approach, and Steppe's entire manner changed; he tensed up and started throwing his weight around.

Sylvester must have smelled it on him—weakness, anxiety—and decided it was time to share the news. There was no going back. Aniuk was dead.

Ritter sniffled and pulled out a clump of his hair.

There was an insistent knock at his door. He thought it was Adoni, come to demand her singing lesson early, to make sure he kept his promise to her and didn't slip away in the middle of the night. "I told you tomorrow, darling," he called out.

"Open the door." It was Theresa.

"What is it?" he asked sharply.

"Open the door, now."

He sneered. "Come to tell me a bedtime story?"

She threw her weight against the wood. "Open the DOOR!"

He rolled out of the bean bag chair, stomped across the floor, and threw the door open.

"*What?*"

She stormed into the room and slammed the door closed behind her. "Who do you think you are, telling him off in front of everybody?" she snarled.

"We were all thinking it and he needed to hear it," he said. "What about that don't you understand?"

"It was low, Ritter. Even for you, it was *low*."

He scowled at her. "By all means, say what you have to say and get out. This room is mine until tomorrow night, whether you like it or not."

"You have no right to say anything to him; after all he's done for you!"

"Fine. Anything else?"

"What is your problem with him? What is it about him that makes you so angry? He's not the only piper you've met to stick to code; he's not the only one who's made mistakes. Why do you hate him so much?"

"There goes my quiet evening."

"You used to be friends."

"Please, don't," he growled. "Don't start with me."

He returned to his nook in the bean bag chair.

Theresa stood between him and the fire. "I don't understand you, Ritter. I try and try to figure you out, and I can't do it. You don't tell anyone anything. Steppe's the one who knows all your secrets, and you stopped telling him years ago. It hurts him, you know that? I can tell it does. He looks at you like one day you're going to come to your senses and see him as an ally. He's wrong, isn't he? It's never going to happen, is it?" Ritter didn't answer. "You might think all this secrecy is cute and makes you fun at parties. It's not. The minute Sylvester showed up all those years ago and started making demands, you didn't get out there and face him down yourself. You let Steppe do it for you. He's up a creek for you and you can't even say thank you."

Ritter rolled his eyes. "And you've got a problem with that, not that it's any of your business."

"He's trying to help you!"

"Because it's his duty, Reese. Because it's code."

"Why should someone else pay for your sins?"

"Why should martyrs be nailed to crosses?" he snapped.

She crossed her arms and frowned.

He closed his eyes, dug his fingers into the sockets, massaged away at the puff and ache. "Steppe knows what happened," he murmured. "He knows why things are the way they are between us. He knows it all, Reese. There's no need to ask me. Why don't you ask him?"

She shook her head. "He won't tell me. He'll negotiate with Sylvester for hours, but…"

Ritter smiled. "Well. That's our Istvan, isn't it?"

Theresa sighed and nudged him with her knee. He made room for her on the bean bag chair, and she settled against his side. He put an arm around her. "I'm sorry," she said. "I shouldn't come down so hard on you. What do I know about it anyway? I'd hide too, if I had the choice."

"Isn't that what you've been doing all these years?" he said sadly.

She chuckled. "Pretty much, eh?" She leaned her head on his shoulder. "Whenever he comes back from Ansgar's fortress, he looks *older*. Like he's been gone for years. He won't tell me why."

"You can't guess why?" She shrugged. He gave her a squeeze. "I wish I could explain it all to you."

"Why don't you?"

"Because you'll like me even less if I do."

She sat up. "Why are we here, Ritter? Why didn't Ansgar make pipers the way she made changelings? Why not create them out of nothing instead of passing her curse on to people?"

"Reese, you can put the loveliest voice in the loveliest throat ever created, but a child can always tell a real person from a fake. Sylvester's brother could tell and it drove him mad. Ansgar couldn't have that. She wanted her pipers, her beautiful ideal, and she needed humans to get what she wanted."

"Ansgar stopped using changelings. Is that because of you?"

"Yes."

"What happened? If Steppe can tell Sylvester what you did to overturn the decree, he'll back off. We won't lose…" She stopped.

"We won't lose anyone else," he finished. "I doubt that." He stretched his legs out. "I told Ansgar she'd start a war if it continued, plain and simple."

"Just like that?"

"They weren't my exact words, but something to that effect."

"The pipers were going to fight against her?"

"They would have, yes."

"Why?"

"Because I had information that would make them want to fight. Pipers are docile creatures for the most part, always singing tributes, to the residents, to Ansgar. But they won't abide deliberate cruelty. It's the one thing that gets them every time. It's the only thing they'll take up arms against. And when she created Sylvester she was… unforgivably cruel."

He waited, hoping she wouldn't ask another question, wouldn't dig deeper. But she did.

"How?"

He sighed. "She made him sentient."

"What do you mean?"

"Changelings weren't sentient. They imitated their emotions based on what they saw others do, how others reacted. They learned it over time. But she made Sylvester differently. She gave him consciousness. She gave him the power to react with real emotion, not just to mimic it. I saw it that night when I left him behind. He smiled at me, and he'd never seen a smile before. Pipers used to make themselves feel better by telling each other that changelings don't feel, don't have souls. Sylvester's existence was proof they were wrong. And if they ever found out about that, there'd be hell to pay."

"You saw what he did to Aniuk," she said. "You think someone like that has a soul?"

"Yes. I do."

"You think *Sylvester* has a soul?"

"*Of course* he does, Reese," he replied, shaking his head. "*Of course* he does."

They lost themselves in the glow of the firelight.

"I can't look him in the eye," Ritter said after a while. "Reese, I can't face him again. Not after leaving him like that. I could have brought him back to the other pipers as proof and renounced her decree. She has the power to kill us all, of course, but we would have gone out with a bang. I chose to bargain instead." He laughed. "Sound familiar?"

"*Sylvester's* going to kill us all," she said. "Every last one of us. We have to do something."

"There's nothing we can do, Reese. Sylvester won't listen. And Ansgar won't listen. This is her favourite game. She hates to lose."

Theresa got to her feet and looked down at him.

"So that's it? We're done for?"

He wouldn't answer.

"You really hurt Steppe tonight," she said.

"I know."

"Please speak to him. Tell him you're sorry."

"I can't."

"Why not?"

"Because he's better off without me, darling. The Welcome is better off without me."

"You're wrong."

"You'll see."

Eventually the fight went out of her. She gathered herself and left the room without another word.

Ritter heaved a sigh. He knotted his trembling fingers together and stared at the fire. He wanted to pick up his saxophone and play until he was too tired to see straight, but the noise would have angered the other pipers and he didn't want to risk their wrath. Instead he stayed quiet and let his mind take him back in time; back to a night in the chalet like this one, a cold night on the eve of a blizzard, before Sylvester came to The Welcome to make his demands.

He remembered the feel of the quilt and stones over his lap, the firm couch cushions, the scent of a candle, newly extinguished, tickling his nostrils. It had been years since he'd worn piper robes. Their texture against his skin that night was a sad kind of homecoming. He didn't know when he would wear blue jeans again, or a trench coat, or leather shoes, or cufflinks. He missed his closet in the city, and all the clothes he'd collected during his roaming years.

It had been a long day, he recalled, filled with morning songs and tributes, filled with evening songs and cups of hot chocolate. The colony had acquired two new residents, had expelled two others, and tension festered throughout the cabins and inside the chalet. Midnight couldn't come fast enough for Ritter. He cherished the midnight hour the most. It meant everything was done and dusted, and he could strike another day off his interminable sentence.

Steppe sat in a rocking chair across from Ritter, closer to the fireplace. He pushed off the warm wooden floor with one foot and kept the other tucked up under his thigh. Ritter was always amused by how much Steppe enjoyed rocking in that chair, and how unaware he was of the fact; he always appeared too deep in thought to register such a simple pleasure. When they first began their daily late night conversations, Ritter couldn't abide Steppe's fidgeting, but after many nights in The Welcome's living room, alone and deep in discussion, he came to appreciate it. Nothing in Steppe's appearance ever made him appear nervous or anxious; his nerves and anxiety manifested themselves in this gentle rocking, back and forth over the braided rug.

"Was it hard this morning, expelling the residents?" Ritter asked.

"It's always hard, particularly when they don't want to go," Steppe said. "Which, granted, is often the case. But it's code. It has to be followed."

Ritter prickled at the thought. "Well, consider it a compliment. It must mean they feel at home here. It's difficult to leave a *utopia*."

Steppe sipped his drink. "The irony's not lost on me, you know."

"I wasn't trying to be ironic. Glib, yes. Ironic, no."

Steppe frowned. "You're making fun of me."

"I'm not, I swear. You're just so unshakably loyal. It's endearing, even if it's misguided."

The rocking chair picked up speed. Steppe sipped his drink and stared ahead absently. Ritter watched him for a while, until he finally had enough, reached out, and put his hand on the wooden armrest, bringing Steppe to a halt.

"So the furies are in the back of your head again, are they?"

"What?"

"What are you thinking of?"

Steppe shrugged. "Just thinking."

"So taciturn," Ritter grumbled. "You can't fool me, Steppenwolf." He settled back against the couch and pulled the quilt up over his chest. "You don't like to be called loyal. Why not?"

"I don't feel it applies."

"That's not an answer. How so?"

"Loyalty requires constancy."

"And?"

"And bravery."

"Unless you give me some examples, darling, the label stays."

He watched as Steppe's leg pushed back against the floor and the rocking resumed, slower than before, measured, meditative. It took him a while to find the right words.

"When I was a boy," Steppe said, "I had a brother."

"Really? I didn't know that."

"A twin."

Ritter gripped his mug tightly. "Twin?"

"We lived with our father in one of the poor quarters in the city. Our house was tiny, two rooms and a corner to cook our meals in. My brother and I practically lived on top of each other for all the space we had. My father made a paltry living doing repairs. There was nothing he couldn't fix, but he specialized in tin. Tin cups, pillboxes, pails. Our neighbours used to bring him their broken wares and he'd fix them in the shed we had out back." He swallowed. "It was difficult for him to take care of us both, but he did it for years. It must have been exhausting."

He scratched the side of his neck.

"Go on," Ritter said.

"My brother took an interest in the trade and my father made him his apprentice. He wanted the same for me. But I've never been good with my hands, not like that. Not like they were. I used to watch them while they were working. My father was so proud of him, I could tell. They had a great understanding of each other. And I know why. My brother was chatty, outgoing. He could carry on a conversation for hours. I was the quiet one. I loved silence. I loved being alone. My father was prouder of him than of me."

"I doubt that."

"It's true. He wanted me to be a tinsmith like him, to start earning some money to help the family. I didn't want that. I didn't want the life of a tinsmith. Mostly I just wanted to be alone."

He put his empty cup down on the floor.

"My father was out one night. My brother too. I was alone for the first time in weeks. I had a peppermint, a gift from a girl. And I didn't want to share it. My brother and I, we shared everything, our clothes, our house, our bedroom, our friends, our family, everything. I finally had something to myself. I didn't know if I'd be able to finish it before they came back home and I wanted it to last. So I hid under my bed and popped it in my mouth. It had almost dissolved when he came home. I heard him call out for me but I didn't answer. I wanted my solitude just a little bit longer. He came into our room and looked around. I'm still not sure why, but he stretched out on my bed instead of his own.

"I tried to get out from under the bed without disturbing him when my father came in. His steps were always heavy, but this time there was something else, something full of dread making them heavier. I could smell alcohol on him, even from under the bed, some cheap moonshine he must have gotten from one of the neighbours. My father only drank when he needed courage; otherwise he was dry as a bone. He sat down on my brother's bed. It was quiet for a time. I heard him say, 'One too many. We'll starve.' Like an apology. Then he stood up. I heard noises, like my brother was getting sick, like he was heaving from the bottom of his stomach. He slid off my bed and ended up on the floor in front of me. My father's hands were around his neck.

"He turned his head and saw me hiding. I was going to reach out and grab him, to pull him away, pull him under the bed with me. He put his hand on my shoulder. Held me back. He held me back. He didn't want our father to find me. And I let him hold me back, Ritter. Does that sound like loyalty to you?"

Ritter saw the hint of wrath in Steppe's eyes.

"His mouth was open, and there was a sound... a single sound... and it came to me. Ansgar's gift. A piper's voice. I felt it come over me like a day dream, like a sickness. I felt it change me, my skin, my blood, my bones. I don't know where he first heard it or how he got it. All I know is he passed it to me right there, at the end of his days. And then my father squeezed the life out of him.

"Just before he died, my brother made a noise. I took it from him. Took it with me. I'll never get it out of my head."

The rocking stopped.

"It's funny," said Steppe, "no one told me how. Something clicked inside me and I just knew I could. My father stooped to lift my brother off the floor and saw me hiding under the bed. He shoved the frame against the wall. I backed away from him. He held his hands up, told me he wasn't going to hurt me. I could smell the booze on him. He told me he couldn't keep the both of us, didn't have the money to care for us, we would starve if he didn't do something, and my brother couldn't possibly make good for himself on his own. He put his arms around me." He clawed at his neck. "He called me my brother's name."

Ritter stared at him. "What do you mean?"

"He called me by my brother's name."

"Your name isn't Istvan?"

Steppe shook his head.

"He killed the wrong son," he said, trembling. "He wanted his apprentice, his hope. He didn't realize he was left with me instead. And I've been Istvan ever since."

The rocking resumed.

"I waited until he went to bed. And I ran. I never saw him again. Spent a few years wandering, singing, until Ansgar called me to the In-Between. You know, to this day I can't stand the smell of peppermint. It makes me sick."

"He must have said the wrong name by mistake," Ritter said. "He was drunk and delirious, he didn't know what he was saying. He couldn't have meant it."

"If he had a son who couldn't do well for himself on his own, it was me, not my brother."

"You can't believe that."

Steppe didn't reply.

Ritter reached over and squeezed Steppe's knee. "I know how difficult it is to speak like this. Thank you."

Steppe lifted a hand and waved lightly.

Ritter murmured, "I have to ask… if it's not Istvan, what's your name?"

Steppe's chin dropped. He looked at the floor.

"Don't make me say it."

Ritter cleared his throat, scratched at his scalp. "Of course."

It all made sense now. This moment in time, this whisper of the past, was the source of Steppe's guilt, his fear of doing too little and saying too much. This was why he always looked as though he had the weight of the world on his shoulders. This was why his face was as solemn as a haunted house, why his voice was a chorus of devils and harpies. Ritter wanted to say something encouraging, something kind, to prove his loyalty, to prove his friendship, to chase the demons from Steppe's heart. But his curiosity got the better of him, and he asked a question instead.

"What does death sound like?"

It didn't take long for Steppe to answer.

"Like praying."

And Ritter thought Aniuk must have prayed as her body burned away and she turned to ashes on the wind. And Sylvester's brother, as the horse's hooves trampled him underfoot. Every piper would know what death sounded like when the changelings returned and Sylvester had his revenge. There was nothing any one of them could do.

Ritter closed his eyes, and waited for the end of the world.

Chapter Twenty-One

In the morning Adoni was curled up on the couch in the front sitting room, tucked beneath a pile of hides. She felt Theresa's eyes on her before the morning songs were supposed to be sung in the music room. The lines in her face were deeper, drawn with soot from the fireplaces. Her brow knotted, and she spoke with a hoarse whisper. "What are you doing here?"

"Ritter wanted to be alone."

"You must be freezing." Theresa pulled the hides away and reached for the girl's hand. "I'll make you some breakfast."

Adoni followed her to the kitchen, where she set about whisking and grilling a plateful of buttery morning biscuits and eggs. Theresa's arms flailed as they reached for ingredients or utensils, and her steps were uneasy, as if she couldn't remember what was where. Adoni waited for her breakfast and ate it slowly as Theresa prepared a tray of baked apple strudel and a pot of strong coffee. Her hands wiped away the sweat from her brow.

When she had eaten the last mouthful of biscuit, Adoni burped and pushed her plate away. "You look tired."

Theresa shrugged. "I didn't get a lot of sleep last night."

She chopped an onion into tiny pieces and threw them into a cast iron skillet. Adoni saw a sob take her by surprise. She put her hand on Theresa's shoulder.

"I'm sorry," she said.

Theresa pulled away.

Adoni left her standing there, alone.

She knocked on Ritter's door and waited for him to mutter "yes" before stepping inside. The fireplace held a bundle of apologetic flames and the room smelled of cedar and smoke. Ritter lay in the bean bag chair with a saxophone on his lap. He wore a loose black smock and pants—stranger, more ceremonial clothing than she thought he wanted to wear. "Ah yes, I forgot about you," he said, and waved her in. "Close the door."

"You play saxophone?"

"I do. My weapon of choice. It's a fairly new instrument compared to most, but I quite like it."

She pushed the stones out of her way and sat down on his bed. "So you can play some stripper music whenever you want, eh?"

"Au contraire. If you play a saxophone with even a little respect, it can sound like a beast, like flowers blooming, like roots driving into the ground. It can whisper and scream. It can beg. It can sneak up behind you and push you through the dark. It can take you by the shoulders and shake you until you see things its way."

She leaned back against the headboard and put her feet up. "So are you gonna play it yet? I know you want to."

He sighed. "You're fierce," he said. "Damn you." He put the instrument to his lips.

His song began slowly, as a steady pulse, barely audible, stirring from the bottom of his belly. His breath warmed the brass and changed the tones vibrating through it from tinny clanging to a rich bass. He tapped the keys lightly and quickly, and the sounds passing through them swivelled around each other, teetered dangerously close to shrillness but never stepped over the line. He stood and let the horn lead him around the room. Its music wove through the air, shredding like an electric guitar, or buzzing like a mosquito in her ear, or wailing like a frightened child, or arching with passion and delight like a river in a storm. Ritter's chest and stomach worked in time with his breath and the notes he played. His muscles shuddered to keep up with the horn, the tendons in his hands rolled with every stanza. He wrestled with the creature clawing through him. When the tune overtook him he bent down low, and the horn hung like a stone around his neck. He screamed into the instrument holding him hostage, his face red and sweating, his voice tangling itself between the notes and frantically trying to escape. He played until his entire body shook and his joints threatened to separate from their sockets. He grabbed onto the song's tail and dug his heels in, forced it to drag him through the mud, slowed it down and calmed it long enough to free himself from its grip.

Adoni took a deep breath and waited until the wave of euphoria ebbed away from her shores. There was strength there in front of her, in the way he gave himself to the music, in the way he wrestled it down to the dirt. There was someone to know, someone to follow, someone to lead her, right there, in front of the fireplace.

"Play any instrument as if it's an extension of yourself," he murmured, "and you can make magic. All right, missus. Let's see what you're made of."

She lay on her back on his bedroom floor, and he called and counted out to her, "Breathe, 2, 3, 4, hold, 2, 3, 4, release, 2, 3, 4, 5, 6, 7, 8." Her chest and stomach filled with air, with the room's inherent muskiness. Ritter circled her and tapped the inside of his wrist in time. "Most women speak in a higher register than their voices want," he said. "And they keep their voices soft, because it's expected of them. Your voice is low and raspy and wonderful. But you're going to have to work if you want to be heard from across a crowded room." He stood over her. "Lovely."

"How old were you when you started being a piper?"

"Don't change the subject."

"Did you really not get to choose?"

"Breathe, 2, 3, 4…"

"How old are you?"

"None of your business," he said.

"Come on man, tell me."

"Why do you want to know?"

"Just because."

"Well…"

He laughed and didn't answer.

He sat on the bean bag chair and tucked his knees up. "Let's hear you hum something," he said. "Don't worry about volume. I want you to warm the bottom of your stomach. I want you to brush away the grit and leave the surface smooth. Get it?" He raised a hand and pinched his fingers together as though holding a conductor's baton. "Go on now."

Her voice was gentle, a cross between a growl and a bell. Adoni let it crawl up the front of her throat, reach into her cheeks, and nestle under her tongue. The smile on Ritter's face grew wider with every note. "You can't hear it, but it's so pure… so honest," he said. "I've missed voices like yours." He straightened up. "Now let's hear you sing out loud. I don't care what song it is, as long as it moves me. Lucky for you it's not difficult to move me these days."

"Just any old song?"

"Old or new, it makes no difference." She scowled. "Don't be shy," he said. "I once knew a princess who could crack a champagne glass at twenty paces. It was *epic*. There's no way you're that atrocious."

Adoni searched for the tune that would leave the greatest impression. Pop songs were too light, too easily lost in a current. Opera was more appropriate—an aria's passionate complaint, a soliloquy in song—but singing an aria to a piper was bringing a slingshot to a gun fight. She needed something to impress, something to get his attention, something to make him consider her greater than she was. She needed answers. So she settled on the first song that came into her head, opened her mouth, and dared the world to hear it. The song that had brought her to The Welcome in the first place.

She was only a few bars into it when Ritter's eyes flashed bright. She let the song fizzle out.

"What's wrong with you?" he asked. His throat was tight; his voice crackled. She smirked. "You think it's funny?"

"No."

"You have no idea what that song means to me."

"How old are you?"

"*None of your business!*"

"Who is she?"

Ritter's bottom lip hung open. He shook his head. "You can't possibly…"

"Sure I can hear her," she said. "I didn't recognize her when I first heard you sing it, but I saw her picture the other day, in Reese's dresser. Reese told me you can just tell when a song's just for you. I can tell that song's just for her. So who is she?"

He stared at her, with the same look on his face as the one he wore in the photograph she had found at the bottom of the pile; the look of someone with a raw and pounding broken heart.

"What's her name?" Adoni asked.

He looked down at the saxophone, the brass useless now without him. "*Was*," he said. "She's gone now."

Adoni crossed the floor and sat down in front of him.

"Belinda," he whispered, trying out the name.

The air stayed still, and the flames flickered.

"She was Steppe's partner," he said. "A great woman. A beautiful woman. She had the most arresting voice, Adoni. Astonishing. And it could carry.

It could carry through the walls, through the forest, it could bring the masses running. I've never heard anything so pure and honest and passionate. Everything else, every other voice, is just… artifice." He brought his trembling fingers to the hollow of his neck and stroked it. "Steppe loved her with everything he had. He and I used to talk about her all the time, when we were friends."

"You guys were friends?"

He nodded. "He used to tell me how inspirational she was. How dedicated she was to being a piper. How moved he was by her love of the residents and her desire to do them good. Poor man. He always was a terrible liar."

"She didn't like being a piper?"

"She loved it at first," he said. "But she loved it because she was told to love it. We're all told to love it. It wasn't dedication. It was knowing her fate and accepting it, because there was no sense in fighting a battle she couldn't win. And he's a terrible liar because, as leader of the miserable bunch of pipers at The Welcome, he has no choice but to praise us for how well we wear the chains. If there's one thing he hates, it's following an immoral code because he has no faith in his own.

"One night we heard her calling from her room up in the attic. Steppe and I went up and found her lying on her bed. She looked terrible. Sallow, as if something was sucking the life out of her."

Steppe bent over Belinda, stroked her hair, begged her to tell him what was wrong. Ritter sat at the foot of the bed and fixed his stare on the fireplace, because he already knew her answer.

"She told us she'd been to see Ansgar. It's a dangerous trip, considering the changeling camp is somewhere in the middle of the forest. She told us Ansgar needed to know the code had failed. The residents—the *people*, who we sang away—deserved better. Our tributes were useless. Our voices *are* useless. She told Ansgar she couldn't follow the code anymore. We couldn't believe it. It was the first time she admitted what Steppe and I had long believed to be the truth about this miserable situation. She asked Ansgar to dissolve the code and let the residents go home." He shook his head. "And Ansgar punished her for it."

Adoni shivered. "How?"

"She lifted Belinda's immortality," he said. "And Belinda was ninety-nine."

Her hair faded from black to white. Age crossed her face; dark brown patches broke from beneath her skin and spread over her cheeks. Her skin loosened and hung over her bones. The breath she drew in barely filled her lungs. Her organs crumbled. As time soldiered on her words grew weaker, her voice thinner. By midnight, she made no sense at all.

Steppe asked her why, over and over; why in the world would she dare to defy Ansgar, on that day over any other day, when she knew what might happen, when she knew there was no better way to advocate for the lives she'd interrupted?

Why would she defy Ansgar without him by her side?

"It was so slow," he said. "So painfully slow. Ansgar's a cruel mistress. She didn't just snatch Belinda from us. She made an example of her. She made it clear what would happen if any one of us defied her again."

It was almost dawn when they felt death was finally in the room with them. Belinda's breath quickened. Her milky eyes darted between the fire, the ceiling, and their agonized faces. Steppe seized one of her hands and pressed it against his chest, over his heart. He clung to her like a shadow, murmuring his regrets, convinced she wouldn't go if he held on tightly enough. Belinda's gaze settled on him for a moment, on his frightened face, on his anguish.

She looked at Ritter.

Her lips moved. Ritter heard her whisper something faintly, an order, or a promise. He bent over her and waited for her last instruction.

She found his hand, opened her mouth, and let her voice pass into his.

Then she closed her eyes, and was gone.

Belinda's sadness ran through the undercurrent of Ritter's voice, louder now that he was close to tears; a tangible unhappiness. It was wings of fire, and a shattering sea.

"It was the look on his face that hurt the most," he said softly. "He looked at me with such betrayal. Like I'd torn out his stomach. Like he should have known better. I can't begin to describe how it feels to be hated like that. Steppe can hate with the force of a thousand men, he's so haunted. He's never forgiven me for it."

"But it wasn't even your fault."

"She dedicated her last moment alive to stabbing him through the heart." He clipped his words. "I hate her memory. I hate her legacy. She cost me my only friend."

Adoni listened to the wood burn in the fireplace.

"What's gonna happen to Steppe?" she asked after a time.

"I'm not sure. I don't know he'll have the guts to report this to Ansgar right away. He'll wait until I'm gone, at the very least."

"Why's he gotta report it anyway?"

"Because it's code. And before you recall his colourful denial of it last night," Ritter said, "you need to understand the code is all that stands between him and an aimless oblivion. He needs it to survive. Pipers do tend to deny the truth when they're having a fit."

"Maybe he's waiting in case you guys make up."

"No, he's not. It's over between us." He touched his throat. "He's never attacked me before. Not like that. He's had enough."

"What happens when he tells Ansgar?"

He spoke carefully. "If she's in a good mood, she'll remove her seal from the colony and leave everyone here to fend for themselves."

"So he's gonna ruin it for everybody?"

"I think he'll try his damnedest to plead his case for the other pipers and for the residents. But yes, there's the risk it won't work."

"How big a risk?"

"Huge."

"Why don't you stop her?"

"No one can stop her, Donny. She's the most powerful entity in the In-Between world. You risk more than your own life when you defy her. You risk the lives of the people around you. You risk the lives of everyone who comes along after you." He reached out and smoothed back her hair. "You've amazed me," he said. "You see everything. And you hear everything. You have me all figured out, don't you?"

She didn't answer.

"I think you do," he continued, a smile inching across his face. "I can hear millions of soldiers marching behind what little words you say. You're some kind of warrior, Donny girl."

She snorted. "Yeah, I'm special."

"No, you're not special. You're wonderfully ordinary. Which means you're hope."

He sat back.

"I think I'll stay in my room today," he said. "While it's still my room. I'd like to listen to some music. Maybe write some before I go. Come up with some plan or other as to where I go from here. Hopefully this time I won't fall in love with a city and want to stay forever. A stone that's stopped rolling is easily found."

Adoni glowered. "Why're you taking this?"

"Because that's my fate. It's Steppe's fate. It's the fate of every piper, past or present, and the fate of the ones who come after. Donny girl… the worst songs in all this unhappy earth are the ones that are sung for no reason. I want meaning for my music. No one in the In-Between can have that."

Adoni didn't speak. She got to her feet, stretched her arms over her head. She looked at him for a long while, studying the resignation in his eyes.

"If you're going, don't forget to say goodbye," she murmured.

"I won't."

She left the room, stood in the shadows on the landing, thought of Belinda, wished she knew more about her, about who she was to Ritter, to Steppe, about why she chose to do what she did, why she sacrificed herself after so many years of service to Ansgar, to the In-Between. Somewhere in the chalet, there had to be answers.

Then she remembered: the key in Theresa's dresser, the pewter box, the old photographs. That was where she needed to start.

Chapter Twenty-Two

She made her way through the music room, past the instruments leaning against the growing shadows and the gathering dust, past the low ticktock of the grandfather clock in the corner, over the patch of light that fell across the floor, and found the cord to pull the attic steps down from above. They slid to the floor, bringing a sprinkle of dust with them that touched Adoni's nostrils and made her sneeze into her sleeve. She crept up the stairs, into the glow of the candles burning together on top of Theresa's wardrobe, and pulled them up behind her.

When she had first gone through Theresa's vanity it was to find the hairbrush, a functional tool, a means to an end. Now that she found herself kneeling before the drawers, searching for something, anything, to give her more insight into the woman whose spirit left so deep a mark on The Welcome, a sickness stirred inside her and made her palms sweat. She slid each drawer open delicately, picked over the contents like bits of broken glass. There were the scarves, the tin bottles, the dried flowers and ribbons, eased aside to check each corner, but the corners were as empty and unimportant as they were those few days ago. The smell, the sweet puff of flower and spice, made her sneeze again, harder this time. She slid the drawer closed more forcibly than she would have liked. *Why does Reese even keep this stuff?* she thought. *You can't use it for anything. It's junk.*

She stopped as soon as the words took shape in her head. Why begrudge anyone who wanted drawers filled with useless things, if they made that person happy? Who knew why some things were held onto and others cast aside? She lifted one of the scarves, put it to her face, smoothed it over her cheek. Some things were kept around because they, too, were a mark left behind by someone in love.

She opened the bottom drawer. The pewter box was still there, the key lying next to it. She put the key into the lock, turned until she felt it click in place and opened the lid, expecting to find the photos bundled together as she'd found them before.

This time, however, the box was empty.

She leaned over and examined the drawer all the way to the back wooden panel. The photographs were nowhere to be found.

Weird. Where'd they go?

She closed the box, put it and the key back. She tried to push the drawer shut once more, but this time it didn't slide all the way back. Something had fallen behind the drawers and kept her from shutting it. She pulled the drawer off its rails and peered into the empty space. The object was lodged between the second drawer and the floor. She yanked it out and set it on her lap.

It was another box, the same shape and size but plainer, made of wood. Adoni thought she'd found the new hiding spot for the photographs. Maybe Theresa knew Adoni had gone through the drawers earlier and wanted to safeguard her memories from prying eyes. The brass hinges squeaked as Adoni opened the lid.

The photographs weren't there; only a few stray hairs lay in the otherwise empty space. Ansgar's name was burned into the centre of the wood.

Adoni decided to hide the box underneath the scarves, where she suspected it had existed for years until she came along to disturb the drawer's contents.

Then out of the silence, "*Well...*"

She leaned back on her heels, knocking the box to the floor, and glanced up quickly, expecting to find Theresa standing at the top of the steps.

No one was there. The voice spoke again.

"*I should keep a journal.*"

Adoni stared at the box, now lying a few feet away from her, its lid propped open at the foot of Theresa's bed.

"*But I know I don't have the patience to just sit down and write,*" the voice continued, muffled somewhat by the ends of the quilts hanging over the edge of the mattress, "*so I'll just talk. This will probably sound stupid when I listen back to it, but that's what they say, isn't it? Your voice always sounds different in your head than out loud.*"

Adoni sat on her hands, stared at the box. There wasn't a single doubt in her mind whose voice was coming from it.

Belinda, speaking from beyond the grave.

Had Theresa known about the box? Had she never bothered to open it? Or had it slipped behind the drawers years ago and been knocked loose by Adoni's rummaging? Did any of the pipers know Belinda kept this diary? Did anyone—Steppe, or Ritter, or even Theresa—go looking for it the night Belinda was taken from them?

Adoni looked at the staircase, made sure it was still in place and no one was eavesdropping. Whether the rest of them knew Belinda had left her voice behind or not, Adoni wouldn't risk springing something so intimate on an unsuspecting audience.

Belinda's voice was rich, with the hint of an accent Adoni couldn't quite place, soft and melodic, the kind of voice that drew people close, made them feel special. Adoni reached for the box, picked it up off the floor so she could better hear Belinda's words. She pressed herself against the foot of the bed, balanced the box on her knees.

"*So how are you today, Belinda? Oh, I'm fine, thank you, just fine!*" She giggled; there was water, trickling down the sides of caves, splashing into puddles. Adoni recognized the current; the same one lay nestled in Steppe's throat. She pictured the two of them walking arm in arm, past some winding brook or some waterfall, pictured them both swallowing slivers of its music to take away with them. "*What do I say? Oh, I know! Steppe played piano for me all afternoon; that was nice. A private concert. He's making up for yesterday's row, I imagine. Doesn't want me to stay cross with him. Every note's an apology. I never can stay cross when he plays for me. Damn that piano!*"

Adoni heard Belinda's smile, her teeth lined up like pearls against her lips.

"*I remember, the first time I met Steppe I thought, he's too young for this. Too young for me. I wonder why that is? Why is it all right for the man to be older, but not the woman? I believed it too, back then. Silly. Maybe that's why it took me as long as it did to finally let him in. He played that piano for me and I thought, here's someone with a true poet's soul. Or maybe I'm just a sucker for rock stars. Ha!*" Adoni smirked. Steppe was many things, but he certainly wasn't any kind of rock star Adoni recognized. "*Still,*" Belinda mused, "*it's nice to know a true poet after so many false ones.*"

Belinda spoke again, more quietly this time; a different tone for a different day. "*Steppe and I went back to bed after morning songs. Of course he's still apologetic about the other day. I don't know why he beats himself up so ferociously like this. He punishes himself if he does the slightest thing wrong.*" Fire crackled, pebbles skipped across the surface of a still lake. "*I don't understand why he doesn't just let it go.*"

The next time Belinda spoke she was lighter, happier. "*It was lovely outside today, nice and warm. Steppe's gone to sing a child away, so I've made myself comfortable and he should be back soon. Well... what's happened? I had a nice afternoon with Ritter. He played his Nina Simone records for me. Actually let me into his room and played them for me. What an honour! Ha! And he went on and on about how wonderful she was, just like Steppe said he would. My word, such passion! They're so similar, those two. Just the other day they got into one of their friendly arguments over who the greater folk singer is: Bob Dylan or Leonard Cohen. Steppe loves Dylan, Ritter loves Cohen. And the imitations, the imitations, just to rile each other up! What rubbish!"* she laughed.

And later, *"Steppe brought a girl back from the city yesterday. She's in a cabin now, probably asleep. He came back late, she's probably tired. I saw them come through the agate last night. Staring out the window at the moonlight, and there they were. This was a little odd, though, because… I swear I heard him speak to her. He's usually so strict with code, and he knows we're forbidden to talk to the residents. Maybe I was imagining things, but… no. No, I wasn't imagining anything. I wonder why."*

Theresa's first night, Adoni thought. *And he broke code.* She listened more intently.

The tone shifted again, this time into even deeper shades. *"Steppe's jealous of Ritter. I can feel it. And he's ashamed of it, too, which makes him angry. Of course."*

Adoni held the box closer.

"Ritter is… Ritter's fascinating. He's not like anyone I've ever met before. That sounds cliché, but it's the only way I know how to say it. My Steppe is familiar. I look at him and I can see parts of myself, all my anxieties and failures, all my strength and love. I've walked where Steppe's walked and seen what he's seen. I understand him. I like to think I understand him, anyway. Who knows how well we understand each other, really? But when I look in Ritter's eyes I can't see my reflection. I don't know where he's been. It's like looking at a thousand different people all at once. Not only do I not understand him, I can't.

"And I've been talking with Ritter, during those restless walks of his, and the more he talks, the more he intrigues me. The other day he said something and, well, it hasn't left me. He said it takes work, hard work, hours of it, to

earn who you are. Not learn, *I didn't mishear him.* Earn. *I don't know what to think about that."*

Adoni didn't know either, though the words were undeniably Ritter's; ephemeral, and undefined.

"*Of course he talks about Ansgar all the time. They both do, Ritter and Steppe. Ritter has no respect for her, but sometimes he speaks of her as though at one point they were friends, colleagues—even equals. He told me they have an understanding. When I ask him what it means, he doesn't answer. Just looks at me and… maybe they were lovers? But that's not it, that's not how it feels. It feels like… like an old wound, like a scar he's so used to seeing that to not see it would mean something's missing. Like the scar on my leg; I can't remember what my skin looked like before it was there. And if it were gone one day, I'd kind of miss it. So Ritter, and Ansgar, it's like… he'd miss her if she were gone, but resents that she's here in the In-Between."* Belinda sighed; the sound carried.

"*And Steppe hates her, every cell in his body hates her, but he listens to her and he obeys. And his hatred doesn't look like hatred, that's what I've noticed. It looks like dedication. It looks like submission. It looks like he's accepted it, like he's good with it. I wonder if Ritter notices. I wonder if he can tell it's fake."*

Adoni remembered Ritter's confession. *He has no choice but to praise us for how well we wear the chains. If there's one thing he hates, it's following an immoral code because he has no faith in his own.*

He can *tell,* she thought.

"*They make me question what I want,*" Belinda murmured. "*And why I'm here. Why I should be here. Why we should stay.*"

Belinda's voice grew heavy, the clang of an iron ball and chain trailing behind every vowel, every consonant.

"*What am I doing here?*"

Adoni held the box tightly.

"*I'm usually… I'm usually all right with this. Years ago, I took a good long look at myself, at who I've become since I was given the gift. And I decided* then, I decided I could do this. I could sing these souls away. What better place for them than a safe place, a place without fear? But it's not without fear, not anymore. I'm ready to talk about it now. I couldn't before, but now I can.

"Some months ago, a changeling addressed one of the residents while she was out by the maple trees. It's called Sylvester. And it's demanded Ritter's life. Ritter won't say why exactly. Sure, he admitted he left Sylvester behind a long time ago, when he sang another child away, but there's something he's not admitting." She let a long breath stream out between her teeth, knocked her tongue against the roof of her mouth. "*Ritter's not talking, but then he never talks about the past with anyone other than Steppe. I'll have to ask Steppe about it later. But I'm not concerned with what set the changeling off. In fact I'm rather surprised it took them this long to start an uprising. God, I'm rambling. Anyway, Steppe reported it to Ansgar, of course, and I thought that would be the end of it, but… she said she's not going to intervene. That's what he told me. She wants Steppe to negotiate with it. To try and keep it happy enough that it doesn't attack anyone else.*

"*Something about that doesn't sit right with me. It wants to* kill *Ritter. And she wants Steppe to… just hold it off. Not summon it to her fortress, not hold court and order it to keep away from the colony, not… not even destroy it, as horrible as that sounds. Just… live alongside it. And* talk *to it.*"

Belinda's confusion reached across the void and took hold of Adoni, who started to wonder, now that she'd been given the words to wonder with.

Talk to it. The words went against everything Adoni knew about the piper code. Why could pipers talk to changelings but not to residents? And why wouldn't Ansgar step in and put an end to Sylvester's warmongering herself? She was powerful enough, from what Adoni knew of her, and had a temper to match. Belinda was right. Ansgar had the power to destroy Sylvester whenever she wanted. She'd punished at least one piper with death for lesser reasons. Sylvester had murdered a piper, and yet Adoni could tell not only would Steppe not ask Ansgar to intervene, he *couldn't*. He knew what her answer would be.

"*I don't know,*" Belinda said. "*I should go to sleep.*"

Her voice was only a hair brighter the next time she spoke.

"*Ritter's terribly defiant in the face of this changeling threat. Am I foolish for admiring him for it? I suppose so, but I do, I admire him for not playing the terrorized victim in all this. I admire him for breaking code, though I'm supposed to condemn him for it. And I wish I could have that kind of courage. And the freedom to be stupid.*" She laughed. "*I hope Steppe doesn't find this. He'd have a heart attack. I'm supposed to be his shining example, aren't I? Dedicated to the code, loyal, all of that. Maybe that's been the problem all along. I'm a fine one to talk, sitting here clucking over his following the code when I'm just the same. I follow code because… it's there, and I have to. Maybe the example I should set is… autonomy and fearlessness.*

"*But maybe that's just wishful thinking. I've seen what Steppe looks like when he comes back from the fortress. I think, out of everything I fear now, growing old is the biggest one. Growing old, and saying goodbye.*"

Adoni picked at the seam of her skirt, rolled the fabric between her forefinger and thumb.

"*Steppe loves me,*" Belinda said. "*He loves me, I know. And I love him too. But the other day we were talking and I… tested him, somewhat. Tested the waters. I asked him what he'd do if one of the pipers reported to Ansgar in his place. It's not explicitly against code for other pipers to ask audience of Ansgar instead of colony leaders. It's an unspoken rule, more tradition than anything else. His reaction was so… he was livid. He started asking me all kinds of questions, demanding answers really, demanding to know if any of the pipers had gone to the fortress, his hands were shaking. The walls were shaking. The windows, the windows were rattling when he spoke. I told him no, not that I knew of, I was just wondering, just asking what he thought is all. He said…*

I've never heard him say anything like this, not ever… he said it would be a betrayal. A betrayal. And it was sad. So sad. Because I think he can tell what I'm planning. And he's afraid."

It took a moment for Belinda to speak again.

"When I was a little girl, maybe four or five years old, my friends and I used to play Kings and Queens. We'd each take turns playing the monarch while the other kids pretended to be servants and jesters and knights and members of the court. And we'd make up little rituals to go along with our rule. Usually it was a bow from the servants or a salute from the knights or a knock-knock joke from the jester. Great fun, really.

"There was one little boy, Kevin… I won't forget that name. When it was his turn, the bowing, the salutes, the knock-knock jokes, weren't enough. He'd make up new rules, then change them without warning. One day he made everyone hop on one foot when they addressed him. The left foot. Then it was the right foot. He sent his invisible food back to the invisible kitchens to be remade because it was too salty, too sweet, too spicy. We kids, we played along. We thought it was funny. We thought it was a fun change from the way we usually played the game.

"Then one day he decided he'd had enough of being a simple bumbling King who was just difficult to please. He decided it would be more fun to be a wicked King. He started to throw fits at the slightest displeasure and order us into the dungeon. We played along, sitting in the dungeon and calling out for his pardon, which he'd eventually grant us, and we'd run free until we forgot to bow to him just right, or turn around three times before we addressed him, and he ordered us back again. Just… for fun.

"One day Kevin was very much the Wicked King and decided he was not only going to sentence his insubordinate subjects to spells in the dungeon, he was going to insult them first. We didn't know what to think. He was always such a good actor, Kevin, we couldn't tell if he was joking or not. He brought one girl to tears, calling her fat, calling her ugly, calling her an orphan that no one could love, telling his other subjects to do the same or face the dungeon. We kids had finally had enough of his bullying and told him we weren't going to play anymore.

"I've never seen a child throw a bigger fit than Kevin threw that day. He screamed and cried and threw punches and said if we didn't play Kings and Queens with him, we'd be sorry. He'd tell his father on us, or he'd tell his big brother to come and beat us up. We were scared. We didn't want to be beat up or get in trouble. So we went along. Eventually, when Kevin came out to play, the game was always Wicked King. Always, always Wicked King.

"Only a child makes up the rules as she goes along and changes them whenever it suits her. Only a child needs this kind of constant, blind devotion. Only a child is amused by pitting one person against another. Only a child is selfish enough to create this kind of hell."

Belinda swallowed.

"I think Ansgar is a child. A selfish, vicious, heartless child. I can't follow an immoral code. And I won't bow down to a child."

There was a long pause.

"Steppe already knows what death sounds like. This... betrayal... it'll break his heart. But I've got no choice. We have no choice. If I give him my voice, at the end of it all... it'll kill him."

The box went silent. Adoni waited a good long while, until she realized she had heard the last secret Belinda had uttered. She closed the lid and stared at it.

She wanted to save him, she thought. *That's all she wanted.*

Belinda was right; the In-Between was hell. For all its incredible beauty, for all its superficial comforts, it was still as dark as any prison ever was, it still held hopes hostage. Maybe that was why Shabnam's brother screamed when she sang that little snippet of Belinda's song to him. Maybe piper music had no hold over happy children. Maybe the only ones who heard it, who understood it, were the broken ones.

Belinda's voice, so sad and little a thing in its wooden box, lit a fire in Adoni's belly. Its fuel was vengeance—for the pipers who'd given up their lives to service, for the children who never made it back home, for the changelings who wanted peace but were lured into war—and it burned hotter as Adoni got to her feet, replaced the box in Theresa's dresser, and pushed the staircase open. She was anxious to leave, absolutely without fear.

She can't lift my *immortality,* she thought.

She decided to go while it was still light out. And she'd ask Natalie to come with her.

Chapter Twenty-Three

The curtains in Natalie's cabin were drawn tightly over the windows. White smoke swirled out from the chimney lip and dissipated in the sky. Adoni hurried towards Natalie's door and knocked lightly. Natalie answered, leaned out of the jamb, and gently kissed Adoni's bottom lip. "Hey. You're welcome."

Adoni stepped inside, but kept her cloak on. "I need you to come with me."

"I was gonna stay in. Where are you going?"

"I'm gonna go see Ansgar."

Natalie frowned. "The place that makes the chests and stuff?"

"No, she's a person. I need you to make me a map." She pointed at Natalie's hope chest. "And then come with me."

"Why are you going there?"

"Because she's messing everything up around here," Adoni said.

Natalie crossed her arms over her chest.

Adoni sat on the bed. "It's just not fair, keeping people here and making everybody do whatever she wants, for nothing. The pipers *have* to worship her or she'll kill them. The changelings can attack us and can kill a piper and she doesn't even stop them herself. If she gets mad enough, she'll take her name off this whole place and no one will get any food or medicine or anything."

"So? We can eat whatever we want in my cabin."

"That won't work anymore," Adoni said, pointing to the hope chest, "and if she gets *really* mad, she'll take away Steppe's magic and he'll get old and die. Maybe she'll do it to the other pipers too. We have to say something to her."

"Why's she gonna listen to you?"

"I don't care if she listens or not, but I'm gonna tell her."

Natalie sat down next to her. "David and Gareth are out there."

"So what?"

"They're pissed off."

"What're they gonna do, if I'm there when they see you?"

"Beat you up too."

Adoni shook her head. "They're a couple of assholes. I'm not even afraid of them." She put her hand on Natalie's knee. "Why didn't you come out last night?" Natalie shrugged and said nothing. "Did you see what happened?"

"Yeah."

"What do you think?"

"It makes me not wanna go out there even more," Natalie said, curling her thumbs into her palms and closing her fingers around them. "That guy and those monsters are out there somewhere."

"That's why we're gonna go in the day when it's light."

"How do you know they don't like daylight?"

"'Cause they're monsters." She smoothed her hand over Natalie's thigh. "Get it to make you some piper clothes too, okay? They keep you warm. Plus they look wicked."

"Why do you care what happens to them?" Natalie asked. "It's not like they care about any of us. They're just doing what they're supposed to do."

"Theresa cares. So does Steppe. He wants to care out loud. He just can't because of the whole stupid code thing."

Natalie wrinkled her nose. "That doesn't make any sense."

"That's what I mean, it doesn't make sense. It's stupid. We need to say something or it'll just be stupid forever, for them and for every kid they bring here."

Natalie leaned her head against Adoni's temple. "I don't get it," she said. "I don't wanna go."

Adoni took Natalie's hand. "But I need you. You make me feel braver."

Adoni stroked the top of Natalie's hand with her fingertips, smelled the oil in her hair and the musk of her skin. She'd found something—someone—worth walking an edge for.

Natalie sighed. "Fine," she said. "Okay. We need a map. And, like, swords or something."

She looked at the chest, leaned over, and opened it.

A parchment, rolled up and secured with purple ribbon, lay at the bottom of the chest, along with a blue piper's robe trimmed with stones and feathers, a grey cloak and hood, a pair of mukluks, and two curved blades, the length of each girl's forearm. Each blade was attached to a sling made of thick animal skins and oiled laces. When the apparatus was strung to a warrior's arm it allowed her to slice as she punched, to gouge as her elbow knocked her foe aside.

"How'd you come up with that?" Adoni asked her.

"I just asked for something badass."

Adoni put the blade against her left forearm and secured the strap. She held her arm up and let the firelight play off the weapon's serrated edge. Natalie slipped out of her sweats and pulled on the piper robes. Once dressed and armed, she went to the window and peered outside.

Adoni looked at the map. There was no legend, no descriptions; only an arrow pointing north to one word, *Ansgar*, written in red towards the top of the page. She recognized the chalet and Natalie's cabin in a cluster of pointed strokes and four illustrated tongues of flame she took to be the pillars in the clearing. "She's north of here. All we have to do is get to this river." She pointed to it with a broken fingernail and traced it up to their destination.

"They're not there," Natalie said. "It's all clear."

They slipped out of her cabin, the map in Adoni's fist, and set out to find the river and follow it to the end.

The folds of the blue piper dress swirled around Natalie's ankles as they made their way through the forest. The stones caught the afternoon light and bounced it off in all directions; the feathers collected snowflakes and little chunks of ice, held them in their tendrils. The cloak, swept up over Natalie's shoulder, gave her a noble aspect that Adoni admired as she walked by her side. She took hold of Natalie's hand and laced their fingers together. "You know that song by that band Led Zeppelin that's all rock and stuff? It goes like this…" She trilled the opening bars of Kashmir through her teeth.

"No."

"It's a good track."

"Uh-huh?"

"That's what goes through my head when stuff like this happens."

"When you go tell people off?"

Adoni blushed. "I don't go tell people off usually, but if I did I'd have this song in my head more. I don't even know what it's about. It's like, some guy on a quest or something, and he's talking with old guys and there's like, wind and things, it's all epic and stuff. It's from the seventies when everyone was on drugs."

"How come you don't tell people off?"

Adoni shrugged. "'Cause they don't care what I think."

Natalie squeezed Adoni's hand.

"Maybe Ritter should have come with us," she said. "No one cares what I think either."

"I do."

Their mukluks swished across the snow like brushes on snare drums. "What are you gonna say to her?" Natalie asked.

Adoni took a moment to spread out every point she wanted to make before reassembling them into a speech. "I'm gonna say she can't turn people into slaves. She needs to dissolve the code, like Ritter said. And she has to make things right with Sylvester and the changelings."

Natalie kissed her teeth. "They tried to kill you."

"They come from a bad place," Adoni said. "It's all they know."

Her words unlocked the door to a distant memory; the memory of a night spent walking through the neighbourhood and looking at Christmas lights with Ida. It had been a long time since they had spent Christmas Eve with travel mugs filled with hot chocolate between their mitts and their faces turned towards all the pretty houses on the other side of the city. "You know what I love most about this time of year?" Ida said. "This is the only time of year when everything looks as magic as I want it to look all the time. How many times can you get away with just leaving lights on your house and wreaths on your door and stuff? Everything's decorated," she said with a nod, "and there's music playing, and there's food everywhere, and everybody's on the same page. And I feel like I'm part of it for once."

"Did you go look at lights with your mom too?" Adoni asked.

"No," Ida said darkly.

"She didn't like the lights?"

"She was too drunk to like *anything*." She looped her arm together with her daughter's. They spent the rest of the evening walking in silence. A firm squeeze of Adoni's arm was how Ida communicated her appreciation from one house to the next.

It struck Adoni, as she walked with Natalie by her side; perhaps all Ida knew, as a daughter, as a mother, was distance, and drink.

Adoni swallowed hard; she missed Ida, more than anything.

The trees grew thinner and further apart until Adoni could see, just ahead of her, the clearing holding Natalie's bedroom apart from the rest of the forest. Natalie's eyes flashed bright with recognition, but her joy soon soured. She freed her hand from Adoni's with a brusque shake and pushed past the skinny tree trunks towards her icy sanctuary. Adoni watched Natalie make her way to the centre and turn around and around, her breath streaming from her in bursts. Adoni stepped into the clearing and surveyed the damage.

There were footprints, broken beer bottles, and cigarette butts strewn all over. Someone had stomped the snow furniture flat, pissed all over what used to stand in for Natalie's bed, kicked and scattered the stones in every direction. Adoni searched Natalie's face, trying to figure out what to say, what to do.

Natalie pinched her lips together and shook her head. "Assholes. They deserve to be here."

Adoni squinted, looking for Natalie's room past the agate. Walls and carpeting seeped into view and cradled the clearing. Everything was still in place in the world they left behind; Natalie's guitar lay on the floor. Adoni crossed the clearing and collected a fistful of stones. Cold in her naked hand, she carried them to the guitar and attempted to place them around its curves. She had outlined half of the instrument when Natalie finally noticed.

Natalie stomped across the clearing, her mouth in a tight frown. Adoni leaned back as Natalie's foot swung out and kicked the stones away. "They're just gonna do it again!" she said. "Leave it!"

Adoni stood and let the image of the bedroom disappear.

Natalie glared at her. "Where's the river? Let's go."

"You snap at me one more time," Adoni said, "you can just stay here and I'll go by myself."

Natalie's mouth hung open. "You begged me to come with you!"

"Don't even say that." Adoni pointed at the stones. "I was trying to make you feel better."

"I can say whatever I like. Actually, I'm the one who got you that map!"

"No," Adoni said fiercely. "You can't talk to me like that. You do it again and I'm going alone."

Natalie glowered back at her.

Adoni stiffened. She knew this kind of anger all too well, knew the kind of fight that was on its way.

"Oh, and I make you feel brave and you care what I think and all that?" Natalie said. "You're so full of shit! Just like Ritter! You think you're better than me?"

"You know I don't."

"You think just because they treat you better that you're better than everybody else?"

"That's not fair!"

"You think you can get there without me? Fine! Go by yourself then!" She turned, her heel squeaking in the snow, and left Adoni standing alone.

"Natalie!"

Natalie kept walking.

Adoni watched her figure recede until hot tears swallowed it up. She played the exchange back, tried to pinpoint where things went wrong. Natalie's voice stuck in her chest like a spear. Her heart sank.

It was too quick, too sharp, and cut too closely.

She took a deep breath and pressed her lips together until her bottom lip stopped quivering. There were greater and more important things to consider on the trek ahead of her.

She unrolled the map and took a good long look.

The river was somewhere ahead, nestled, from what she could tell from a series of markings, between two thick forests on either side. She stuffed the map into one of her wide pockets and continued through the clearing. The trees grew bigger and older as she made her way. The sky above turned grey, and soon a heavy snow covered her footprints. Pellets of ice stung her face.

She pulled the hood of her cloak down lower and forged ahead. Wherever Ansgar was, she assumed a roof hung overhead.

Chapter Twenty-Four

Adoni broke past a particularly knotty tangle of roots and saw the river running along before her. It was silver in the afternoon light, decorated with pointed rocks jutting up from the riverbed. The snow fell harder and faster and melted to obscurity as soon as it hit the water. She pulled her hood back and tried to discern which way the water flowed; the map told her to walk against the current, and she couldn't tell from her perch between the trees whether to head left or right.

The walk had made her thirsty; she stepped out of the forest and walked to the water's edge. Her fingers skimmed the river and a chill went through her body, and as she cupped the water with both her hands, she found it flowed from left to right. She drank as much as she could, stood up, and gazed across the raging current, where the trees from the other half of the forest loomed.

The wintry stillness stepped aside and the city faded into view. The river lay just beneath Yonge Street near Dundas Square; she could see the tacky gift shop, adult store, and seedy strip club between the trees. Patrons stormed past each other without so much as a grin or a nod of the head.

She watched them enter these establishments, noticed how deftly they sidestepped each other, the surly faces they deliberately pulled on to avoid having to exchange pleasantries with strangers. Tubes of neon light and thousands of bulbs flashed away. The darkening afternoon, the thickening snow, made it all seem so much more depressing than she remembered it being when she left it behind.

I don't wanna be like that, she thought. *I wanna be happy. I'm gonna be happy, when I go home.* She turned to her left, to follow the river to Ansgar's estate.

Instead of a horizon filled with water and trees, she came face to face with a smiling, hissing thing with hair and eyes as black as her own. She sucked in her breath and stumbled backwards.

Right into the many waiting arms of a changeling gang.

Fingers gripped the back of her neck, her hair, and the snarling army of changelings pulled her up and dragged her alongside the river. She twisted and fought, trying to free the arm her blade was strapped to, trying to figure out which way to aim and slice. The wind picked up speed and slapped her in the face so violently she couldn't breathe; without breath, there was no way to scream for help across the forest.

She sputtered and choked as the changelings yanked her first in one direction, and then another. It was impossible to tell which way they were headed as steps turned in on themselves, as the same trees and rocks were passed three, four, five times in the space of a few fleeting moments. Her stomach started to give, and the bile rose in her throat.

The changelings kept her swept up in their undulating mass until they reached an enclave thick with trees, where they came to a halt and threw her, face first, onto the ground. Adoni dug her fingers in the snow and finally succumbed to vertigo; she arched her back and wretched a yellow acid, then rolled onto her side, her cheeks burning with humiliation, desperate for the world to stop spinning.

A pair of boots stepped into her view, and she heard a voice speak gently to her kidnappers.

"Give her a minute," Sylvester muttered, "then bring her in."

They pulled her to her feet, and she found herself surrounded by a collection of ramshackle huts. The changeling shantytown was built among the trees; branches and roots stuck out of holes cut into the flimsy aluminum siding walls. The changelings burst through a door and dragged Adoni through a twisting corridor. The cold dirt floor had been beaten smooth by hundreds of footsteps, and the air was heavy with an earthy, livestock smell. The light beaming down from the low-slung ceiling was stronger than the light from the wall lamps at The Welcome, and buzzed as it spilled over their heads. Adoni stole a glance at them as she was pulled through the corridor; the slum, dilapidated though it was, hummed with electricity.

The changelings arrived at a closed door and shoved her inside. Adoni stumbled forward and fell onto her hands and knees. She heard the flimsy door shut and the changelings retreat.

"I hope you're not damaged."

She looked up and there he was, standing eerily still before of a web of Christmas lights and electric plugs.

The lights hung on nails and ran the circumference of the room, past a collection of rickety shelves, and splashed a rainbow's palette onto the earthen floor. Sylvester stood next to a sink and a narrow stove. A single yellow bulb overheard cast a dim light on the burners. Something was sticking out from between the red hot coils.

"I hope you'll forgive my brethren for the way they brought you here," Sylvester said. "They're not in a position to ask anyone nicely." Adoni stayed low and held the blade in front of her. Sylvester tilted his head. "Tell me about yourself," he said. "I want to know you."

Adoni didn't answer.

"You'll regret that silence, when it's all that's left of you," he said as he turned away. "I'll make some tea."

He raised his arm in a slow arc, spread his thin fingers and reached for a kettle on one of the dusty shelves. Adoni watched him fill it with water and set it to boil on the stove. There was something contrived about the way he moved, from the way he turned to face the sink, to the way he held the kettle under the water tap, to the way he set it down on the burner. There appeared to be hours of dumb show built up on his shoulders, hours of rehearsal spent trying to strike the right chord of domesticity. Mimicry kept the vacant, placid look of a satisfied maître D on his face, but the expression played out too tightly, too falsely.

The backs of Adoni's legs stiffened and shook.

"I wonder why you've come to the In-Between," he said. "It's obvious you're not one of those who were taken from their homes, taken from their lives. They give you their piper clothes to wear, for one. They grant you access to where they sleep, where they eat." He took a teapot off of another shelf and filled it with several scoops of loose-leaf tea. "Perhaps they chose to bring you here on their own, without Ansgar's decree. Defying Ansgar is a rare occurrence at The Welcome. But it's happened in the past. I was surprised to see an unfamiliar face at The Welcome's door. When I knock, Steppe answers me. He welcomes me in, even though it sickens him to do so. I know The Welcome's pipers well. And I knew you weren't one of them, even at first glance. So I wonder, Ambassador, why you would be here in this place, when there are so many other places you can be."

She didn't move, didn't make a sound.

"That night on the steps, I asked you a question," he said. "You answered it, though you didn't say a word. You know there's a time and a place for revenge. Somewhere, you and I have an understanding. I wonder why you don't let that persuade you of the righteousness of my actions."

The coloured lights danced over his cheeks, his pointed nose, and the lips he kept frozen in a sinister half smirk. He peered over his shoulder at her, his eyes just a little too bright. "You're wondering why I killed the piper twin."

Adoni's blood froze. Sylvester's sweetly malicious voice gripped her ears. "Aniuk was a useful bargaining chip," he said. "Her death was leverage."

The kettle came to a boil with a high-pitched whistle. Sylvester took it from the stove and poured the boiled water into the teapot. "I'll let that steep," he said lightly; the echo of a happy homemaker. "Luring her to her end was simple, you know. I just pretended to cry."

He leaned back against the Christmas lights. "I haven't cried in years, you understand. Hundreds of years. It was foreign, feeling tears on my face again. Crying runs away with you. The louder, the harder, the faster it runs. Give it long enough, and it's almost real. It was... odd. Not since my brother died. Did you know I had a brother?"

Adoni shook her head. Withholding the truth was the only ace still up her sleeve.

"A twin sibling. Like Aniuk. She was walking in the clearing. My sobs brought her to the edge of the forest. She couldn't help herself, I suppose. She must have thought I was a resident. Pipers are forbidden to interact with residents once they're brought to the colonies. Pipers are filthy hypocrites. They'll break their code if it suits them. It suited her to do so. As it suited me to drag her through the forest. It suited me to strap her to a tree. It suited me to light the pyre. It suited me to collect the ashes. Steppe ordered me to return to The Welcome, you see. *Ordered* me. It's rude to show up at someone's home empty handed."

He poured the tea into a cup and held it under his nose. "Do you think my story is an isolated case? That I'm the only one who's died so many hundreds of times, in dreams, since serving my sentence? For every blow to my body, my brethren have endured countless more. For every scar I have, they have three times as many. Blows and scars are common among us. They're totems of our shared experience. The life of one piper means nothing to me. We are thousands. *Thousands.* Our bodies are temples of violence. Our demons can never be outrun."

He put the cup down and unceremoniously pulled off his shirt to reveal a chest, shoulders, arms, and torso covered in thick, ugly scars, whip marks and burn marks. He turned around; five long, angry gashes ran down the length of him. "That one," he said, "is from a rake. During a very cold night." He dropped the shirt onto the ground. "Scars are the language of the changelings who made it back to the In-Between. Their language is written all over their bodies."

He picked up his drink and took a long swig. "They wanted to build houses in the forest," he said. "A colony of their own, near the lake. They wanted to bond with each other. Like friends. To tell their stories to each other. To commiserate, and make some attempt to heal. My brethren didn't understand the evil that befell us all. How heinous it was. How heinous it remains, because those pipers who chose for us, judged for us, went on to live their lives, free of pain and fear. I'm the only one who understood this. You see, Ritter left me on the doorstep to my destruction on a cold night, as cold as the one on its way. And my hatred for him will never subside, no matter how many nights pass, from that one to this."

He moved towards the stove. "You must know by now that Ansgar's name is the most powerful in all the In-Between. Put it on a hope chest, say, and put the chest in a resident's room, and tell the resident the room is hers, for a while at least, and that chest will give her whatever she wants. It's why no one else can ask something of it, once it's given away. Ansgar's name means possession. *Control.* It's a license to covet, to reach out, and to take whatever you want.

"Do you know how to get someone to see something your way? To get them to accept your terms unequivocally? To get them to follow you beyond the fourth dimension, beyond the In-Between?"

He didn't wait for a response.

"You take away their voices. You remove the only thing they have left. Do you know how to do that?" He set his cup down. "Ansgar shows us favours, sometimes. She gives us electricity, running water, things the pipers don't have. She doesn't interfere when I tell her I'll destroy her chosen messenger. She lets me judge for those who refuse to judge for themselves. And she lets me take her name in vain, whenever I see fit."

He took what Adoni could now see was a brass seal from between the coils on the stove. He held it up. "I branded them one by one. They have no voices to speak with, or to sing with, or to scream with. I wanted *silence*, you see. I coveted *silence*. So she gave me her name, and I silenced them.

"They're silent, and easy to control."

He took a step towards her, the seal—Ansgar's name, spelled backwards—glowing hot between his fingers.

Adoni held the blade out and curled her lip.

He stepped close enough for her to take a swipe at him. She let the blade fall across his chest, slicing him open, spilling the terrible black blood beneath his skin.

She felt the walls closing in on her, felt the air turn dense with violence. For a moment, she couldn't breathe.

Sylvester stopped and let the blood gush down the front of him.

Then his skin stitched itself back together, leaving a jagged scar behind.

He ran his hand over the sewn-up wound. "Stupid girl," he said. "A weapon is only weapon if you know how to use it."

His hand shot out and he seized her face, covered her eyes, dug his fingers into her cheeks. She screamed as he twisted her bladed arm behind her back and pinned her against the floor with a knee between her shoulder blades. He flung her cloak aside, tore her robe away from her left shoulder and said, "This is going to hurt."

He pressed the seal against her skin.

And pain, pain was all she could feel, pain through her shoulder, through her arm, up her neck and down to her stomach. The most incredible, insisting, searing pain she had ever felt in her life.

She tried to scream, but had no voice to do it.

He released his grip and ripped the seal away from her skin. She pulled her knees to her chest and curled up as tightly as she could, closed her eyes, and felt his fingers undo the knots keeping the blade on her arm. He picked it up and stood over her, his smile a feral gnash of exposed teeth.

"Take comfort," he said. "Even if you had tried, you couldn't have persuaded me not to hurt you." He tossed the blade into the corner and put his shirt back on. He brought the teacup to his lips again and sipped deeply, gratefully. "Your words will be my words now. Your actions will be my actions. You'll fight it for a while, I'm sure. You'll try to keep it from seeping into your every thought. But eventually the anger, the hatred, the regret... especially the regret... they'll ravage your mind, destroy your memories, tear apart everything that makes you who you are. You'll go *mad*, Ambassador. Absolutely mad."

He took his time and drank his tea with the ease and tranquillity of someone on holiday.

"For every night Steppe defies me," he said gently, "I'm going to take one of his residents. I'm going to brand each one of them, just as I've branded you. I'm going to turn his allies against him, and I'm going to destroy them all." He leaned forward to get a better look at his prey.

She pushed herself up, opened her mouth, and tried as hard as she could to scream. All that came out was a strained wheeze.

Sylvester slung the blade over his shoulder. "I told you you'd regret it."

Chapter Twenty-Five

Theresa sat at Steppe's piano and pressed her sore fingers against the sides of a mug of hot chocolate. The afternoon sun had descended, the sky dark and heavy with clouds. A snowstorm was imminent.

She took a breath and let the smell of sweet chillies clear her head. The night before still held her thoughts captive; all she could think about was Steppe's head, bowed in misery, and the echo of his beautiful voice, splitting with anguish as he wailed with failure at her feet. No matter what she said, he wouldn't be comforted. So she listened, waited, soothed him with slight caresses of his neck. He gripped the back of her dress so tightly, when he finally opened his fists and let go, the material was damp with his sweat.

He got to his feet. She spoke his name softly. But he shook his head and left the room.

One hour after an empty sunrise, many years ago, Theresa found herself at the back door of the chalet's kitchen. She had only ever seen the chalet from her cabin window and couldn't imagine what it looked like inside. Pipers were still strange creatures to her then, with an odd beauty she didn't understand. Steppe hadn't said a word to her once her cabin door closed shut behind her three months before, on the night he brought her to The Welcome. She wanted a chance to see him and the other pipers, to steal glimpses of them eating and drinking and singing their melodies. Certain she wouldn't get caught, she opened the door and peeked in.

Steppe sat at the table with his head in his hands, sucking in his breath as he choked a coughing fit into submission.

She stood still and listened to him fight for composure.

Lost somewhere between the chalet walls and the world beyond, he didn't notice her presence. He started when her hand touched his shoulder, and he looked at her with red, swollen eyes and a nose wrung raw from sniffling.

It was the only time he ever dove straight for the truth.

"Belinda's dead," he said.

A greasy tear fell over his cheek. His nostrils flared as he grabbed hold of another sob, another assault on his composure. They stared at each other for a long time.

"I don't know what I'm going to do without her," he said at last.

She folded her hands together.

The smile he gave her was a sad one. "You're not supposed to be here," he said.

By the time Steppe emerged from his bedroom his face was raw and real, without the mask of stolidity he usually wore. He appeared in the music room on a squeal of rusty door hinges. He noticed Theresa and tried to smile, but couldn't keep it up for long.

"You and me have to talk," she said.

He crossed the room and picked up one of the violins. "I'm not going to change my mind about him," he said.

"I'm not talking about Ritter."

She threw the pewter box into the centre of the room. It hit the floorboards with a hard thud.

She had discovered the box was empty late in the morning, after she'd lit the fires and put the day's bread in the oven to bake. She wanted to look into the past, to find answers to her questions; to find the picture of Ritter and stare at it until she could make sense of it. Instead she found her things pushed back and rumpled in their drawers. The photographs were gone.

"You went through my dresser," she said.

"It was her dresser first," he replied, without a pause, without consideration.

She stood up. "I don't know how many times we have to have this discussion."

"And we don't have to have it now," he said brusquely. "Those pictures are mine."

"You could have asked me, instead of busting in when I wasn't looking. I would have given them to you. I knew they'd depress you!"

"So what?" he snapped. "What is it to you?"

The flames in her eyes rose quickly. "Nothing at all. Is that what you wanna hear?"

"I don't want to talk about this." He sat down at the piano, snatched an angry breath through his nose, and struck the keys all at once.

Silence.

Theresa tossed the wire cutters onto the muted instrument. "You're *going* to talk about this."

A clammy sweat broke out on his forehead. He shook his head. "I can't."

"I'm waiting."

Beyond the music room, Theresa heard a growl of mourning and knew it was Paj, conjuring her sister in song, sticking the ashes back together. Elsewhere, Finnur's head lay against Roxanne's chest, and he let the steady beat of her heart take him back to the home he loved, the home he left behind to serve his piper's sentence. Roxanne wanted the ocean back, wanted the rocks and the waves that lapped the sand on quiet mornings and crashed against the cliffs on stormy nights. Theresa heard Ritter's saxophone, its plaintive song sawing through The Welcome's wooden beams, and recognized the need, the want, the desire for freedom.

She needed Steppe to speak.

"I knew Belinda kept those pictures in her dresser," he said. "Of course I knew you'd look at them from time to time, over the years. It was my way of letting you get to know me. My way of explaining how things were with Belinda and me, without having to say the words. Last night, for a minute, I lost myself in front of you. I just wanted my secrets back."

"If you want your secrets back, we have a problem. Don't you think?"

"Haven't you ever wondered why you've never had to be welcomed past the front door?"

Theresa cocked an eyebrow at him. "When I was a resident…"

She remembered stealing into the chalet unannounced, remembered him hunched at the kitchen table. Her answer stuck in her throat.

"You're not supposed to be here," he said.

His confession came out on a whisper, as if a lower volume could soften the blow.

"I tried to save a boy all those years ago," he said. "I was so self-righteous. I thought everything I said was so important, and every song I sang was a masterpiece. I saw myself as a kind of guardian angel, visiting him whenever he was alone, encouraging him to talk, offering him all sorts of useless advice. Advice he already knew. But he resented my coming to him every day with all my empty words. Eventually he let me know exactly how much he resented me. He screamed at me. Right in my face, nose to nose. And I let my anger get the better of me. I let my frustration take me back to when I was his age, to dark times I fought hard to forget. I thought he was ungrateful, that he didn't know real pain, and I lashed out. I never told you just what I did to him, did I?"

She shook her head. "I figured it was too painful for you to talk about."

He leaned forward and knotted his palms together. "I tore his eye out," he said. "I snarled at him, just once. Just *once*, Reese. Like a beast."

He took a breath.

"The night you and I met, I was supposed to make contact with another girl in trouble," he said. "She lived near the school. I thought I'd cut across the playground to get to her. And then I heard you. And I saw you there, with your knife, looking… familiar. Looking like I did once. Fourteen looks the same all over, I suppose. I wanted to save you. I wanted someone to understand where I'd been, without words or music. I wanted forgiveness. So I took you with me, and I begged Ansgar to let you stay. She said yes. Without condition, she said yes. She granted you access past her name, whenever you wanted. Sometimes she's… benevolent, I guess.

"You were my last attempt to save a soul without the code. You became a part of us. The older you got, the more capable you were of taking care of yourself. I thought you were my first success. I trapped you in this life, and I had you convinced it was all you ever wanted."

He reached for her abandoned mug of hot chocolate, stole a sip.

"Last night when I told Ritter we were in this mess because of him, I faced my own hypocrisy. If I hadn't abused my authority and violated your trust, you might have made a life for yourself beyond the In-Between. But you're here because of me. And you stay because of me."

Theresa bit her bottom lip. When she finally spoke, her voice was a lump of coal.

"Because of you," she said. "Not because I love hiding from the cold in this beautiful old place. Or because I love how the snow falls every single day and makes everything sparkle. Or because the maple trees are right there and I can always have real syrup on my pancakes. Or because the river shines in the sun and the water's always fresh. Or because I'll never hear music like piper music anywhere else. Or because I love the magic around me. Or because I love you. Not because I want to be here. Because you wanted me to be here. That's what you think."

Steppe stood up and reached for her.

"Don't touch me," she said.

They heard a thump on the chalet's front door. Outside, two fists pounded urgently on the wood and bolts. The hallways rocked with muffled sobs, with words so warped with fear they came out as gibberish.

Theresa swooped down the staircase. Paj, Finnur, and Roxanne opened their bedroom doors and followed her descent from their perch on the landing. She threw the door open and found Natalie—petrified, skin red from running in the cold, hair and clothes covered in sticky winter weather. She shook her arm and her blade landed on the porch with a clang.

Theresa gasped. "What happened? Come in, you're welcome."

"Reese, she's not to pass over…" Steppe began.

"Oh shut up!" She pulled Natalie over the threshold and knelt before her. "What happened?"

Natalie wrapped her arms around herself. "Me and Adoni went in the forest to go to that Ansgar place…"

"What? Why?"

Natalie sobbed harder.

Theresa put her hands on the girl's shoulders and gave her a squeeze. "Did something happen to Adoni?"

"She and me had a fight," Natalie said, "and I told her to fuck off, but I followed behind her anyway, to make sure she was okay…" She looked up and caught sight of the pipers staring down at her from the landing, locked eyes with Paj.

Paj nodded.

"The changelings got her," Natalie whimpered. "They found her at the river and they got her."

"Which way did they go?" Theresa asked. "Did you see where they went?"

"I wasn't fast enough..." she croaked.

Theresa put her arms around the girl. "What are we gonna do?" she asked Steppe.

He put his hands over his face. "Sylvester's planning on using her as a hostage, I guarantee it," he said from behind his fingers. "We'll have to negotiate for her return. There's no other way around it. I'll have to get a message to him somehow. We'll have to agree on a place to meet, and a time..."

Ritter's bedroom door swung open and slammed against the wall. All eyes were on him as he stomped down the stairs in a pair of heavy boots.

"Where are you going?" Finnur asked.

"To get our girl back." He grabbed a coat from the closet and threw it around his shoulders, stuffed his arms into the sleeves, and reached for the front door. Steppe clapped his hand over the knob and held it fast.

"This isn't your concern anymore, Ritter."

"It is until midnight, darling."

"You're a hero all of a sudden?"

Ritter gave him a poisonous smirk. "I brought her here, didn't I?"

"You'll bring the entire changeling colony down on us. I need to handle this delicately."

"You'd handle a raging inferno *delicately*."

"Let him go," Theresa said. She held Natalie close to her chest. "You're always calling him a coward."

Steppe was about to launch into another useless diatribe when Ritter, almost tenderly, reached out and took his hand. "She's just on the brink of something fantastic. For all we've put her through, it's our duty to help her realize it. None of us can afford to lose her. If you're afraid of what you might do to him, let me go instead. I've lived for myself for almost a thousand years. I'd like to live for someone else, for a change."

Silence.

"I never asked her for it," Ritter whispered. "I never wanted her voice. You know that, somewhere, don't you? You've got to."

Steppe shook his head. "Don't." He straightened his back. "Can you manage alone?"

Ritter shrugged. "If you're worried about *forsaking* me, don't." He raised a mocking, dramatic hand and waved once. "I absolve you of your duty. Of everything."

He opened the chalet door, stepped onto the porch, picked up Natalie's blade, and strapped it to his arm.

The pipers watched the storm swallow up his silhouette.

Chapter Twenty-Six

Adoni stayed on the floor, her breathing shallow, legs curled up against her chest. Sylvester sipped his tea and watched her for a time. He didn't move except to bring the edge of the cup to his lips for another taste. When his cup was empty he set it down on the counter, picked up the Ansgar seal and Adoni's blade, turned, and left her lying there.

She lay still until she heard the click of a latch falling into place. He'd locked her in.

She slowly drew herself up and stretched her limbs. The pain in her shoulder relaxed to a throbbing ache. She pulled her robe away from her skin and craned her neck to view the damage. Six black letters spelled out her fate across her brown skin. She shuddered and tears sprang to her eyes. Natalie would never know how sorry she was for sending her away. Ida would never know where she was and why she went. She raced through her thoughts while she still had them, determined to hold on to them for as long as she could.

There beyond the pain, beyond the silence, was Ritter, sitting in his bean bag chair and gazing at her with infinite respect and dignity.

You're wonderfully ordinary, he'd said. *Which means you're hope.*

So she got to her feet.

She crept up to the door and peered through the crack in the jamb. The latch was thick and made of iron, but loose enough that she could lift it out of its cradle by sticking something thin, like a stick, through the door. The kitchen didn't have much in the way of projectiles, but the tin walls seemed flimsy enough to peel off a sliver of scrap metal to put through the crack. She went to the opposite wall to search for a loose corner, a bent panel, anything to bend away what she needed to escape.

She spotted a splinter sticking out of the wall, close to the floorboards; a curl of metal about a centimetre long that had formed when the walls cracked with the change of season. Adoni got down on her hands and knees and gripped it tightly, worked it back on itself as if she were opening a can of tuna. The sharp edge slipped through her grip once and sliced her skin open. She sucked her breath in through her teeth and held up her hand. Blood pearled up on her thumb and looked like purple beads under the Christmas lights. She wrapped her shirt around the wound and tried again, working the sliver of metal millimetre by millimetre away from the wall. When it was long enough, she twisted it around and folded it back and forth until the metal was hot from the friction and the scrap came loose. It wouldn't hold up as a knife, but it was long enough to lift the latch and sharp enough to cut through cloth. She held it up and allowed herself a moment of triumph before turning around and searching for something to protect herself with.

The only wood in the room came from the shelves that stood on either side of the kitchenette. One of the shelves was particularly broken down, dried out and splintered from years of abuse. She carefully took away the cups and saucers and set them down in the sink. She listened hard for the slightest hint of changeling activity beyond the walls, and when her silence was returned with silence in kind she put one hand against the side of the shelf and pushed back until it slid free from the rusty nails holding it tenuously in place. She freed the other end of the shelf in the same manner and propped it up against the wall. With a swift kick she broke the plank in two, so that each half was thin enough to grip in her fist. She swung it back and forth; it wouldn't hold up forever.

She found the Ansgar tag that was sewn into the collar of her cloak and gripped it with her unharmed fingers. The fibres tore apart as she pulled the slice of metal back and forth over the material, sawed away at it until she'd severed half the fabric, took the makeshift blade to the other side of the tag and did the same. The result was a long, thin strip of material that she knotted around one end of the plank. She found the tag in her robe and ripped it out with the same ragged finesse, and wrapped the scrap of material around the other end of the plank. She swung it again; the Ansgar name renewed its strength and kept it from crumbling in her grip.

She went to the stove, turned the burner on full tilt, and put the wrapped end of the plank against the coils. First there was smoke, and then the irrefutable smell of burning, and Adoni watched a flicker of orange flame rise up from the bundle. The flame divided into two tongues, three tongues, and then wrapped itself around and became one blazing torch. She held it up and swung it around, watched it lick the air, waited for any sign of decomposition. Ansgar's name kept the fire from failing, kept the wood from splitting. She went to the door, poked the strip of metal through, and lifted the latch.

She heard the changelings' ragged breathing deep in the tangle of halls, heard scratching at the walls, hissing and snapping, punches and slaps. Adoni held the torch out in front of her. No special moves were required; all she had to do to use this weapon effectively was touch the flame to the clothes of whoever was unfortunate enough to get in her way. She thanked Sylvester for showing her the error of her ways and stole forward on gingerly steps.

The lights bore down on her, lighting her way with a green, asylum-like glare. Based on what she could remember of the changelings' movements, she reckoned the kitchen was right in the middle of the maze, the room furthest away from the world outside as possible. She had to make her way diagonally from that point on. When she reached the end of the hall she turned left, away from another naked bulb and towards a rank-smelling darkness. She took the next rightward corridor, and then turned right again. Every so often she stopped and listened carefully for the whisper of clothing against the walls or the crackle of a dry throat in the musty air. If there was so much as a hint of movement or sound, she went in the opposite direction. She knew she was close to the exit when she could feel the winter chill seep through the walls. She turned left again and rushed to the end of the hallway, mistaking a shadow for the final turn to escape. Her fingers pressed against the wall instead—a dead end. She shrunk away and turned to retrace her steps.

A changeling stood at the other end of the hallway. It turned its head and glared at her.

Adoni froze and clung to the torch as her mind raced for leverage, to find some advantage.

The changeling curled its lip and hissed at her. It pointed its toes towards her and headed down the hallway, hands up, prepared to strangle her when it reached her.

Adoni thought quickly; without a voice, it couldn't call to its brethren for backup. She had to cloak her movements somehow, to get past them all when they finally got wise and organized themselves into another heaving mob. The light bulb overhead flickered with a surge of electricity.

It was just the sign she needed.

She raised the torch over her head and swung out, smashing the bulb into a thousand little pieces.

The changeling sneered at her. She pushed past it and ran towards the next corridor, the next pool of light. Another swing of the torch shattered a second bulb, and a third, until she left every twisted corridor she came across blanketed in darkness. She heard the changelings stir in their nests, heard doors swing open and footsteps beating their way towards her. Adoni stormed through the hallways, her thick legs burning as she tore along the paths. She heard the wind whistling through the forest branches and saw the slightest flicker of snow between the slats of a broken doorway. She dove for it, threw it open, and flung herself outside.

There was no mercy for her in the darkness, no chance to prepare—without Ansgar's name sewn into her clothes, she could feel every angry winter wail, every gust of wind, right through her skin, through her blood, through her nerves and bones. She gripped her robe close to her throat and pressed on, fistfuls of snow battering at the wound on her shoulder. Wind screeched between trunks and branches, ice pellets hit the trees and stuck to the bark. She heard the lonely howl of wolves a hundred miles away.

She could barely keep her eyes open as the storm flung itself at her, so she held the torch out and felt her way forward until her hands were swollen with cold. As the adrenaline drained away and the weather seeped into every pore the muscles in her legs began to fail her, and soon she was limping heavily along. The scrap metal slipped from between her fingers and was lost in the snow, and the torch dipped and sagged in Adoni's weakening grip until she could only hold it out at her waist.

The frigid air sucked the last drop of moisture from her throat. She collapsed and released a silent groan; though it had no power to reverberate across the forest she still felt it boiling inside her, and the first twist of madness reached in and violated the deepest recesses of her thoughts.

Somewhere in the dark, past the swirling winter abyss, she heard her name floating over hills and around trees. She peeled her eyes open.

Ritter stood a few yards away with Natalie's blade strung tightly to his arm. His body bent forward in the storm, every inch of him on the verge of lunging. He called out for her again, his voice singeing her ears.

With no voice to scream with and no strength left, she squeezed a handful of snow into as hard a ball as she could, raised her arm, and threw it at him. It sailed over his shoulder and splattered against a tree trunk.

He turned and caught sight of her on the ground with the torch, still burning, lying next to her in the drift. Staggering forward, boots slipping on the ice, he threw his arms around her.

"You're a stupid girl!" he hissed. "A very brave and a very stupid girl! Whatever possessed you to come out here? You're insane! Are you hurt?"

She looked at him, imploring him from across a great divide. He pulled off his coat and threw it around her shoulders.

"We have to get out of here," he said. He couldn't resist making a joke. "No doubt your adoring fans are on their way. I don't know about you but I'm certainly not in the mood to sign any autographs."

Autograph.

She pulled the coat away from her wounded shoulder, grabbed hold of his arm, and offered him the raised and blackened scar.

He squinted at it through the snow and sleet, his nose wrinkling at the faint odour of her burned flesh, and recognized the angles of the letters, their malevolent arc and slash. A scowl sneaked its way onto his lips.

"Damn her. I knew I couldn't trust her."

Adoni tightened her grip and gave him a shake. He cupped her face in his hands. He might have told her everything then and there, if another voice hadn't seeped through the dark and the storm.

"What are you doing?"

They turned.

Sylvester stood a little way off, dressed in the suit and hat he'd worn a few short days before, holding a steel bucket brimming with water. He tilted his head, and his eyes settled on Ritter with the weight and finality of a guillotine.

Adoni gripped her torch and waited for Sylvester to move a single inch, take a single step towards them. She waited for him to explode. He didn't.

Not until Ritter, with spite and fury spinning in his bright green eyes, opened his mouth and said, "*I'm your brother!*"

Adoni's stomach curdled; it wasn't Ritter's searing tenor anymore. It was someone else's voice, someone younger, someone irreparably damaged by life and by time, someone desperate and begging.

"*I'm your brother!*"

It pierced her ears and split every last one of her nerves. She recognized it—its softness, its hint of something sour, the fine line it walked, its villainous edge.

It was Sylvester's voice, plucked from somewhere beyond the agate; his voice, from a time when his throat was no older than a child's.

Ritter's vindictive simper cut across his face.

Sylvester opened his fingers; the bucket hit the frozen ground, spilling the water at his feet. His lip quivered. His knees bent.

Ritter puts his lips against Adoni's ear and whispered, "Come on."

And they scrambled to their feet and flew between the trees, like bats out of hell.

Chapter Twenty-Seven

Ritter seized Adoni's wrist and yanked her along behind him, pulled her off of the beaten path and shoved her towards a thicket of trees. They lifted their knees up high and tore through snow drifts several feet deep, tripping over hidden roots and slamming their shins against buried rocks. A branch whipped across Adoni's cheek, drawing blood.

Sylvester followed their tracks with an agility she didn't know he possessed, taking his cues of when to dodge and when to jump from their every stumble. Adoni heard Ritter's lungs falter, heard the cadence of his footsteps start to slow. She looked back at him. He wheezed and pressed on against the wind.

The forest came to an abrupt stop at the edge of the river, now raging as the wind and snow picked up momentum. Adoni searched the horizon for a place to cross; the rocks were too far apart to provide any decent footing, and there were no ice floes to grab onto.

So she grabbed Ritter's hand, hauled him towards the water, took a deep breath, and hurled herself into the current.

The shock of the cold nearly sucked her breath out of her. Piper clothes were useless when fully submerged in frigid waters; the waves pushed her robe up over her waist, exposing her legs to an unforgiving chill. Ritter's coat tangled up under her arms and over her head. She felt his fingers stiffen in her grip and tried as hard as she could to keep hold of him, but a shift in the current sent her tumbling end over end, and the force ripped his hand out of hers. Eyes closed, mouth pinched shut, she flailed her arms and kicked her legs, desperate to be tossed back to the surface before instinct took over and forced the river into her lungs. Its icy clutches bore into her sinuses and set them throbbing in her skull, seized her chest and brought her to the brink of submission.

The water shifted again, tossed her high enough to break the surface.

She tore a gasp from the frosty air. There was no sign of Ritter; all she saw were the pointed silhouettes of trees and the snow piled up along the riverbank. She coughed once, and the water pulled her back in the undertow and darkness enveloped her. She fought to keep her head up, stretching her limbs out as far as they could go with the hope of hitting a boulder and slowing her descent. Her fingers grazed their craggy surfaces a number of times, but the current flung her past them too quickly for her to grab hold of one.

Drowning was supposed to be the most peaceful way to die; when the fight for life was finally thrown, the following calm was a kind of gift. Frozen to the bone, surrounded by blackness, Adoni knew it for the kind of death it was: a crushing, lonely death; an unfair death. She kicked at the darkness with every ounce of strength she had left, her body twisting like a fish on the end of a line. She wouldn't let it win. Death would have to drag her, kicking and screaming, from the bottom of the river if it wanted her so badly.

One last push from the whirling waters rocketed her forward and dragged her down to the rocks below. Adoni dug her heels in and straightened her back; the water was finally shallow enough to let her stand up straight, tilt her head back, and poke her nose up over the chipped surface. She steadied herself against the current. A sliver of moon peeked out from behind the thinning clouds; the storm was breaking up. She looked to her left—the forest stood there in silent glory, and four curls of smoke eked into the sky from between their dense branches. She stepped towards the riverbank carefully, sliding her feet together and apart until it grew shallow enough to hold her head upright.

Ritter stood on the riverbank with his arm outstretched, drenched and shivering. "Grab my hand!" Adoni reached for him. He took hold of her forearm and lugged her up onto the shore. The wind hollered through their soaked clothes and set their teeth rattling in their heads. "The colony isn't far," he hissed, his jaw tight with cold. "Come on. And if you're going to do that again, *warn me*."

Adoni nearly wept with relief when she saw four flames flickering in the sky. She needed warm, dry clothes, a fire at her feet, Theresa's hot chocolate, solace. Ritter took her arm and brought her up the front porch steps. He put his hand on the doorknob and turned.

It didn't budge.

"It's after midnight," he murmured.

Adoni raised her exhausted arm and brought it down on the wood.

Ritter rested his chin on top of Adoni's head. They shuddered and clung to each other.

Theresa threw the door open. "You're welcome, *get in here!*"

Adoni was barely over the threshold when Theresa gathered her into a tight embrace. Theresa slapped a hand over the girl's wounded shoulder, oblivious to the pain she was in, and heaved a long and grateful sigh against the girl's cheek. "You're drenched! You're freezing! What the hell happened to you? Are you all right?"

"No, she's not," Ritter said.

He pulled Theresa's hand away and tugged Adoni's robe down, exposing the angry burn.

She looked from Adoni's wounded flesh to Ritter. "What the hell is that?"

"A seal," he said.

"The changelings have a *seal?*"

"Apparently."

Theresa glared at the brand. "Come on kid," she said before turning to Ritter. "Steppe's in his room."

Ritter wiped his dripping chin with his arm.

Theresa led Adoni to the kitchen, pulled a chair away from the table and pointed at it. Adoni sat down. Theresa filled a pot with water and set it on the stove, reached for a boning knife, and held it up to inspect its edge. She caught Adoni staring at her and shook her head.

"I don't know what to say, kiddo," she muttered.

Ritter made his way to Steppe's bedroom. He knocked and waited, but no one called out to ask who it was. He opened the door and peered inside. The room was vacant, the space, immaculately clean. He let the stillness take him away; he hadn't set foot in Steppe's room for more than a decade, and it looked the same as it always had, with furniture lined up neatly along the walls, with nary a speck of dust on his night stand or dresser, with every single bed stone lying on the pressed quilt in the perfect shape of a snowflake.

Ritter used to sit on the floor in front of the fire and admire the way the flames danced in Steppe's blue eyes. He took a breath and could smell Steppe between the walls, a sweet smell, like a honeycomb.

"Ritter?"

Steppe was sitting on Ritter's bed, peering through the door at him. Ritter approached him cautiously. Steppe didn't get up. Instead he stared at him as if unable to believe he had actually made it back in one piece.

Ritter looked around at the tiny room he used to call his own. His CDs and records and tapes were in wooden crates. His clothes sat folded on the end of the bed, ready to be packed into a suitcase that stood open on the floor at Steppe's feet. He swallowed and smirked at him. "I see you haven't wasted any time."

Steppe didn't answer.

Ritter turned towards the fire. He tore off his soaked shirt and dropped it in a sopping heap on the floor. He went to retrieve a dry one from the pile on his bed when he noticed a glossy piece of paper in Steppe's hand. He squinted at it.

Steppe tilted it, to give him a better look.

Ritter blinked and let out a soft, sad chuckle. "I haven't worn my hair like that in years," he said. "I should grow it again." He picked up a dry shirt and slid it over his head. "Our girl's downstairs…" he said.

"I found it with the rest of Belinda's pictures," said Steppe.

Ritter poked his head and arms through the shirt and slowly drew the fabric down to his waist.

"It makes sense now," Steppe said. "Why you were the only one she recognized, at the end."

"What on earth do you mean? She took a picture of me, so what?"

"You're lying down."

"And?"

He heard something in Steppe's voice, a heavy suspicion lurking in the undercurrent. An accusation.

Ritter thought he would never have to say it out loud again. "I was your *best friend!*"

"You were *everyone's* best friend. You always knew just what to say."

Ritter's heart knocked against his ribs. He turned away; cast his eyes towards the fire.

Then he turned, and slammed his fist into Steppe's jaw.

Steppe lunged at him, knocking him against the wall. He landed the second, third, and fourth punch, his fist whacking Ritter squarely in the face. There was no pain—the chalet protected them from pain, from bleeding, from split skin and broken bones—but ire drove them to lash out as hard as they could nonetheless. Ritter grabbed Steppe around the waist and tried to fling him off. Until that moment he'd had no idea how solid Steppe was, how strong he was. Steppe dug his heels into the floor and flipped Ritter onto his back as though he weighed nothing at all, threw himself on top of him and slammed his fist into Ritter's cheek again and again, hardly pausing for breath.

Even if they had taken their fight to the clearing, Steppe wouldn't have a single scratch on him.

They shoved, punched, kicked, until Roxanne and Finnur, hearing the scuffle from their rooms, stumbled onto them and pulled them both apart.

Roxanne held Steppe around his waist as Finnur crouched between him and Ritter, ready to spring into action should either man raise another fist. Ritter snatched a breath and nodded, his lips curling with an indignant smirk. "Sylvester has an Ansgar seal," he said flatly. "And he's burned it into Adoni's shoulder."

"*What?*" Steppe growled.

"You heard me. Why don't you get down there and show me how easy it is to be a hero?"

Steppe flew from the room, leaving the photograph, the half-packed boxes, Roxanne, Finnur, and Ritter behind.

He burst into the kitchen and rushed to Adoni's side. "Which shoulder is it?" Adoni pulled her robe away and showed him. He clenched his teeth as Ritter's frame filled the doorway. "Why would she do this?"

"To get even," Ritter said.

"With who?" Theresa asked. "With Steppe?"

"With me."

They waited for him to continue.

"Steppe was going to speak to her about Donny being here. It's code, after all. I wanted to get to her first. Soften the blow, so to speak. Ansgar and I have a kind of understanding, after all these years."

Steppe's jaw hung slack. "What did you tell her?"

"I told her we had a stowaway among us. I told her she can hear piper music, can even hear the different endings of all our evening songs. I asked for reprieve from the code."

Stupefied, Steppe shook his head. "She didn't lift your immortality for it."

"I told you. We have an understanding."

"But..?" Theresa said.

"She wanted to even the score," he said. "I asked her for a favour, she gave Sylvester a seal of his own."

"We have to get rid of it," she said.

"It should heal enough by tomorrow," said Steppe. "Maybe we can cover it up."

"You can't cover it up."

"It might fade in the night. The chalet's still protected, it might heal. Or we can tattoo over it..."

"Why don't we pierce her bellybutton too, while we're at it?" Theresa snapped. "We can't tattoo over it, or cover it up. It's gotta come off."

The pipers looked at Adoni as frightened tears inundated her eyes. Ritter took her hand and squeezed it firmly. It was cold comfort in her clammy palm.

Steppe nodded weakly. "All right. Go on."

Theresa took the pot of boiled water off of the stove and shuffled towards the outside door. "There's a pile of clean napkins on the shelf," she said over her shoulder. "Grab a bunch and meet me outside. I'll try and do it as quick as I can."

Steppe's brow wrinkled. "The residents can't see this."

"We can't do it in here."

"Why not?"

"Why not?" She set the pot down on the floor with a thud, raised her hand, and thrust the boning knife through her palm without so much as a flinch. "*That's* why not." She pulled the knife out again and held her bloodless palm out to Adoni.

Adoni shrank back. Not a single one of them had mentioned giving her something to numb the inevitable pain. She looked from Theresa to Ritter to Steppe; each of them stared numbly at her. She shook her head and looked around frantically, searching for a pencil and a piece of paper, so she could write down what she needed. The only thing she could think of that was quick enough, thorough enough, was chloroform.

Theresa went to Adoni, put an arm around her waist, nudged her towards the door. Adoni twisted away from her and flung her arm over her head, desperate to get her attention, Ritter's attention, Steppe's attention. She pushed Theresa away and lunged for the cupboards, pointed at them hysterically.

"It's all right," Steppe said as he grabbed her wrist and turned her around, urging her back to Theresa's side. Adoni went slack in Theresa's arms, tried to make herself as heavy as she could, hoping one of them would finally notice where she was pointing, finally understand, finally think about what they were about to do. She mimed fainting, covered her mouth and nose with her hand.

"I know, honey, I know," Theresa said, heaving Adoni up from the floor.

Steppe and Ritter closed in. Each of them took up one of Adoni's arms or legs and eased her back to her feet. She struggled, tried to grab onto their collars, tried to get them to look at her, so she could mouth the word *chloroform*.

So she could mouth the word *anesthetic*.
So she could plead, *don't do this to me.*
But they weren't listening.

Chapter Twenty-Eight

An eerie silence had smothered the wind. The cabins stood quietly in the calm, their roofs heavy with snow, their windowpanes caked with ice. Theresa and the pipers brought Adoni out to the side of the chalet, their hands smoothing circles over her back, over her hair, trying to calm her.

Adoni's eyes searched desperately for Natalie, but she was nowhere to be seen.

So Adoni stopped fighting.

Theresa brought her to a tree stump a few feet from the kitchen door. She glanced over her shoulder to see if any of the residents were watching and confirmed they were alone. She held up the knife. "It's an Ansgar blade, it's gotta be sharp enough. Even out here." She glanced at Adoni.

Adoni shook her head.

Theresa crouched down in the snow and put the edge of the blade to one of the stones on the hem of her skirt. She slid the blade across the stone like a bow over violin strings. The sound she drew was a metallic slice, a sound befitting a lamb's slaughter.

Steppe and Ritter emerged from the chalet with the clean napkins and boiled water. Steppe held the napkins, wadded, in two unshakable fists and stood beside Theresa. He leaned forward and watched her work the steel back and forth over the stone. He didn't say a word.

Ritter set the pot down next to her and turned to Adoni, who cowered a few feet away and shivered in her wet clothes. He knelt down before her in the snow. "You're going to be fine. It's going to hurt like hell, but you'll come through. Donny." He took her hands in his and squeezed them tightly. "I tried to convince myself it was your own fault, for following me through the agate, for staying when you should've gone, for going out on your own like a lunatic and getting caught. But it's not your fault, it's mine. If I were a better piper, I would've never dragged you into this. If I were a better person…" He swallowed the lump in his throat. "I'm so sorry, girl. Forever."

Her lips formed the words, *I wanna go home.*

Theresa stood up, the blade undoubtedly sharp, and reached for one of the napkins in Steppe's hand. "Something to bite on," she said, twisting it until the fibres squeaked against each other. "Donny?"

Adoni peered around Ritter's frame and the tears sprang up once more. She slowly walked towards Theresa, towards the tree stump, her entire body shrinking in anticipation of the knife against her skin, the blood. Theresa handed her the napkin. "You have to put your shoulder flat against the wood," she said. "I need you to stay as still as possible, so I can get it all at once. I won't do it until you're ready, so when you're good, spread your arms out wide. Okay?" She cupped the side of the girl's face and stroked her cheek. "It'll be over soon."

Adoni put the napkin between her chattering teeth and knelt down in the snow. Her fingers slid along the bark as she leaned forward. She pressed her shoulder onto the stump just as Theresa asked, squeezed her knees together tightly enough to send an ache through her thighs, curled as closely into herself as she could, and struggled for warmth. Theresa bent over her and held the knife ready.

Adoni's breath came through her nose in quick gasps now that she was so close to the edge. Passing out would have been a mercy, but consciousness held her awake and at attention. There was no perfect moment to go through this, no exact moment when she would be all right with having her skin carved off of her body, no matter how caring and loving the hand that brought down the blade.

She sucked in her breath, closed her eyes, and threw her arms out wide.

There was a flash beneath the sliver of moon. Adoni screamed.

Theresa leaped away as the girl roared through her clenched teeth. Adoni grabbed hold of the stump, clawed at the wood. Blood sprang from the wound, coursed over her shoulder and down her back, seeped into the fibres of her torn robe and into the frozen wood.

Ritter snatched a handful of napkins from Steppe and flung himself onto the ground next to her. He pressed them against the wound, shaking with relief at the sound of her voice scissoring the night air.

Theresa tossed the knife into the pot of water and wrung her trembling hands together. Steppe wrapped his arms around her and held her against his chest.

"I missed..." she muttered, barely audible. "I missed... I didn't get all of it..."

"It's enough," he said, his hand on the back of her head, his fingers in her long black hair. "Thank you..."

"The A's still there... I didn't get it... my hand... something stopped my hand..."

"It's all right."

"It's *not all right!*" She pulled away and rushed to Adoni's side. "I'm so sorry," she said. "Let me look at it..."

Adoni's mouth opened. The rag fell onto the snow.

She shrieked.

"NO!!!"

The force split the tree stump in half and sent everyone around her spinning in all directions.

Theresa ended up flat against the chalet wall with the wind knocked clean out of her lungs. Steppe landed a few feet away from her and clutched his head. Ritter flew into the clearing and slammed into the stone well.

Adoni scrambled to her feet. Soaked with river water and with blood, wracked with pain and exhaustion and wrath, she took in a deep breath, clenched her fists, and shrieked.

"Can't you see this place is *miserable?*"

She stumbled into the middle of the clearing, a bedraggled spectacle in ripped clothes, as the residents dashed out of their cabins and stood on their porches. The residents watched her take a place between all four burning pillars. Ritter pulled her back towards the chalet. He hissed in her ear. "What are you doing? Are you crazy?"

She let him scoop her back into the kitchen and sit her down at the table. Steppe and Theresa, gasping, followed.

Ritter sat Adoni down at the table and pulled her robe back to look at the wound. It was sealed under The Welcome's enchantment, and only a smudge of puckered skin remained next to a black letter *A*.

"What's going on?" Theresa demanded.

"The spell's broken," Ritter said.

"What do you mean, the spell's broken? Did you hear her? I've never heard anyone scream like that. Not any piper. Not even Steppe!"

"The first initial's still there. There must still be a bit of the enchantment left."

"So, what? She's as powerful as Ansgar now?"

"How am I supposed to know?" he snapped. "I'm not a bloody psychic!"

"No, it makes sense," Steppe said. He nodded. "She's not a slave to Sylvester's will anymore, but Ansgar's name isn't gone completely. What's left has got to be part of her now."

Theresa threw her hands up and let them fall, slapping against her skirt. "I can't believe this. She split that trunk in half, Steppe. *In half.* Is she a piper now?"

He looked at Adoni and muttered, "God, I hope not."

Adoni twisted away from Ritter. "Sylvester's coming," she growled. "When he gets here I'm gonna kill him."

"No you won't," said Steppe. "You're not sabotaging everything we've worked for. I'll handle Sylvester."

"Sylvester's had the seal for years!" she yelled. "Years!" The word coursed through the floor and set it rumbling. "Ansgar gave it to him! He branded all the changelings, and they lost their minds! They're zombies! Slaves! And Ansgar doesn't care!" She held up her arm, drenched with her blood, and pointed at him. "You guys do everything she says, but she's a monster! Don't you understand? She's a *monster!*"

"He told you he branded the changelings?"

"Yes!"

He opened his mouth as if to speak, closed it again, his eyes darting around the room. "I don't understand," he said. "Why would she help him build an army and then tell me to keep him from attacking the colonies?"

"Because he asked her nicely," Ritter said. "It doesn't take much."

Steppe shook his head. "You knew Ansgar could do this?"

Ritter gave him a pitying, despairing look. "Come on, Istvan. You knew it too. Sylvester's first attack happened just after Reese arrived. Didn't it?"

Theresa's face was blank.

"It's all irrelevant then," Steppe said. "Her code… her decrees… these senseless motions she puts us through. She's on the take, just to hear us beg. It can all change at any moment… for her amusement."

"She's a monster, Steppe," said Ritter. "Amoral. Illogical. In a thousand years, I've never known her to be anything else."

Silence.

"No," Steppe muttered. "No." He turned his back to them, thrust his hands against his scalp and grabbed handfuls of his hair.

Then he pulled back his arm, made a fist, and punched the chalet wall, hard.

The bones in his hand cracked as he slammed it against the wood. He punched it again, again, again. And when it looked as though he'd had enough, he tilted his head back and screamed violently.

The entire chalet shook as though a quake had caught it in its grasp and tore it loose from its foundation. The nails twisted, the bolts snapped, the floorboards cracked, and doors blew open and swung shut.

Steppe screamed with outrage, screamed with frenzy, screamed for blood. Adoni, Theresa and Ritter each grabbed hold of what they could to keep from falling over—the doorjamb, the table, a corner of the wall. Seal or no seal, his rage threatened to split their skin, rupture their organs, suck the air out of their lungs. He had to be stopped, or he'd kill them all.

Finnur and Roxanne stumbled into the kitchen, holding on to each other. Paj pushed past them, approached Steppe as he howled away, put her hand on his shoulder, turned him around; red face, flushed skin, the veins in his neck sticking out, his temples pulsing. She put her hands on his cheeks.

"Stop," she said. "It's time to stop."

He trembled in her grip and glared back at her, looking for a moment as though he'd reach out and try to snap her neck. He stole deep, anguished breaths through his nose, through his teeth, his chest heaving. But she was calm and gentle as a pool of water, and eventually his breathing stilled, and the angry flush in his cheeks drained away. He looked away and nodded.

Adoni turned to Ritter, her lip curled. "How can you be so good with it?" she asked him, brimming with menace, putting into words what Steppe could not. "You knew this whole time Ansgar'd play both sides and you didn't tell anyone. You let Steppe have his meetings and you knew it wouldn't make a difference if Ansgar didn't want it to. Because you didn't want to face Sylvester after what you did to him. Is that why?"

Ritter didn't answer.

"What's the point of this place?" she demanded. "Why does it even exist? You know and you're just not telling, aren't you? Who is she?"

She slammed her fist on the table, and they jumped.

"*Who is she?*"

There was a knock at the front door.

Adoni stiffened.

"Donny," Ritter whispered.

She shoved her chair back and bolted from the kitchen.

He yelled her name again, but she didn't bother to turn around. The lamps flickered as she flew past them. She slammed her hand down on the knob and threw it open.

Sylvester stood on the porch with Adoni's blade strung on his arm.

He smiled at her as though he hadn't been the administrator to her humiliation only a few hours before. But when he caught the look of impending violence in her eyes, his smile quickly fell.

He hadn't had enough time to turn away before Adoni drew in a breath and shrieked, forcing him from the porch and onto his back in the clearing.

Her cheeks flushed; the power was exhilarating. Finally, she wasn't helpless anymore. She stalked towards him as he must have stalked towards the chalet, on determined, measured steps. Not running, but walking, as if she had all the time in the world to make him pay for what he had done.

He scrambled to his feet as she opened her mouth again. Her next scream sent him hurtling against one of the cabins. His body hit the wood with a thud and sent a shower of icicles down around him. Adoni caught a pair of eyes peeking out from the cabin windows and smirked. They would all know what she was capable of now.

Sylvester pulled himself up and ran towards the woods. She drove her voice into the snow and watched it buckle at his heels. He disappeared between the trees, and she went after him. Ritter called to her but she ignored him. Sylvester had to suffer the way she had, the way Aniuk had. Vengeance was only thing in the In-Between that could satisfy her now.

She stopped in the middle of the blackness and listened for him. He wouldn't run forever; his arrogance would eventually get the better of him and he would try to corner her the way he had before, descend on her somehow when she wasn't expecting it. She walked carefully, assessing what she could do to him once he was found. She could force him to the river's edge and shove him in, keep his head under water until he drowned. She could drive him face first through the snow until he suffocated. Finally, she decided on what to do: scream as loud as she could and, hopefully, break him in two.

Before each step she stuck out her foot and felt the ground ahead of her, wary of clipping her pace on a root or a dip in the earth. The watery smell of rocks and snow would make it easier for her to find him. All she had to do was detect the slightest doll-like odour in the air, something plastic and sour, and she would know Sylvester was near.

She heard footsteps behind her and turned quickly, ready to let her voice fly. Ritter's silhouette appeared against the light from The Welcome's pillars. "Get back to the chalet," he ordered.

"No."

"It's dangerous to be out here. For you and for me. Come on."

Adoni held a finger to her lips and shook her head. He continued to speak.

"You don't know how many of them are out here. You won't be able to take them all on at once. You may have a slip of Ansgar's power but you have no idea how to use it. Now get inside before you get us all killed."

"Why didn't you tell anyone about her?" she asked, throwing silence and caution to the wind. "Why didn't you tell anyone she's a traitor?"

"Because I didn't want to give it all away!" he snapped. "All right? Everyone here is so eager to play his part, piper or resident or *whatever*, so what good is it telling them they've all been had? I *liked* being the only one who knew the truth. Whenever I heard another lecture about the way things are supposed to be here, that truth gave me comfort. I knew it was all for nothing. I was the *only* one who knew."

The flame of a torch, held aloft in Steppe's hand, appeared between the trees.

"Adoni," he said, his voice its usual detached timbre, "please come back."

"So you're just selfish?" she asked Ritter, ignoring Steppe's request. "You just wanted to be the guy who knows something we don't?"

"So black and white," Ritter said, shaking his head. "Just the kind of thing a kid would say. Yes, if it makes you feel any better, yes, I'm selfish. I wanted the truth all to myself. It's all I had. It made me better than everyone else. Is that what you want me to say?"

"Come back, both of you," Steppe said. "We can't stay out here."

"I wanna know whose side you're on," she said.

"My own," Ritter replied. "Always my own."

She sneered at him and turned away, moving deeper into the forest. "Adoni, come back!" he demanded. She ignored him.

She was a few more paces ahead when his hand fell on her shoulder and gripped her hard. She whipped her arm away.

"I don't believe you," she said. "You're lying."

"Fine, just come back before you catch death."

"He's gonna pay for what he did!"

"And who's next to pay up, eh? Who comes after him?"

"Ansgar!"

"Not if you're keeping score. Next in line is me. I brought Sylvester to the farmer's doorstep. I didn't know it would stain me the way it has. This evil doesn't end with him. It plays out on a much larger stage than you know."

She frowned. "You didn't know," she said. "You didn't know what you were doing."

"That's not true. I knew exactly what I was doing."

"She tricked you! She made you think you were doing something good, singing all those kids away! I'm not gonna let her get away with it!"

Her new powers coursed through her, as much a part of her now as her own spit and blood. She tried to turn, but he thrust his arm in front of her and blocked her escape.

"You'll never take Ansgar down," he said. "Never. You think that puny voice of yours is going to leave a scratch on her? You're going to get hurt, you stupid girl! You're going to get yourself killed! And I won't be able to save you, don't you understand? Don't you understand anything at all?" Tears filled his eyes. "I didn't want to remember," he said miserably. "I'm up against too much, and I'm too tired to fight it. How many times would I have to explain Ansgar's evil over a thousand years, to the old pipers, to the new ones? How many wars would there have to be to finally take her down? I can't bear to see this through to the end. It's so much easier to be a pawn than a hero."

Adoni's bottom lip quivered. He was right; she wouldn't have been able to lead the pipers, the changelings, the residents all to victory against Ansgar. But her legs stiffened, and she clenched her fists, and said, "I'm not going back. I'm not gonna hide. I'm gonna fight."

Just as the words left her lips, she felt Sylvester's long fingers grab hold of her ruined collar. Too late to turn around, he yanked her back against him and laid an arm across her chest.

Steppe thrust his chin forward and raised his fists, but stopped when Sylvester snapped at him like a dog and held the blade against Adoni's throat.

"What war is this for you to fight?" he said to her coolly. "It's not you I want." He pointed at Ritter. "It's him."

He dragged her down to the ground, knelt behind her and gripped a fistful of her hair. She reached across her body and tore at his face with her fingernails. He jerked her head back further until she thought her spine would snap. She was powerless, she realized, unless he was in front of her.

Sylvester smirked at the pipers. "Her or you, Ritter," he said.

"Neither," Steppe said. "Let her go."

"That's not an option."

"Ansgar wronged you, Sylvester, just as she wronged us. You have no quarrel with Ritter. It's Ansgar who made you all slaves."

"Ansgar rules the In-Between and no power here can possibly destroy her," Sylvester said. "Whose choice was it to follow her every whim? If I can't kill her, I'll kill the thing she loves the most. Or I'll kill your ambassador. Whichever you prefer."

Steppe glared at him. "Don't make me hurt you, Sylvester," he growled.

Sylvester chuckled. "You wouldn't hurt me," he said. "I wouldn't be able to visit you day in and day out if you had the stomach for it." He raised the blade higher. Adoni winced. "I doubt you'd be able to manage a clear shot at this point."

"Do you really want to find out?"

"Don't," Ritter said. He held his hands up, took a step forward. "I deserve what's coming to me. Let her go."

Sylvester held her tighter. "You enjoyed leaving us behind, didn't you?" he asked.

"It was my duty," Ritter replied. "It's what I was made for. You were the last changeling I left on someone's doorstep. You made me realize how evil it was. I ran from her after that. Of course she found me and had me brought back."

"How wonderful, to be your rebellion's cipher," Sylvester said through his teeth. "There's something I've always been curious about. Indulge me. She never punished you for running. She punishes Steppe in your place. Why is that?"

"We have an understanding."

The words fell around them like dead leaves. But Adoni heard something in the back of Ritter's throat; one last secret he was afraid to reveal.

And this time she wasn't the only one who recognized it.

Sylvester's cheeks went pale, his eyes opened wide. He sprang to his feet and let the blade fly, slicing Ritter's cheek.

Ritter grunted and stumbled back, pressed his hand against the wound. Sylvester pointed the blade at him. "Move your hand."

Ritter glared at him.

Sylvester put the blade back to Adoni's throat. "MOVE IT!"

Ritter straightened up and dropped his hand.

They saw it in the torchlight; the long, angry gash, spilling black blood, sewed itself up before their eyes.

Sylvester tossed Adoni aside and lunged at Ritter. Steppe let a snarl fly. It threw Sylvester back against a tree and knocked him silent. Adoni threw her arms around Ritter as Steppe turned and stared at him.

"It can't be true. It *can't* be."

Ritter shook his head.

"You're a changeling?" Steppe asked him. Ritter didn't speak. "*What are you?!*" he roared.

"Don't make me say it," Ritter answered weakly.

"You didn't tell me! Why didn't you tell me?"

"You were my best friend," he said, holding Adoni tightly. "My only friend! She put you in charge of the most forsaken place in the In-Between and ordered you to make it right when she knew you couldn't! What good would it possibly have done?"

"You don't have to take this!" Adoni said to them both. "She's the one who's playing us! She's the one we should be fighting against!"

She caught a blur of movement out of the corner of her eye.

Sylvester slammed her against a tree and wrapped his hands around her neck. The force of his fingers opened her mouth and wrestled a distorted gurgle from her throat. She reached up, seized his wrists, and faced the boundless hatred in his eyes. Beyond the borders of the In-Between she saw the city, moving back and forth after midnight, its lights, its cars, its buildings and their yellow windows, its life. She saw Steppe move towards them, teeth gnashed. She saw him open his mouth and felt him take in a breath so deep it sucked the sound of the woods out of their ears.

He was going to kill Sylvester himself. He was going to make things worse.

She didn't let him finish. She drew in a breath of her own, and released a twisted, petrifying shriek.

She heard a *squish*, and a *pop*.

Sylvester let go of her and screamed. Both of his hands flew to his face and clapped themselves over his right eye. Adoni watched a stream of black blood trickle out from between his fingers. He fell into the snow, hissing in pain. Free to breathe again, she sputtered, coughed, and looked down at him, waiting to witness the quick heal, the split-second sewing up of his wound. When he looked at her again his skin had indeed healed - in a thick, pink scab over a now hollow socket.

"You little *bitch!*"

She stared at what remained of his obliterated eye, no longer the frightened creature his changelings stole in the afternoon, no longer a cringing thing at his feet. But there was no rush of adrenaline, no warmth in her cheeks, no satisfaction or pride as she watched him snivelling in the snow.

"You and I are enemies, Ambassador," he sneered. "I may not be able to defeat you alone anymore, but all whims in the In-Between belong to Ansgar. I'll return with an army of thousands, who suffer the way I suffer, and we'll have our revenge."

"Then I'll fight your army," she said calmly. "And I'll win."

He stared at her.

Then, he gathered himself up to his feet, straightened his jacket, and brushed the snow from his pants. His lifeless eye cast itself on Steppe, Ritter, and finally, her. His lips parted.

Steppe stood next to her and took her hand, linking his fingers with hers.

Sylvester gave her a smile so menacing it lingered on the backs of her eyes. He went away into the woods, in silence.

They stood still, listening for his return, for the sound of an army lying in wait behind the trees. The night held nothing but a frigid peace, the wisp of a breeze, and the occasional howl of a wolf in the distance. Sylvester wasn't coming back; not then.

Adoni fixed her gaze ahead, her eyes unblinking even in the cold, dry air. "Are you all right?" Steppe asked her.

She shook her head, took up Steppe's torch, and followed the footprints back to the clearing.

When she arrived, she went to every cabin door and knocked as hard as she could. It took a few moments to bring everyone out onto their porches. She stopped in front of the well and turned around to address them all, her blood caked on her arm, her face filthy, her black eyes filled with lightning.

"You think Ansgar's just some magic thing that gives us food and clothes and whatever. But Ansgar's a person, and she doesn't care about you, or me, or any pipers, or any changelings. She doesn't care what happened to you before you got here. She doesn't care what happens when you leave. She just wants to put us through her system to watch us all suffer, every day, forever. And someone's gotta stand up to her and say *no*." She held up the torch. "I don't want these clothes, or a room in the chalet, or a cabin of my own with a magic chest, if it means I have to live the way Ansgar thinks I should live. I'm going home. Who's coming?"

Each resident looked at her bloodied, broken figure in the clearing.

One by one, they turned their backs on her, went into their cabins, and closed their doors behind them.

Chapter Twenty-Nine

Adoni looked up at the sky and blinked her tears away before they fell over her cheeks. Ritter stepped out of the woods and joined her in the clearing, put his hands on her shoulders and pressed his lips against her temple. The gesture was so simple, so elegant, she thought she'd start to cry right then and there. She leaned against him and would have given in to sobbing, if a tiny figure hadn't chosen that very moment to appear between the cabins.

She wiped her eyes with the back of a grimy hand and watched the child approach. He wore Batman pyjamas, undoubtedly a gift from his hope chest.

Adoni smiled at him. "Missed you, Tyler," she said when he was close enough. He wrapped his hand around one of her fingers and tugged.

With Tyler's hand in hers, she turned back to the chalet and stepped up to the kitchen door. "You're welcome," she said.

And by her own authority, she crossed the threshold.

Theresa was sitting at the kitchen table. She saw them enter, safe and sound, and got to her feet. She put her arms around Adoni. "Did you kill him?"

"No."

"Where are the others?"

They came through the door, and she sighed. "What happened to your cheek?" she asked Ritter when she noticed the silvery scar.

"I need to speak to everyone," Steppe said to her. She let her question go unanswered.

They followed Steppe to the foot of the staircase, where he called for the rest of the pipers. Roxanne, Paj, and Finnur slowly came out of their rooms and stood on the landing.

"The Welcome has abandoned the code," Steppe said to them. "Effective immediately. No one here answers to Ansgar anymore."

They looked at each other, and then looked at him.

"Just like that?" Roxanne asked.

"Why?" asked Finnur.

"Because we've suffered for it for too long. And the residents have suffered for it for too long. And the changelings have suffered for it for too long. I've had it with this slavery. I can't in good conscience force anyone else to abide by it. Ansgar may rule the In-Between, but she won't rule me. And I won't let her rule the souls on this colony any longer."

"You realize you'll start a war when she catches wind of this," Ritter said.

"I'm used to war," Steppe replied.

"What about the kids?" Adoni asked.

"The kids," he said, smiling at the word, "don't have anything to worry about while they're here. I've got a few favours to call in from the other colonies. Their leaders won't disappoint me." But he couldn't look at her as he spoke. "What will you do now?" he asked.

"I gotta get my uniform. I can't go back in these."

She mounted the grand staircase slowly, to give Tyler enough time to raise his awkward, pudgy legs one after the other and climb up alongside her. The pipers gazed at her; the closer she got to the top of the stairs, the more able she was to register their wonder. Their eyes brimmed with respect and intimidation. She nodded, and saw they could barely contain their pride.

"Wait here for me, okay?" she said to Tyler when they stood at the top of the stairs.

He stopped and glanced shyly at the pipers.

"Hello," they said to him, in one timid voice together.

Adoni crossed the music room floor and climbed up the ladder to Theresa's bedroom. There was the vanity in the corner, the wardrobe on the other side of the room, the slanted ceiling and animal hides and polished stones and low, wide bed.

And sitting on the bed was Natalie, still dressed in her piper robes.

Adoni knelt in front of her, took up her hands, and stroked her knuckles with her thumbs, leaving a smear of blood behind that Natalie didn't bother to wipe away. Natalie leaned over to examine Adoni's shoulder.

"I'm sorry about before," Adoni said.

"Me too."

"You told them what happened, eh? That's why Ritter came."

"Uh-huh."

"How'd you know?"

Natalie looked down at her lap. "I followed you."

"Thank you."

Natalie's song—its earth and bells and promise—moved Adoni to her feet. She went to the wardrobe and found her school uniform hanging neatly among Theresa's clothes. She pulled off the ruined, worthless robe and left it lying on the floor, slipped on the white buttoned shirt, the grey slacks, and the itchy blue cardigan. She turned back to Natalie.

Ida would like her, she decided, once she got to know her, once she sobered up and saw past the hair and attitude. They could hang out after school in Adoni's room and listen to music, or go to the movies or for walks in High Park, or have a picnic on the Island and take the last ferry home. She had to get Natalie's number. She had to know where she lived. She had to have a plan in place on nights when Natalie didn't want to be at home. Or Natalie could come and live with her. Ida wouldn't mind. They could get part time jobs to help out, and Ida wouldn't worry about money anymore and would get back on the wagon and be the mom Adoni knew she was, and the three of them would be happy.

"Are you gonna go back in those?" she asked.

The question didn't seem to register at first; then Natalie pressed her lips together and swallowed hard. "I'm not going back."

Silence.

"Why?" Natalie didn't answer her. "Please?" she asked.

Natalie shook her head and said nothing.

Adoni dove to her knees and grabbed Natalie's hands again. "Please?" she said, as steadily as she could. "Please? Please come back with me? Please?" Natalie pulled her hands away and shook her head, over and over again. "Please? Please come back with me? Please, Natty? Natty? Natty?" Adoni reached her Natalie's face, for her burning cheeks.

Natalie turned her head and leaned back out of her reach.

Adoni's brow bent, and her chest heaved, and her voice leaked out of her like acid burning, like lava boiling. "You can stay with me, okay? You don't have to go back home. You can stay with me and I can take care of you. I'll always believe you. Always, always, always. Come back with me, Natty. Please come back with me."

Natalie leaned forward and pressed her lips against Adoni's twisted mouth. Adoni tried to regain her composure long enough to feel Natalie's warmth and smell her skin one last time. It was too late.

Natalie pulled away before Adoni could feel that beautiful, aching smack against her lips; all she kissed was a chance goodbye.

Natalie stood up, went to the ladder, climbed down, and disappeared.

Adoni stared at her filthy hands. They seemed small and useless, ten fingers that let things slip through them all the time, important things, things she could never get back. She reached out and filled each empty palm with a polished stone, squeezed them in her fists until the muscles in her arms shuddered.

She hurled the stones against the wall, sank to her knees, and sobbed.

And put her hand over her mouth.

And sobbed.

And punched the floor as hard as she could.

And felt her world shrivel and die.

A hand smoothed itself over her hair, over her back, with care and consideration. "Donny?" Theresa said. "You okay?"

Adoni turned around and pressed herself against Theresa's chest, hid in the folds of her clothes. "She won't come with me! She doesn't even love me!"

Theresa held her close. "She's just not ready to leave," she said.

"I thought she loved me too!"

"It's not about love, kiddo. It never is."

Adoni clung to the woman with all her strength, sobbed with the force of a tidal wave, a thousand wild horses.

She cried until every inch of her body emptied itself of loss and loneliness, until weakness seeped into every limb and finally stilled her, and Theresa's heartbeat took away the sting.

"That little boy's waiting for you downstairs," Theresa murmured.

Adoni nodded and got to her feet. She wrapped her arms around Theresa's waist and hugged her tightly.

"I'll meet you outside, okay?" Theresa said.

Adoni took one last look at the room, then made her way down the ladder.

Tyler stood next to Steppe's piano, shuffling from foot to foot. Adoni sniffed and held her hand out to him.

He looked at her weary face and said, "Sad?"
Adoni nodded. "Yeah."
Tyler took her hand. "Yeah," he said.

Ritter and Steppe stood next to the well, staring down into the black water. The air was no longer thick with pain and dread but light and crisp, like a sketch in pencil across a blank page.

"So she made him sentient," Steppe said.

"Yes."

"It's so..."

"Cruel?"

Steppe turned to him and nodded. "She made you sentient too."

"Don't be daft," Ritter chuckled. "It took me decades to cultivate this stellar personality."

"You hid it well. I had no idea. The way you mimic us..."

"No," Ritter said, cutting him off. "We're not mimics. We have emotions, Steppe. *I* have emotions. I have a soul. I just had to earn it. It took me a thousand years, but I earned it."

Steppe's grin was sad. "Don't we all."

Adoni and Tyler emerged from the chalet. Both pipers came towards her with bowed heads and stopped a few feet away from her. "You're ready," Ritter said. "Natalie must be in her cabin. Packing, I assume."

"She's not coming."

Ritter frowned and shook his head. "She wants to stay?"

Adoni shrugged and looked down at her running shoes.

Ritter sighed. "I can't say I'm surprised."

"I'll take care of Natalie," Steppe said. "All of them. Don't worry."

"And Sylvester?"

Steppe levelled his gaze on the trees across the way. "I can deal with Sylvester."

"You were close, tonight," Ritter said. "The closest I've ever seen you come to destroying him."

"Yes," Steppe replied. But he didn't continue.

"I wanted to tell you," said Ritter softly. "So many times. But you're right, I'm a coward." He put his hand on Steppe's shoulder, gripped it in earnest. "I didn't want you to think that I can't really feel anything. That I'm just an empty shell pretending. That at any moment I'll betray you. That I can't be loyal. That I don't have a soul."

"Nothing could convince me of that," Steppe said. "Changeling or not. Sometimes I think you're more human than I am."

Each man looked down at the snow, at his boots. Finally, Steppe asked, "Who's Ansgar?"

Ritter looked out across the clearing. "It's funny. I never thought we'd ever get to this moment. You were never one for asking questions, and I never had to explain myself. Match made in heaven." He smiled a desolate smile. "Ansgar is a demi-goddess who's always existed in the In-Between. She's impulsive. Vindictive."

"She's a little kid," Adoni said. "Right?"

Ritter cocked an eyebrow at her. Finally, after a considerable pause, he nodded. "No matter how many years pass, she's always five years old."

He ran the tip of his finger along his new scar.

"She's a child?" Steppe asked.

"A lonely child," Ritter said. "And her loneliness makes her cruel. She wanted a playmate. So she created me. And then I wasn't enough. She didn't want puppets; she wanted real children to play with. So she had me go fetch them for her. And they were fun, for a while, until they started begging to go home again. So she had me fetch the lowliest children I could find, children who wouldn't want to leave her. And they were fun for a while, too, until they got too old and she got bored of them. And then she decided she didn't want *playmates*. She wanted a *kingdom*. She wanted to rule. So she cursed people with piper voices and wrote her name on their souls and turned them into slaves, and filled the In-Between with children from all over to serve as her subjects. Sylvester was a delightful distraction for her. I'm sure she'd love nothing more than to see her changelings wage war against her pipers. I'm sure she'd love to watch until one side is completely annihilated. She loves to see her dollies dance. And when she gets bored, she'll change the rules again. That's who Ansgar is."

"Wicked King," Adoni muttered.

Steppe shook his head. "Everything I believed was a lie. And I let myself believe it, because I didn't have the guts to ask for the truth."

"So we're both cowards?" Ritter asked with a smirk.

"Don't tell me any…" Steppe began. He took a breath. "I don't want to hurt anyone."

Ritter hesitated, then put his hand on Steppe's shoulder.

Steppe reached up, wrapped his warm hand around his friend's cold fingers, and squeezed.

Ritter looked up at his former bedroom before speaking again. "I won't be back," he said, facing Steppe full on.

"I didn't think you'd ever risk anything for anyone," said Steppe. "But you did. Everything, actually. I'm… You'll always have a place here. You don't have to go, if you'd rather stay. I was…"

Ritter chuckled. "You're a true poet, Steppe. As flattered as I am by your offer, I'm afraid I can't accept it. I miss the way I spend my nights when I'm free to decide what to do with them. And I'd like to get a tan once in a while."

"What about your things? They're still upstairs."

"I'll leave them. They never really felt like mine anyway. I'll collect new things. Or maybe I'll forgo owning things for a while. Be romantic."

"Listen," Steppe said. "About her… About Belinda…" Ritter stopped smiling. Steppe put his hands in his pockets. "Whatever words I say…" he began.

Ritter leaned into him, kissed his lips, and whispered, "I know, darling."

He crouched down in front of Adoni, green eyes sparkling as the dawn began to break. Adoni opened her arms and hugged him fiercely.

"Thanks," she said quietly.

Ritter held her for a while, listened to her breathing, listened to her heartbeat. He gave her one final squeeze, and kissed her cheek. "We'll see each other again, you know."

"I know."

He stood and looked into the distance. Words circled in his head, overwhelmed him with their demands to pass his lips and enter the stratosphere. He pushed them aside and opened the agate.

None of his words were worth more to him than the sound of Adoni's voice—muskets and trumpets and the purr of a lion—reverberating in his ears.

He stepped through, and the agate closed behind him.

Adoni looked at Steppe. He kept his eyes on the spot where Ritter disappeared; they never wavered.

"You know Theresa's drawers upstairs?" she asked. "With the mirror?"

"Yes."

"She has a bunch of stuff in it, like scarves and bottles and stuff. There's a box up there…"

"With old pictures in it," he finished. "I know."

"Not that one. Another one. It's a wooden box. I was going through the drawers because… I was snooping," she said. "And I found this box, and when I opened it, I heard Belinda's voice."

She waited, thinking for certain she'd see a flash of Steppe's temper in his eyes at the mention of his dead lover's name.

"Go on," he said softly.

"You can go upstairs and listen to it if you want. It's her journal. I know it's not good to read other people's journals, but… I mean, it's important you know what she was thinking and stuff."

"Tell me what she said."

Adoni stuffed her hands into her pockets. She couldn't blame him for not wanting to hear Belinda's voice himself just then—not after so many years of silence. "A lot of it is her asking herself why things were the way they were. The one thing you need to know is why she didn't pass her voice on to you. Because that's what pipers do, right? They're supposed to pass their voices on to the people they love the most. I don't know why you would. If you love the person, why make them a slave? I don't know. But Belinda, she said if she gave you her voice, you wouldn't be able to take it. She thought it would kill you. Maybe if you got mad enough you'd, like, explode. Maybe it would've made you crazy. And I get it, you know? Because you're... *intense*."

Steppe chuckled bitterly. "I guess so."

"She didn't want to hurt you. She loved you. You can tell, just by listening to her. She respected Ritter a lot, but she didn't love him. She loved you." She looked up at him.

He hung his head and tapped his toes against the frozen ground. "It's hard," he said at long last, "to admit when you're wrong."

Theresa joined them in the clearing. Her steps were lighter, as if whatever weight plagued her before was lifted from her shoulders. She stepped up next to Adoni and gave her a smile. "Okay," she said. "Time to go." She looked at Steppe.

He stared at her. "You're not..."

"I am," she said. "I'm going too."

He shook his head.

She reached for him. He backed away from her.

"I'm gonna see what I've been missing," she said, slowly drawing her hand back down by her side. "There's a whole world I need to get reacquainted with. It's been a long time."

"If this is because of what I said earlier..."

"This is because you think of me as a part of you," she said. "And while I'm here, that's exactly what I am. It's not enough anymore." She looked at Adoni. "I want more."

"Reese," he said. "I wanted you to decide to leave on your own, I know, but I don't know…"

"Steppe…"

"I don't think…"

She put her hand on his face. "This is what I want. Okay? It's what I want."

The sky turned from green to yellow, from yellow to brilliant gold. He fought to look at her, to see her standing strong and beautiful against the lightening sky, to not have his last glimpse of her be tarnished by a furrowed brow and eyes filled with longing.

So when his eyes finally lifted, he gazed at her with esteem, like a gift.

After everything he had seen and heard, there was nothing left to say. He nodded, releasing her from The Welcome, and from his side.

She beamed at him, opened her arms, and leaned against his chest. She tilted her head up to find his lips and kiss them. And he kissed her back, gently, urgently, savouring every moment of her touch, keeping that part of her a secret in his heart forever.

"God, I love you," he whispered.

"Steppe…" She held him as close as she could. "You mean the world to me."

She turned back to Adoni and said, "Okay."

Adoni put her hands on her hips. She looked up at the rosy sky, committed its colour and the way it shimmered over everything and everyone in the clearing to memory. She squinted and looked past the In-Between, into the city, shivering with imperfect beauty, just outside her reach.

She raised a hand, pointed her finger, and traced a line in the air from the top of her head to the soles of her shoes. The halves peeled away, into the agate doorway.

She turned around, took one last glimpse at The Welcome, at the cabins, at the chalet, at the glowing bedroom windows, at the burning pillars, and finally, at Steppe.

He nodded, and waved goodbye.

Tyler held onto Adoni's hand, his eyes wide. Theresa trembled, pressed her fingers against her temples and struggled for deep, even breaths. Adoni heard a frightened squeak come from the back of Theresa's throat.

She took the woman's hand in hers and squeezed as tightly as she could. "It's okay," she said.

She stepped forward, holding onto them both. She didn't let go until the three of them stood, together, on a corner, underneath a streetlamp, in the rain.

Chapter Thirty

Adoni looked around at the run-down convenience stores, the newspapered windows and graffitied brick walls, and smelled car exhaust and the hint of something burning in the wind. She recognized where they were—at an intersection a few streets over from her home. It was early in the morning, before the traffic hit its stride and deliveries were made to the merchants foolhardy enough to operate in this part of town. She looked up at Theresa, who gazed about her in confusion.

"I don't remember this," she said, shaking her head.

"I know where we are," Adoni said. "I live around here."

"Jeez." Theresa walked a few paces, her piper skirt swaying as she moved. She put her hands on her cheeks and turned around in a circle. "I haven't seen a store in…" She sniffed the air. "Do you smell that?"

Adoni grinned. "There's a coffee shop over there, see?" She pointed down the street.

Theresa laughed. "Wow. What I wouldn't give for a double-double right about now."

"Me too. Want a bagel, Tyler?"

Tyler nodded. Adoni lifted him up to keep his feet from getting wet in the puddles.

They strolled towards the coffee shop, passing the stores and narrow doorways leading to second floor apartments. Theresa's eyes were alight as they drank in the appliance and electronic rental places, the repair shops, the makeshift places of worship. By the time the three of them reached the coffee shop her eyes were glazed over, and she stared at the floor while they stood in line.

Theresa ordered herself a double-double and one for Adoni, a carton of milk for Tyler, and two buttered, toasted bagels. Adoni pulled out the crumpled fifty dollar bill she had stolen from Ida. Her stomach sank. "I have to pay mom back later," she said.

"I should have used Ansgar's cupboards one last time before I left," said Theresa. "I got used to handouts. Shit." She dug the toe of her boot into the tiled floor.

They took a seat near the window so Theresa could watch the world she was about to re-enter go by for a while. More and more people filled the streets as the morning wore on. Theresa gave Tyler the top of her bagel and took a bite of the remaining half. She closed her eyes and sighed. "Man, that's good. Real bread, real butter."

Adoni bit into her own bagel. Theresa was right; there was no artificial flavour to speak of. "But I still like what you make," she said quickly.

"Thanks."

"What're you gonna do now?"

Theresa finished her bite and swallowed. "First I'll need to find an apartment or something. It'll be tricky. No one's rented to me before so I'm not sure if they'll be willing to. I can tell them I've been out of the country, some place that doesn't speak English so they won't ask to talk to references or anything. The credit history'll be a problem too." She rubbed her eyes.

"But what about after?" Adoni asked. "What're you gonna do for life?"

"You know," Theresa said, "I want to start a business. Like a food truck or something. Something small."

"You'll be good at that."

"Thanks. What about you?"

"I'm gonna bring Tyler home and let my mom know I'm okay."

Theresa nodded. "That's what I should've done," she said. "But I was too scared. When I realized I didn't have to go back, I thought I was lucky." She chuckled. "In a way I guess I was. In a way I wasn't. Funny, huh?"

Adoni looked up from her coffee to the city whirling away beyond the coffee shop window. She couldn't remember what day of the week it was, whether it was the weekend or if she had school. Assumption's halls would be as dank as they were before she left, the classes just as boring and confusing, the kids as gossipy as ever, even Monica, with her greasy skin and stringy hair and cartons of uneaten fries slathered in gravy. Shabnam would be waiting at Adoni's locker, a receipt for a new phone in her hand, her belligerent demands loud enough for everyone to hear.

Adoni sighed; no matter how good, or how bad, things would be from that point on, her only option was to knuckle down and get through it.

They finished their bagels and sipped their coffee until the paper cups were empty. Adoni picked Tyler up and they stepped back into the street. They stood in front of the coffee shop for a moment, neither one knowing which way to head.

And then Adoni sucked in her bottom lip and bit down hard.

Possibility lay right in front of her—an entire city filled with experiences, old and new, around every corner. But there was no such future for the residents of The Welcome. When they finally woke up that morning in the In-Between, the only possibilities afforded them were the ones that could fit between the four sides of their hope chests. The only decisions they had to make were what time to rise from their beds and which way to turn on their way through the trees, simple decisions doled out to pass the time. The only friends they had would be shunted off as soon as they reached that magic number of eighteen years and became *adults*—too old to play Ansgar's game.

Then there were the pipers, doomed to follow Ansgar's orders, to collect her broken children and stash them away on her colonies, to throw them away when they no longer amused her. Pipers sentenced to sing Ansgar's praises, though they knew she wasn't worthy of them, because they were afraid of what would happen to them if they didn't. The pipers of The Welcome knew the truth about Ansgar, and Steppe would do whatever it took to protect them from the wrath she would raise when she found out those subjects had deserted her. But there were other colonies—other pipers, other residents, who were still slaves to Ansgar's will, and Steppe couldn't protect them all, on his own, if they deserted her too.

Adoni clenched her jaw and glared at the sidewalk, scratching at the scab on her shoulder. "I made a mistake," she said.

"What?" Theresa asked, too absorbed in the noise of the street to hear what Adoni had said.

"I have to go back," she said. "They can't do it without me."

She took Theresa by the wrist and hurried them into the narrow space between the coffee shop and the laundry next to it. Ansgar's moniker surely meant she could find the portal and tear it open, the way Ritter had when she laid eyes on him that night. She tried to remember just how he'd done it. It seemed like a lifetime ago, and she couldn't recall the tune he'd used, or the tone, or the timbre, to summon the agate from the In-Between. Finally, she took a breath, opened her mouth, and let Belinda's song fly.

Her voice was definitely stronger, definitely huskier. She sang until the tune ran right out, waited for the agate to seep into view.

Nothing happened.

"Why isn't it working?" she asked.

She tried again; nothing.

She tried Natalie's song, with its earth and its bells; nothing.

She raised her finger, as she had in the In-Between, waved it around; nothing.

"How do you open the agate?"

"You're asking me?" Theresa shrugged. "I can't open the agate."

"But I should be able to open it. It should work for me. Why isn't it working?"

Theresa put her hand on Adoni's shoulder. "I don't think it will."

"What do you mean? You heard me before. I've still got the *A*. Why won't it work out here?"

"Because you don't have a piper's voice."

"Yeah I do! You heard me!"

"What you've got is an initial on your shoulder," Theresa said. "It may be powerful in the In-Between, but it's not enough out here. You heard Ritter; pipers have Ansgar's name written on their souls. They're the only ones she wants opening the agate, not you."

Adoni gaped at her. "I can't go back?"

Theresa shook her head. "Sorry, kid."

"But Steppe needs me! Sylvester's gonna attack again, you know it. And Ansgar too. I can't let him fight them alone!"

Adoni clasped Tyler close to her. Theresa stepped in front of her and knelt down, looked up into Adoni's face. "Donny, believe me, it's for the best."

"No it's not! There's all those kids! There's all those pipers! He can't be everywhere all over the In-Between!" She let go of Tyler and started to pace, kicking a dented can out of her way. "I'm so stupid! I left too quick! Look how quick I just gave up, just like that! What about Natalie? I just left her there! I should've stayed!"

"Donny, you need to let it go."

"I can't just pretend like it never happened!"

"Steppe knows what he's doing. They'll be fine, so long as he's there to protect them."

"What if Ansgar goes after the others? What then?"

"Don't worry."

Adoni wrapped her arms around herself and shrieked. She turned and kicked the side of the coffee shop as forcefully as Ritter had kicked the wall of her apartment.

She heard a cry of shock and caught Tyler's large eyes staring at her.

She frowned and returned to his side, pulled him in close. To Theresa, she muttered, "If you think it's so easy, don't you worry either."

Theresa shook her head. "I didn't say it'd be easy."

Adoni licked her lips and tugged at her cardigan.

"Come on," she said after a time. "There's a shelter around here."

She led Theresa and Tyler over uneven sidewalks and winter puddles, past the storefronts and shoddy road work. They passed another divvy joint and smelled bacon frying and bitter coffee floating on the breeze. A car horn blasted in the distance, an ambulance raced to someone's aid. They passed a rotisserie place with its doorway painted tacky shades of orange, red, and green, and heard a woman's plaintive melody, sung in a language they couldn't understand, spill into the street over a pair of cheap speakers.

There was the shelter, right on the corner. Adoni stopped in front of it; she could still hear the music from the rotisserie a few doors down. It was an appropriate melody—mournful, but not completely without hope.

Theresa stared the place down. "I haven't been to one of these since…"

"Want me to stay until you know for sure?"

"I'll be okay. These places don't ever really leave you. I'll manage." She stooped and hugged the girl tightly, then murmured in her ear, "Thank you so much."

Adoni gave her a kiss on the cheek. She pulled away as Theresa wiped a few rogue tears off her cheeks. "I'll come by later, okay?" she said.

"Okay. I'll be here."

Theresa winked at her, turned around, and made her way through the shelter's front door.

Adoni took a deep breath when she and Tyler reached the front door of their building. She smelled a wonderful bouquet of garlic, onions, and spice rise from a cast iron skillet in someone's kitchen. Theresa would make a fantastic food trucker; there was no doubt about it. Adoni wanted to be there when it hit the city streets.

She led the boy up the stairs and into the foyer. Someone had carelessly left the front door open on its latch. The landlord would draft one of his spiteful letters if she left the door as she'd found it—they passed into the main hall, and she closed it behind her. Tyler took the lead, bounding up the stairs and over to the splintered front door of his parents' apartment. Adoni crouched down in front of him and levelled with him. "You and me are buds, okay? Your mom's gonna be mad. She's gonna scream and maybe cry too, because that's what moms do. But if you need anything, I just live here. Knock loud, okay?"

Tyler nodded and put his hand on the knob, turned it, and found the door open. He walked into the apartment and closed the door behind him.

Adoni waited; silence. His parents were probably still asleep, if they were there at all.

She bent and found the spare key Ida kept under the loose floor board, put the key in the door quietly, turned it, and went inside.

The air was stale, the windows shut tight. She slipped off her running shoes and looked around at the old furniture, the empty box of crackers on the counter, the magazines on the couch and coffee table, the bottles lined up next to the sink. The sour funk of breath laced with alcohol was gone.

"Mom?"

Silence.

"Mom?"

She heard the creak of a mattress and feet on the floor, one, two, three, four steps pounding towards the bedroom door. It flew open and Ida bounded into view. Adoni's heart leaped into her throat. She had a split second to prepare herself for what might be a hug or a slap in the face.

Ida's mouth opened, and she flew into her daughter, pulled her down to the floor, and wailed, and wailed, with relief.

"BABY!"

"Hi mom."

"MY BABY! MY BABY!"

"I'm sorry, mom. I took your fifty bucks and…"

"BABY!"

And she pulled Adoni into her lap, stroked her hair, and rocked her back and forth as she sobbed against her neck. "My little girl!" she cried. "My little girl!"

Adoni stayed curled up on the floor next to Ida, who had sobbed herself to sleep on her shoulder and only opened her eyes when Adoni shifted into a more comfortable position. She looked at her mother's tired, broken face and saw a version of herself that she loved, feared, understood, and wouldn't dare become if she could help it.

"Mom?"

"Yeah?" Ida's voice was raw and thin, the voice of someone who had just been through a war.

"You gotta stop drinking."

Ida didn't speak. So Adoni kept going.

"You gotta stop drinking, okay? Because when you get drunk you scare me. It's scary. Okay? And I like when we're hanging out and looking at pictures. And when we look at the Christmas lights. And when we go for burgers because even though we're moving again at least we get to pack together. Okay? And we don't get to do those things when you're drunk, because you go away and some other person comes and takes your place, and it's hard to remember I love you then. Okay, mom? Please?"

Ida lifted her head and looked into her daughter's black and endless eyes. Her voice was almost too small to hear. "It's so hard... when you're alone..."

"But I'm right here."

Adoni couldn't think of anything else to say. She looked at her mother's face, into her mother's eyes, and waited.

Ida shuffled onto her knees and brought herself up to her feet. She went to the windows, unlatched them, and pushed them open as wide as they could go. The superintendent must have come in and fixed the stubborn pane that always gave them trouble. The cool air streamed in and ruffled the magazine pages. The city murmured with promise beyond the glass.

Ida took a breath and closed her eyes. When she opened them again they were filled with fear, with fight, and with hope.

Adoni watched her disappear into the kitchen and let the sound of the city take her away, let the light and the air refresh her tired skin and soothe her heart. She hoped the residents, past and present, were okay. She hoped Natalie would be ready to leave before she forgot about her.

Adoni bit her lip; Steppe wouldn't be able to fight the war alone, and he'd let her go without telling her there was no way back.

Then she remembered.

Ritter.

Ritter was somewhere in the city, on his way to music and meaning. Ritter, who had brought her to the In-Between in the first place, who knew all its secrets, all its lies, who told her she was brave, and stupid, and hope. He could open the agate for her, and bring her back.

Adoni took a breath, and a silent vow; she would search for Ritter in every corner of the city if she had to. One day she'd find him. One day she'd return to the In-Between. One day, she'd shout the whole thing down.

She heard Ida unscrew the bottles on the counter and, one by one, tip the contents into the sink.

When the last bottle was empty, Adoni wrapped her arms around her legs, laid her head on her knees, and bathed in a beautiful, fleeting, golden silence.

Epilogue

"He's abandoned the code," Sylvester said. "I've heard the pipers talking. No one at The Welcome answers to you anymore. That's what they say."

He sat on the chair in the centre of the chamber, swaddled in darkness, his hands clasped tightly together. The fire played off his pale skin, lit him up like a poltergeist. The pink scab was covered with a black felt patch.

He got no response, and sneered.

"Your chosen messenger has abandoned the In-Between. He's back to roaming the cities and ignoring your decree. Other pipers will follow, mark my words. They'll discover what Ritter really is and what you've done to The Welcome for his sake, and they'll revolt against you. Steppe has the power to lead them; you know full well he does. They'll no longer be your precious, gentle slaves. How long will you go on protecting them?"

Silence.

"You owe me your allegiance," he growled. "After all you've done to me. After all you've done to us. You gave Ritter a piper's voice, and you've given me nothing but scraps. I've played by your rules for decades, tit for tat, just as you ordered. It's brought me nothing of use."

Silence.

He rose from his seat and threw his glare against the pitch. "Will you just sit there in the dark and do nothing? Will you sit there in silence and let it all come down around you? I thought the great Ansgar was more than that! I thought the great Ansgar was no one to trifle with! I thought the ruler of the In-Between would bring her enemies to their knees and make them cower before her! Am I so wrong? Are you nothing but a shadow? Are you nothing but a whimpering ghost?"

Silence.

"I've lost an eye!" he screamed. "I demand an eye in its place!"

He heard a step.

And another.

And a third.

Ansgar's voice slithered out of the darkness.

"I know what death sounds like, Sylvester."

Then, "Want me to show you?"

END OF BOOK ONE

Acknowledgements

Thank you...

...for taking a chance on a new writer and reading in between the lines—Halli Villegas and Tightrope Books

...for expert editing and limitless enthusiasm—Jessie Hale

...for an epic beta read and great advice—Tim Ford

...for support while I was writing—Nathan Berman, Laurie Bulchak, Istvan Dugalin, Joanne Harrison, Simon Leclerc, Sara Mohammed, Karim Morgan, Anna Narday, Birgit Nowatzki, and Katja Werner

...for being my dear (and patient) family—Victor, Violet, Louise, Victor, Christine, Alex, Rachel, Alexandra, and the Challengers

...for their generosity, and the privilege of experiencing their work—Samantha Beiko, Leah Bobet, Alyx Dellamonica, Catherine Hernandez, Jocelyn Shipley, and Caitlin Sweet

...for the adventures I've had from that day to this—Toronto, New York, Chicago and Uncle Chach, Bay Roberts, Brampton, and Brigus

...for being my best friend, my constant champion, and the love of my life—Russell Challenger